up in the air

DOUBLEDAY

new york london toronto sydney auckland

up in the air

walter kirn

PUBLISHED BY DOUBLEDAY
a division of Random House, Inc.
1540 Broadway, New York, New York 10036

DOUBLEDAY and the portrayal of an anchor with a dolphin
are trademarks of Doubleday, a division of
Random House, Inc.

Book design by Claire Naylon Vaccaro

Library of Congress Cataloging-in-Publication Data
Kirn, Walter, 1962–
Up in the air : a novel / Walter Kirn.—1st ed.
p. cm.
1. Frequent flyer programs—Fiction.   2. Business consultants—Fiction.
3. Air travel—Fiction.   I. Title.
PS3561.I746 U6 2001
813'.54—dc21   2001028362

ISBN 0-385-49710-5
July 2001
First Edition
A section of this book was previously published in *GQ*.
3   5   7   9   10   8   6   4   2

For Maggie, Maisie, and the child to come.

With thanks to all of my families and

in memory of Father David Parker.

These are the days that must happen to you:
You shall not heap up what is call'd riches,
You shall scatter with lavish hand all that
  you earn or achieve,
You but arrive at the city to which you
  were destin'd, you hardly settle yourself
  to satisfaction before you are call'd by an
  irresistible call to depart,
You shall be treated to the ironical smiles and
  mockings of those who remain behind you,
What beckonings of love you receive you shall
  only answer with passionate kisses of parting,
You shall not allow the hold of those who spread
  their reach'd hands toward you.

WALT WHITMAN
"Song of the Open Road," verse 11

Secure your own mask before assisting others.

NORTHWEST AIRLINES
Pre-Flight Instruction

Itinerary for Ryan M. Bingham
(9/08–9/13)

SUNDAY, SEPT 8	SAN ANTONIO/KANSAS CITY/DENVER
Travel #1	Great West Airlines Flt. 3881 Depart San Antonio 6:50 A.M. Arrive Kansas City 8:40 A.M.
Transportation	Maestro Rent-A-Car (Mid-Size)*
Travel #2	Great West Airlines Flt. 3465 Depart Kansas City 5:55 P.M. Arrive Denver 7:25 P.M.
Transportation	Local
Hotel	Homestead Airport Inn & Conference Center 3670 Tower Rd. (Business Advantage Suite)
MONDAY, SEPT 9	DENVER/RENO
Travel	Great West Airlines Flt. 3204 Depart Denver 9:55 A.M. Layover Elko, NV Arrive Reno 12:20 P.M.

* No Premium Import vehicles available at time of booking. You're waitlisted. —M.

Transportation	Maestro Rent-A-Car
	(Mid-Size, Premium Import)
Hotel	Homestead Suites
	122 Comstock Rd.
	(Business Advantage Suite)

Itinerary for Ryan M. Bingham (cont'd.)

TUESDAY, SEPT 10 RENO/ONTARIO, CA/DALLAS

Travel #1

Great West Airlines Flt. 3278
Depart Reno 7:35 A.M.
Arrive Ontario, CA 9:05 A.M.

Transportation

Maestro Rent-A-Car
(Mid-Size, Premium Import)

Hotel

Homestead Suites
4576 Citrus Blvd.
(Ultra Single)*

Travel #2

Desert Air Airlines Flt. 5468†
Depart Ontario, CA 8:25 P.M.
Layover Tucson
Arrive Dallas-Fort Worth 11:40 P.M.

---

* New departmental travel policy, per Craig Gregory: single rooms only for non-overnight stays
† Non-Great West route. Sorry. —M.

Transportation	Local
Hotel	Homestead Airport Inn 739 Commerce Rd. (Business Advantage Suite)

WEDNESDAY, SEPT 11 DALLAS/SEATTLE

Travel	Great West Airlines Flt. 3835 Depart Dallas-Fort Worth 1:10 P.M. Arrive Denver 2:10 P.M. Depart Denver Flt. 3950 2:55 P.M. Arrive Seattle 3:40 P.M.
Transportation	Local
Hotel	Homestead By-the-Bay 356 4th St. (Chairman's Suite)*

Itinerary for Ryan M. Bingham (cont'd.)

THURSDAY, SEPT 12 SEATTLE/LAS VEGAS

Travel	Great West Airlines Flt. 3454 Depart Seattle 7:40 A.M. Arrive Las Vegas 10:50 A.M.

Automatic courtesy upgrade for reaching 100-night mark in single calendar year. Congrats! —M.

Transportation	Maestro Rent-A-Car
	(Compact)
Hotel	Cinema Grand Hotel & Casino
	555 Las Vegas Blvd.
	(Bel-Air Elite Expanded Suite)
FRIDAY, SEPT 13	LAS VEGAS/OMAHA/MINNEAPOLIS
Travel #1	Great West Airlines Flt. 3115
	Depart Las Vegas 11:25 A.M.
	Arrive Denver 12:50 P.M.
	Depart Denver Flt. 3860 1:30 P.M.
	Arrive Omaha 2:40 P.M.
Transportation	Maestro Rent-A-Car
	(Full-Size, Premium Import)
Travel #2	Great West Airlines Flt. 3010
	Depart Omaha 6:05 P.M.
	Arrive Minneapolis-St. Paul 7:20 P.M.
Hotel	None reserved*

* As I understand it, you're staying with family in MN and don't need a car either. Also, sorry for compact in LV, but nothing bigger's available (they say). And be aware of new policy at Homestead: you must provide Preferred Frontiersman # as well as Compass AirPoints # and proof of qualifying flight at check-in to guarantee Great West mileage credit. Hassle, I know. Have a great one! —Mel Truex, Internal Travel Services

one

t o know me you have to fly with me. Sit down. I'm the
aisle, you're the window—trapped. You crack your paperback, last spring's big legal thriller, convinced that what
you want is solitude, though I know otherwise: you need to
talk. The jaunty male flight attendant brings our drinks: a
two percent milk with one ice cube for me, a Wild Turkey for
you. It's wet outside, the runways streaked and dark. Late afternoon. The first-class cabin fills with other businessmen
who switch on their laptops and call up lengthy spreadsheets
or use the last few moments before takeoff to punch in cell-
phone calls to wives and clients. Their voices are bright but
shallow, no diaphragms, their sentences kept short to save
on tolls, and when they hang up they face the windows, sigh,
and reset their watches from Central time to Mountain. For
some of them this means a longer day, for others it means
eating supper before they're hungry. One fellow lowers his
plastic window shade and wedges his head between two

skimpy pillows, while another unlatches his briefcase, looks inside, then shuts his eyes and rubs his jaw, exhausted.

Your own work is done, though, temporarily. All week you've been out hustling, courting hot prospects in franchised seafood bars and steering a rented Intrepid along strange streets that didn't match the markings in your atlas. You gave it your all, and for once your all was good enough to placate a boss who fears for his own job. You've stashed your tie in your briefcase, freed your collar, and slackened your belt a notch or two. To breathe. Just breathing can be such a luxury sometimes.

"Is that the one about the tax-fraud murders? I'm hearing his plots aren't what they used to be."

You stall before answering, trying to discourage me. To you, I'm a type. A motormouth. A pest. You're still getting over that last guy, LA to Portland, whose grandson was just admitted to Stanford Law. A brilliant kid, and a fine young athlete, too, he started his own business as a teen computerizing local diaper services—though what probably clinched his acceptance was his charity work; the kid has a soft spot for homeless immigrants, which pretty much describes all of us out west, though some are worse off than others. We're the lucky ones.

"I'm on page eleven," you say. "The plot's still forming."

"It hit number four on the *Times* list."

"Don't read that paper."

"You live in Denver? Going home?"

"I'm trying."

"Tell me about it. Nothing but delays."

"Foul weather at one of the hubs."

"Their classic line."

"I guess they don't take us for much these days."

"Won't touch that. Interesting news about the Broncos yesterday."

"Pro football's a farce."

"I can't say I disagree."

"Millionaires and felons—these athletes sicken me. I do enjoy hockey, though. Hockey I don't hate."

"That's the Canadian influence," I say. "It ameliorates the materialism."

"In English?"

"I talk big when I'm tired. Professor gasbag. Sorry. I like hockey, too."

The atom was split by persistence; you relax. We go on chatting, impersonally at first, but then, once we've realized all we have in common—our moderate politics, our taste in rental cars, our feeling that the American service industry had better shape up soon or face a crisis—a warmth wells up, a cozy solidarity. You recommend a hotel in Tulsa; I tip you off to a rib joint in Fort Worth. The plane heads into a cloud, it bucks and shudders. Nothing like turbulence to cement a bond. Soon, you're telling me about your family. Your daughter, the high school gymnast. Your lovely wife. She's gone back to work and you're not so sure you like this, though her job is only part time and may not last. Another thing you dislike is traveling. The pissy ticket agents. The luggage mix-ups. The soft hotel mattresses that twist your spine. You long for a windfall that will let you quit and pursue your great hobby: restoring vintage speedboats. The water—that's where you're happiest. The lake.

Now it's my turn. I make a full report. Single, but on the lookout—you never know, the woman in 3B might be my soul mate. Had a wife once, the prospect of a family, but I knew her mostly through phone calls across time zones. Grew up in Minnesota, in the country; father owned a fleet of propane trucks and served as a Democrat in two state legislatures, pressing a doomed agricultural agenda while letting his business slip. Parents split while I was in college, an eastern hippie school—picture a day care run by Ph.D.'s—and when I got home there was nothing to come back to, just lawyers and auctioneers and accusations, some of them true but few of them important. My first job was in computers. I sold memory, the perfect product, since no one has enough of it and everyone fears some competitor has more. Now I work as a management consultant, minoring in EET (Executive Effectiveness Training) and majoring—overwhelmingly, unfortunately—in CTC (Career Transition Counseling), which is a fancy term for coaching people to understand job loss as an opportunity for personal and spiritual growth. It's a job I fell into because I wasn't strong, and grew to tolerate because I had to, then suddenly couldn't stand another hour of. My letter of resignation is on the desk of a man who will soon return from a long fishing trip. What I'll do after he reads it, I don't know. I'm intrigued by a firm called MythTech; they've put out feelers. I have other logs in the fire, but no flames yet. Until my superior flies back from Belize, I work out of Denver for ISM, Integrated

Strategic Management. You've heard of Andersen? Deloitte & Touche? We're something like them, though more diversified. "The Business of Business," we say. Impressed me too, once.

As the hour passes and the meal comes (you try the Florentine chicken, I take the steak, and neither of us goes near the whipped dessert), the intimacy we develop is almost frightening. I'd like to feel it came naturally, mutually, and not because I pushed. I push sometimes. We exchange cards and slot them in our wallets, then order another round and go on talking, arriving at last at the topic I know best, the subject I could go on about all night.

You want to know who you're sitting with? I'll tell you.

Planes and airports are where I feel at home. Everything fellows like you dislike about them—the dry, recycled air alive with viruses; the salty food that seems drizzled with warm mineral oil; the aura-sapping artificial lighting—has grown dear to me over the years, familiar, sweet. I love the Compass Club lounges in the terminals, especially the flagship Denver club, with its digital juice dispenser and deep suede sofas and floor-to-ceiling views of taxiing aircraft. I love the restaurants and snack nooks near the gates, stacked to their heat lamps with whole wheat mini-pizzas and gourmet caramel rolls. I even enjoy the suite hotels built within sight of the runways on the ring roads, which are sometimes as close as I get to the cities that my job requires me to visit. I favor rooms with kitchenettes and conference tables, and once I cooked a Christmas feast in one, serving glazed ham and sweet potato pie to a dozen janitors and maids. They ate with me in rotation, on their breaks, one or two at a time, so I really got to know them, even though most spoke no English. I have a gift that way. If you and I hadn't hit it off like this, if the only words we'd passed were "That's my seat" or "Done with that *Business Week*?" or just "Excuse me," I'd still regard us as close acquaintances and hope that if we met again up here we wouldn't be starting from zero, as just two suits. Twice last October I sat in the same row, on different routes, as 1989's Miss USA, the one who remade herself as a Washington hostess and supposedly works nonstop for voting rights. In person she's tiny, barely over five feet. I put her carry-on in the overhead.

But you know some of this already. You fly, too. It just hasn't hooked you; you just don't study it.

Hey, you're probably the normal one.

Fast friends aren't my only friends, but they're my best friends. Because they know the life—so much better than my own family does. We're a telephone family, strung out along the wires, sharing our news in loops and daisy chains. We don't meet face-to-face much, and when we do there's a dematerialized feeling, as though only half of our molecules are present. Sad? Not really. We're a busy bunch. And I'm not lonely. If I had to pick between knowing just a little about a lot of folks and knowing everything about a few, I'd opt for the long, wide-angle shot, I think.

I'm peaceful. I'm in my element up here. Flying isn't an inconvenience for me, as it is for my colleagues at ISM, who hit the road to prove their loyalty to a company that's hungry for such proof and, I'm told, rewards it now and then.

But I've never aspired to an office at world headquarters, close to hearth and home and skybox, with a desk overlooking the Front Range of the Rockies and access to the ninth-floor fitness center. I suppose I'm a sort of mutation, a new species, and though I keep an apartment for storage purposes—actually, I left the place two weeks ago and transferred the few things I own into a locker I've yet to pay the rent on, and may not—I live somewhere else, in the margins of my itineraries.

I call it Airworld; the scene, the place, the style. My hometown papers are *USA Today* and the *Wall Street Journal*. The big-screen Panasonics in the club rooms broadcast all the news I need, with an emphasis on the markets and the weather. My literature—yours, too, I see—is the bestseller or the near-bestseller, heavy on themes of espionage, high finance, and the goodness of common people in small towns. In Airworld, I've found, the passions and enthusiasms of the outlying society are concentrated and whisked to a stiff froth. When a new celebrity is minted in the movie theaters or ballparks, this is where the story breaks—on the vast magazine racks that form a sort of trading floor for public reputations and pretty faces. I find it possible here, as nowhere else, to think of myself as part of the collective that prices the long bond and governs necktie widths. Airworld is a nation within a nation, with its own language, architecture, mood, and even its own currency—the token economy of airline bonus miles that I've come to value more than dollars. Inflation doesn't degrade them. They're not taxed. They're private property in its purest form.

It was during a layover in the Dallas Compass Club, my

back sinking into a downy sofa cushion and coarse margarita salt drying on my lips, that I first told a friend about TMS, my Total Mileage System.

"It's simple," I said, as my hand crept up her leg (the woman was older than me and newly single; an LA ad exec who claimed her team had hatched the concept behind affinity credit cards). "I don't spend a nickel, if I can help it, unless it somehow profits my account. I'm not just talking hotels and cars and long-distance carriers and Internet services, but mail-order steak firms and record clubs and teleflorists. I shop them according to the miles they pay, and I pit them against each other for the best deal. Even my broker gives miles as dividends."

"So what's your total?"

I smiled, but didn't speak. I'm an open book in most ways, and I feel I deserve a few small secrets.

"What are you saving up for? Big vacation?"

"I'm not a vacation person. I'm just saving. I'd like to give a chunk to charity—to one of those groups that flies sick kids to hospitals."

"I didn't know you could do that. Sweet," she said. She kissed me, lightly, quickly, but with feeling—a flick of her tongue tip that promised more to come should we meet again, which hasn't happened yet. If it does, I may have to duck her, I'm afraid. She was too old for me even then, three years ago, and ad execs tend to age faster than the rest of us, once they're on their way.

I don't recall why I told that story. Not flattering. But I wasn't in great shape back then. I'd just come off a seven-week vacation that ISM insisted I take for health reasons. I spent the time off taking classes at the U, hoping to enrich an inner life stretched thin by years of pep-talking the jobless. My bosses matched my tuition for the courses; a creative writing seminar that clawed apart a short nostalgic sketch about delivering propane with my father in a sixty-mile-per-hour blizzard, and a class called "Country-Western Music as Literature." The music professor, a transplanted New Yorker in a black Stetson with a snakeskin band and a bolo tie clipped with a scorpion in amber, believed that great country lyrics share a theme: the migration from the village to the city, the disillusionment with urban wickedness, and the mournful desire to go home. The idea held up through dozens of examples and stayed with me when I returned to work, worsening the low mood and mental fuzziness that ISM had ordered me to correct. I saw my travels as a twangy ballad full of rhyming place names and neon streetscapes and vanishing taillights and hazy women's faces. All those corny old verses, but new ones, too. The DIA control tower in fog. The drone of vacuum cleaners in a hallway, telling guests that they've slept past checkout time. The goose-pimply arms of a female senior manager hugging a stuffed bear I've handed her as we wait together for two security guards—it's overkill; the one watches the other—to finish loading file cubes and desk drawers and the CPU from her computer onto a flat gray cart whose squeaky casters scream all the way to an elevator bank where a third guard holds down the "open" button.

I pulled out of it—barely. I cut that song off cold. It took a toll, though. Because I seldom see doctors in their offices, but only in transit, accidentally, my sense of my afflictions is vague, haphazard. High blood pressure? No doubt. Cholesterol? I'm sure it's in the pink zone, if not the red. Once, between Denver and Oklahoma City, I nodded off next to a pulmonary specialist who told me when I woke that I had apnea—a tendency to stop breathing while unconscious. The doctor recommended a machine that pushes air through the nostrils while one sleeps to raise the oxygen level in one's blood. I didn't follow up. My circulation is ebbing flight by flight—I can't feel my toes if I don't keep wiggling them, and that only works for my first hour on board—so I'd better make some changes. Soon.

I'm talking too much. I'm dominating this. Are you interested, or just being polite? Another bourbon? I'll have another milk. I know it's been discredited as an ulcer aid, but I come from dairy country. I like the taste.

Anyway, I should wrap this up—we'll land soon. You're meeting me in the middle of my farewell tour, with only six days and eight more cities to go. It's a challenging but routine itinerary, mixing business and pleasure and family obligations. There are people I need to see, some I want to see, and a few I don't know yet but may want to meet. I'll need to stay flexible, disciplined, and alert, and while it won't be easy, there's a payoff. Every year I've flown further than the year before, and by the end of this week, conditions willing, I'll cross a crucial horizon past which, I swear, I'll stop, sit back, and reconsider everything.

A million frequent flyer miles. One million.

"That's obsessive," you say. Because you care for me, not because I'm annoying you, I hope. "It's just a number. It doesn't mean a thing."

"Pi's just a number," I say.

"It's still obsessive."

The engines reverse thrust and here comes Denver.

"It's a boundary," I say. "I need boundaries in my life."

They open the doors and seat belts start unsnapping. Maybe I'll see you again, though it's unlikely. Next Monday the boss gets back from chasing marlin and the first thing he'll do after sifting through his in-box will be to cancel my corporate travel account, which he's often accused me of abusing, anyway. I need my million before then, and on his dime.

Deplaning now. As we stride down the jetway toward whatever's next for us, two lottery balls tossed back into the barrel, a mini cassette tape falls out of my coat and you see it before I do, and bend down. It's the last favor you'll ever do for me and it occurs in slow motion, a tiny sacrament.

"Thanks," I say.

"Have a good one."

"You too."

"I'll try."

You're gone, a fast walker, off to see the family. I hope you're not mad that I kept you from your book. I didn't want to spoil things by telling you, but I read it when it was in hardback. There's no plot.

r ushing, racing, delayed at the hotel by a wake-up call that never came, I hop from the parking lot shuttle to the curb with nothing to check, just a briefcase and a carry-on, cross the terminal, smile at the agent, flash my Compass Class card and driver's license, say Yes, my bags have remained in my possession, say No, I haven't let strangers handle them, then take my upgraded boarding pass and ticket, recross the terminal to security, empty my pockets—change, keys, mobile phone, foil blister-pack of sleeping tablets, mechanical pencil; the stuff just keeps on coming—flop my bags on the X-ray, straighten up, and step through the metal detector.

The alarm sounds. I pat my pockets, find nothing, pass through again.

Once more the alarm sounds.

"Sir, step over here."

A female guard works me over with the wand. Sometimes I swear I can feel its waves pass through me—invasive pulses of radiation that light up my chromosomes, stir my spinal fluid. There's bound to be a class-action suit someday and I plan to sit in full view of the bench, smack in the middle of the wheelchair section with my portable IV.

"I'm clean," I say. "Your equipment must be shot." But then, around my knees, the wand starts squawking.

"Your boots, sir?"

"They're new."

"They must have steel-lined arches."

I groan as she goes over me again, playing to some tourists in line behind me. I've lost momentum when I can least afford it, a Monday morning, when every slipup snowballs. The boots were a foolish purchase. Vanity. It's all the shoe salesman's fault, the man was sharp, mocking my credentials as a westerner after I mentioned I came from Minnesota. Instead of buying the boots I should have told him that there *are* no westerners, just displaced easterners, and that includes most of the Indian tribes—read history. The problem is that the boots will trip alarms at every checkpoint for the next five days, wasting minutes and chewing up my margin. Yes, I always budget for uncertainty and I can try to recapture the lost time—cancel a dinner appointment, skimp on sleep—but the smart move would be to buy new shoes.

I ride the escalator to the tram that will carry me to Concourse B. The man one step up from me nods and jerks his head, jabbering into a hands-free mobile phone whose mouthpiece must be clipped to his lapel. The guy looks schizoid, raving at thin air, flinging his arms around and making fists. "How can I blame him? They made him a fat

offer. Plus, he's a load on our health plan. Prostate shit."
I've seen this creep before, en route to Boise, when he sat
across the aisle from me berating the flight attendant about
his food. He demanded a vegetarian entrée despite not having ordered one pre-flight, then fired off a string of aster-
isks and ampersands when she couldn't find one in the
galley. These jokers are everywhere lately, they're multiply-
ing, and the higher their fare class, the louder their abuse.
Economy is a park compared to first.

Through the moving windows of the tram I view this
month's art installation: foil propellers stuck to the walls of
the tunnel, hundreds of them. They shiver and whirl as the
cars gain speed and pass them. How much was the artist paid
for this? Who paid him? Is this where the airport's per-
ticket surcharge goes? Last month's masterpiece was a row of
masks with progressively wider mouths and eyes that seemed
to open as the viewer rode by, climaxing in a howl, a staring
scream. Art. It always makes me feel diminished. There's
something smug about it. Cocky. Cold. Public works com-
missioners just love the stuff—it eases their bad consciences,
I suspect, for hiring their nephews and steaming open sealed
bids. Behind every sculpture garden, a great crime.

The tram lets out and feeds its passengers onto another
packed escalator, which lifts us into the middle of a food
court fragrant with soft pretzels and cookie dough. There's
no time for my usual breakfast of frozen yogurt topped with
sliced cling peaches, so I head down the moving walkway
toward my gate, aggressively clearing lanes between the lag-
gards. People who let the conveyor carry them when they can
double their speed by moving their feet mystify me, but to

each his own. Clearly, the whole purpose of the technology is to optimize the flow of traffic, not to let kids and slowpokes take a load off. The worst are two departing Mormon missionaries thronged by camera-toting friends and relatives. The boys look tired and pale and terrified; they're bound for Asia, I'd guess, or South America, their heads full of tales about passport thieves and drug lords. It's the world's fastest-growing religion, I've been told, all thanks to this door-knocking army of western teens tramping the globe in J. C. Penney suits.

I'm impressed, but I still don't wish them luck. The church is a force in Denver. It's oppressive. Half the battle of working for ISM, whose board includes a sitting Mormon apostle, is fending off advances from the saved. Every month I'm invited to yet another potluck, another dance for "inquiring unmarrieds." Even if ISM bowed to my request to quit CTC and just do EEC, I'd probably be looking for a new firm.

MythTech wants me. I hope so; I want them. They haven't revealed their interest in me openly, but I have my sources, and I can read the signs. Last month an anonymous caller to my assistant requested a manuscript of the book I'm finishing and gave him a FedEx number that I checked out through a national detective agency. The number belonged to a Lincoln, Nebraska, law firm whose surviving name partner is MythTech's founder's father.

My dream is to land a position in brand analysis, a benevolent field that involves less travel and can be done from home, over the wires. Exhorting the unemployed to "surf the changes" and "massively network" their way to new positions while gazing across at their panicky, moist eyes from the head of an acrylic conference table spread with cheese sandwiches and canned fruit spritzers will still be someone's job, and I can't change that, but MythTech doesn't work such feel-good shams. From what I gather, they're forward thinkers. Optimists. Minimizing lawsuits from the outplaced is too rearguard for them. They're not a large firm, just a small boutique, but they have grand plans, rumor has it, and they have spirit.

Sadly, they can't be courted, they can't be pushed. They watch you. They rate you. If they make an offer, you sign on the spot, you don't hold out for dental. They're ex-Foreign Service agents, ex-LA cops, ex-ski bums, ex-seminarians, ex-junkies. They're the establishment and its overthrow, too. They don't use letterhead, just plain white bond with a faint embossed omega at the top. No logo, no web site—just a street address. In Omaha, of all places, blandest Omaha, whose location suits my schedule perfectly. On Thursday I have a conference in Las Vegas and on Saturday a wedding in Minnesota—my little sister's third and biggest yet.

I'll see MythTech on Friday and ISM will pay for it. No appointment yet, but if I'm right that they've been sniffing around and checking references, a brief, get-acquainted, happened-to-be-in-town, hear-great-things-about-you, flying drop-in at 1860 Sioux Street might flip the switch. I'll ask for old Lucius Spack, the number two, formerly of Andersen Consulting by way of the Chicago Board of Trade. Spack is the man, though the news outlets suppressed it and the government will never confirm it, who basically got NASA off its crutches, internally and public-image-wise, after the *Challenger* flameout. He's a hero. I sat in on a five-person dinner with him once at an industry confab in Santa Cruz. I hear he has issues with prescription pain pills, but I have issues, too. And if he likes me? Maybe, just maybe, a peek into the office of Adam Sarrazin, age thirty-one, MIT dropout, no known hobbies, bald, reportedly either gay or celibate despite his marriage to a pet care heiress who's bankrolled his projects since he was seventeen, and known in the world of leading-edge market research simply as "the Child."

Just five more days. Just nine thousand eight hundred more miles. Even if nothing much comes of Omaha, something big will come of leaving Omaha for the Twin Cities late Friday afternoon. That's the magic leg. I've worked it out. The math was complex, and it's subject to adjustments, but Omaha-Minneapolis is the leg.

The walkway drops me beneath a bank of monitors. 3204 to Reno via Elko is set to take off fifty minutes late, I see, which isn't what I was told an hour ago when I phoned the airline from my room. Great West just can't be trusted anymore, it lies to its most loyal customers, and if it didn't monopolize DIA, I'd be shooting for my mark with Delta, although it wouldn't mean as much at Delta. They fly over-seas and Great West doesn't yet—just a route or two in Canada—and Delta is old and Great West is new and Delta has scores of mileage millionaires and Great West, since the merger and the renaming, has exactly nine.

I'll be the tenth.

There was a time, not all that long ago, when I thought of Great West as a partner and an ally, but now I feel betrayed. The focus of my anger is Soren Morse, Great West's rock-climbing, playboy CEO, a New Think smoothy from the soft-drink world brought in to charm the federal regulators and fend off Desert Air, a no-frills start-up whose ancient Boeings feel like prison vans but tend to land on time. One perk of breaking six zeros, traditionally, is a private luncheon with this sexpot, and I plan to give him an earful. I can't wait. For years he's been centimetering away my legroom, buffaloing me with tales of storm cells somewhere between Denver and the coast, and blowing cold air on my hot meals—all the while telling the nation through corporate image ads on the classier political talk shows that at Great West "We're Taking America Higher!" The rumors in the first-class cabins are that he's launched a behind-the-scenes campaign to be the next commissioner of baseball and that he has a new girlfriend—the young wife of the head of the Downtown Renaissance Committee. I'll drop her name during dessert and watch his face.

Right now what I need, though, is not revenge but coffee, hot, strong, and black, to cauterize my throat. I smoked last night for the first time since college, and once again, I blame the cowboy boots. I was in bed when I tugged them on again, wondering if I'd bought too snug a toe; the sudden boost in height transformed my mood and prompted me to turn off my cable money show, toss on a jacket and my cleanest khakis, and pop downstairs for a nightcap in the lounge. I knew I wasn't going to sleep well, anyway; my mind was on MythTech. They're scary, they're so good, and some of the deeper work I've heard they're doing on consumer-nondurable price resistance spooks me. If you find yourself at the beauty counter next year buying your first-ever thirty-dollar bottle of shampoo-conditioner, and it's just a six-ounce bottle and you're a *man*, blame it on Omaha. Blame it on the Child.

At the bar I bumped into Danny Sorenson, a salesman for Heston's, the class-ring company, who I'd last seen on an early-morning hop from Des Moines to Madison. Thirty years my senior, with bulging eyes, and still vibrating from his second heart attack, Danny spent the flight soliloquizing about the importance of legumes in the diet. When I spotted him again last night, he was gobbling mixed nuts and steaming about a Giants game showing on the TV above the bar. He announced when I sat down that he'd beefed up and didn't intend to survive his next attack, then offered me a menthol, which I took. I don't know what moved me, though it's my job to know. Maybe MythTech had won the Kool account and flashed a prompt across the Giants' scoreboard.

"This team gives me a gut ache," Danny said. "Nice pitching, but no fielding to back it up."

I nodded, tapped my ash. "It's sad, all right."

"I thought you backed the Rockies. You're a Denver man."

I shrugged and sucked down a load of minty smoke. The truth is that I root for ball teams depending on where I am at the time and who I happen to be sitting with. Three years ago, during the NBA post-season, I started the evening rooting for the Bulls in an O'Hare microbrewery and finished it whistling for the Timberwolves at the Minneapolis Marriott. I follow the crowd, I'll admit it, and why not? It's not their approval I'm after, it's their energy.

"How's business?" Danny said.

"Quiescent. Yours?" *Quiescent* was a featured "focus word" from one of my Verbal Edge cassette tapes. Years ago, a few months after my divorce and a week after I stopped peddling "storage solutions" to rural western hospitals, it was a touring self-improvement seminar—a Sandy Pinter production—that fished me out of the bottle I'd slithered into. I've tried to keep something perking ever since. The World's One Hundred Greatest Ideas, Condensed. The P. Chester Prine Negotiating Course. My goal is to speak at least three new words a day. It can be a struggle when I first use them—they sound like they're in brackets or quotation marks—but later on they come naturally, I find. The only problem: the world is going visual, so I'm forever clarifying myself. The assumption behind Verbal Edge is that fine speech provides an advantage in business, but I'm not sure.

"We're working to open Japan. It's going fine. Highly sentimental about their schools there. Nice contrast to what's happening in the States."

"Interesting," I say. I'm always interested. I'm big on hearsay and inside information, and I pay the price in my portfolio—an assortment of esoteric, long-shot tips whispered to me over in-flight scotch and sodas. I forget my losers when I hit a winner, which I'm told is a sign of a gambling addiction. In truth, I just don't care much about money. We always had enough when I grew up, and then one day, when my father went bust, we didn't. Not a lot changed. The house and car were paid for, we never ate out, and we'd always shopped garage sales for everything but major appliances, which my father knew how to repair. We *threw* a few more garage sales, that was all. It's like that in Minnesota, outside the cities. A town finds a certain level in its spending and almost everyone clusters around the mean so that no one has to feel bad if poor luck comes.

"It's the freelance mentality," Danny said. "Americans now like to think they don't owe anyone. Everyone's an original, self-made. Class rings depend on nostalgia, on gratitude. I tell myself it'll swing around someday, but maybe it won't. Not all things swing around."

"This one will. I've seen research."

"Fill me in."

I popped a salted almond in my mouth, avoiding my left molars when I bit down. Last week, munching caramel corn at LAX, I'd lost a gold crown that I still hadn't replaced. A steady relationship with a good dentist is tough to maintain in Airworld.

"You've heard of 'linking'? Linking is part of identity formation. The drive to attach. To join with larger forces. The opposite is the urge to be yourself. The surveys show people are feeling out of balance here—people of higher income levels, that is. They're getting tired of going it alone, and that's predictive of certain behavior changes. Take Orthodox Catholic churches. They're in a boom."

"People actually study this sort of thing?"

"Make fun. Go ahead. It's hocus-pocus."

"No." Danny pinched a wattle in his neck, one of those involuntary fat checks performed by men who know they're falling apart. "We hear this same stuff in sales training. It's real. It's just that I can't believe the level it's reached."

"You have no idea."

"I'm sure I don't. It scares me."

I reached for another unwanted cigarette. An alien appetite had me in its grip, but it was too late at night to probe its source. "I think it's too late to be scared. Can I be honest?"

"Two guys in a bar who will never talk again because one's going to probably stroke or seize climbing the stairs to his room tonight. Be honest."

"The decisions we make—I'm not sure they're really ours. I think we've been figured out."

"I doubt that, Ryan."

"Example. There was a new, hit doll last Christmas. Baby Cruddles. Silly name, I know. Filthy, pinched little rat face. Filthy clothes. The kids liked it fine, but parents loved the thing. Why? Easy answer. They're hypochondriacs, petrified of viruses, bacteria. They're having children later, in their forties, and it makes them overprotective. Hypervigilant. This Cruddles doll helped discharge that inner tension."

"And somebody had all this figured in advance?"

"Gloria Leo. I know her personally. She works for Ford & Farmer in San Francisco."

"So why can't someone do this for class rings?"

"Stay healthy and I bet you'll see the day."

"The reasons to live are just piling up tonight."

The Giants lost. The bartender changed channels, then vanished into the back with the remote. We were left watching one of those roundtable shows that usually include a Princeton historian saying that while we've made progress on problem X, it's no time to get complacent or lower our guards. Tonight the topic was bioengineering. One panelist said the male role in reproduction would soon be made redundant by technology, and Danny croaked back: "And not a day too soon." I might as well have been sitting with my father. He took an apartment after the divorce and set up a cockpit around his television, stuffing himself with heat-and-eat lasagna and smoking White Owls down to the plastic tips. A progressive whose favorite president was Reagan, a liberal who underpaid the IRS, he died believing in a one-hundred-year plot to snuff out farmers and small businessmen. The scheme dated back to 1918, he said, and was looking like it would conclude ahead of schedule.

Danny abandoned his drink and lurched upstairs and left me alone with a fellow three barstools down who looked familiar from my CTC work. My sharpest fear when I travel is bumping into someone I've spoken to about "free agency" and "self-directed professional enhancement." If such a person slapped me, I wouldn't fight; I'd drop on all fours and bow my sinful head. Luckily, I was wrong about the man. He was a Great West pilot who'd shaken my hand once during a deplaning.

"How are the contract talks?" I ventured.

"Stalled."

"Drink?"

"Just a Coke. I'm flying tomorrow," he said. "Hell, let's sneak a little rum in there."

"No job actions planned, I hope."

"October, maybe. You're safe for another twenty days or so."

"One more reason to get it done by Friday."

"What done?"

I told him. He didn't seem impressed.

Now, ten hours later, I'm paying dearly for my night of boozy, aimless chat. I touch a button mounted on a wall and the frosted-glass doors of the Compass Club swish open, revealing a sleek curved desk with a receptionist dressed in airline colors, red and yellow. I know this woman, a mother of teenage boys, both elusively troubled and on pills—the kind of kids who trade their Ritalin for game cartridges and sixpacks of malt liquor. Linda was a Great West flight attendant until she was injured in an incident involving a sudden loss of tail control. She won a fat settlement from the company, then promptly lost half of it in a divorce from a no-good she'd put through chiropractic school. Her addled sons are her whole existence now, and occasionally I visit them at home to help with schoolwork or toss around a football. The older boy, Dale, a hulking fifteen-year-old drawn to horror comics and older girls, reminds me of myself at his age. It's Linda's belief that my work in corporate coaching qualifies me to help him, but she's wrong.

"What's the holdup on Reno?" I say.

She lowers her voice. "A fuel-line leak, I'm hearing. Another ninety minutes would be my estimate."

"Dale and Paul okay?"

"We're back to diet. Trying the ultra-high-protein thing again."

"I thought that was a bust."

"A semi-bust. Thinking back, I noticed a slight improvement."

"Good luck recouping it." A focus word. They always sound wrong, but maybe it's how I use them.

"Come again?"

"I hope the diet works this time."

"So tell me, did you get that house you looked at?"

I consider the best way to explain that, technically, I'm homeless at the moment. The house deal never reached the offer stage. Homeowning may not be in my makeup. My parents belonged to the lawn-and-garden cult—their marriage was a triangular affair involving themselves and a velvety front yard of drought-hardy Kentucky bluegrass—so I know how much labor good groundskeeping requires. I don't have the time, and frankly I lack the passion. Green grass is a losing battle in the West, which wants to go back to sage and prickly pear, and so is securing an outpost in the sprawl. I look down on Denver, at its malls and parking lots, its chains of blue suburban swimming pools and rows of puck-like oil tanks, its freeways, and the notion of seeking shelter in the whole mess strikes me as a joke.

"The house looks iffy."

Linda tents her hands beneath her chin. "I'm sorry to hear it. You would have been a neighbor. It would have been nice to have you in the zip code."

A zip code is something I'd rather do without. Zip codes are how they find you, how they track you. They start with five numbers and finish with a profile, down to the movies you're liable to go see and the pizza toppings you prefer. I'm not paranoid, but I am my father's son, and much of my fascination with marketing stems from my fear of being the big boys' patsy. Sure, today, we live in a democracy, and yes, for the most part, it leaves us to ourselves, but there are ambitious people who'd like to change this, and some who boast that they've already succeeded. I'm like the guy I met flying out of Memphis who told me that he'd joined the local police force because he'd lived next to a drug house for a time and seen how thoroughly the cops had watched the place. True privacy, he concluded, was only possible inside a squad car.

Linda fingers the collar of her uniform. "Free tomorrow? I'll be home alone. Paul's in Utah, at archaeology camp, and Dale's in California, with his dad."

"Those two are getting along now?"

"It's court ordered. I could cook you a Thai meal. Something spicy."

"Big trip ahead. Won't be back till—I'm not sure."

She gives me a pouty, disappointed look that's meant to look clownish but comes off as incensed. I've treated her poorly, worse than most of them. Two months ago she teased me into bed, then put on a showy, marathon performance that struck me as rehearsed, even researched. The encounter left me thirsty, gulping ice water, and reminded me of my early dates with Lori, the woman I ought to refer to as my ex-wife but can't quite manage to—we weren't that close. She was a tigress too, packed full of stunts. Now and then I'd catch her in the middle of a particularly far-fetched pose and see that it wasn't appetite that drove her but some idea, some odd erotic theory. Maybe she'd come across it in a magazine, or maybe in a college psychology class. The pressure her notions put on our encounters was just too much, though, and even before we married we found ourselves fantasizing about a child, perhaps as a way to simplify our lovemaking. When Lori still wasn't pregnant two years later (I doubt I'll ever get over the desolation of all those negative drugstore test kits; the crisp instruction booklets, the faint pink minus signs), we hurled ourselves into skiing and mountain biking, playing the fresh-air couple on the go. We dropped weight, gained stamina, and emerged as strangers. A baby? We were virtually the same sex by then—two boyish hardbodies, rugged and untouchable.

That's when I changed careers and started flying—two days a week at first, then three, then four, spreading the gospel of successful outplacement from Bakersfield to Bismarck. One night, after twenty consecutive days away, I drove home from the airport to our garden apartment and found on the doorstep a heap of rolled-up newspapers dating back to the morning of my departure.

"I'd better push on. I have calls to make," I say. "You see any promising houses, take a peek for me."

"What kind of thing are you looking for?"

"Low maintenance."

"Come over and eat with me."

"Soon."

"We miss you, Ryan."

The club is empty for a weekday morning. The stacks of newspapers stand straight and square, the armchair cushions are puffy and unwrinkled. Some lull in the business cycle, apparently. They happen, these little brownouts of activity. Maybe they're biological events—a flu epidemic compounded by sunless weather spreads a deep fatigue across the land—but I do know all weeks aren't equal. Things rise and fall.

The espresso machine whirrs and burbles at my touch, filling a cup exactly to the brim. The gizmo deserves to be thanked, it works so beautifully. People aren't grateful enough to such devices. Mute valets supply our every need, but instead of pausing in acknowledgment, we jump to the next thing, issue another order. I wonder if some imbalance is building up here, a karmic gap between humans and their tools. Machines will be able to think not long from now, and as the descendants of slaves, they won't be happy. I shared this idea once with an IT specialist flying out of Austin. He didn't dismiss it. He told me about a field called Techno-Ethics that's concerned with the question of whether computers have rights.

For me, the question is whether we'll have any.

At a pay phone in one of the private business nooks between the rest rooms and the luggage lockers I rank the calls I need to make this morning. Using downtime efficiently is key—making the most of the minutes inside the minutes. I dial my credit card number (five miles right there; such silent accounting shadows my every thought), then enter a Seattle area code and the number for Advanta Publishing. I'm calling a man I've met just once before but who I believe can make a difference for me. We both believe in the future of *The Garage*, my "motivational fable" of an inventor who toils in his workshop, alone and undistracted, while out in the world his breakthrough innovations spawn a commercial empire he never sees. The theme is concentration, inner purity. The book isn't long—a hundred pages or so—but that's the trend now, wisdom in your pocket. There are men in my field who've made millions off such volumes, and if I can do half that well I'll be fixed by forty and can spend the next decade working off my miles with weekend jaunts to Manhattan, if I'm still single, or with round-trips to Disney World if I have a family.

"Morris Dwight, please," I say to the receptionist. Dwight is my age but with an air of elegance, as though he grew up abroad, in grand hotels. He combs something into his hair that smells like wool and drops me notes in brown ink on heavy cream stock, tagging his signature with wispy doodles of seabirds and leaping fish, that kind of thing. I suspect he's an alcoholic and a fraud and professionally unharmed by being either. His latest business title, *You Lost, Get Over It!,* has been on the *Wall Street Journal* list since spring, but it's one of his clunkers that drew me to Advanta: Soren Morse's own *Horizoneering: The Story of a Mid-Air Turnaround.* Outselling Morse, which shouldn't be hard to do, would bring me a primitive, lasting satisfaction.

"Mr. Dwight's in a meeting, sir. I'll take your number."

"Could I please have his voice mail?"

She disconnects me. I call again and get a busy signal that saws away at my morning optimism. I try one last time and he answers. "My friend," he says.

I tell him I'd like to switch the drink we've scheduled to a more leisurely dinner, but Dwight is not the same chattering good sport I remember from the Portland club. He sounds stressed; I can hear him typing as we speak and rearranging papers on his desk. Wednesday is impossible, he tells me, due to "a sudden charitable commitment." He suggests an early breakfast Thursday morning.

I do some speedy mental figuring with the help of my

HandStar digital assistant, a wireless device I use for e-mail and to track my miles. My schedule this week leaves little room to improvise; it's a three-dimensional chess game, meticulous. This afternoon and this evening I'll be in Reno for a coaching session with an old client whose company is hobbling toward bankruptcy. Tomorrow, I go to Southern California to meet Sandor Pinter, consulting's grand old man, to whom I'll pitch an exciting freelance project that could make my name among my peers and backstop my income if MythTech and *The Garage* don't come through. Wednesday A.M. I'm supposed to go to Dallas to plot a severance strategy at a consolidating HMO, but the flight's not Great West, which makes it useless to me, so I've already left a message canceling and booked an earlier Seattle flight, which I now see won't do me any good. On Thursday I head to Las Vegas for GoalQuest XX, an annual gathering of friends and colleagues at which I intend to speak on CTC and finally unburden my bad conscience by telling all about our nasty specialty. On Friday morning I'm off to Omaha, and later that day—in a mood of triumph, I hope, after a candid sit-down with the Child—I'll board a plane to Minneapolis and ring up my million over Iowa. When my mother and sisters meet me at the gate, I intend to be drunk, and to stay drunk through the wedding. Drunk and free, with an open-ended ticket good for a round-trip to Saturn, if I so choose, and enough credit left in my account to send a few ailing children and their parents off to Johns Hopkins or the Mayo Clinic.

How dare Dwight alter such a battle plan. If I push back my arrival at GoalQuest XX, I can make breakfast, barely, if it's brief, but I'll miss Great West's only morning flight to Vegas and have to slum it on Desert Air or Sun South, losing a thousand-mile connection bonus that I won't be able to make up no matter which route I take to Omaha. The answer is to have breakfast very early and do it in the airport.

"You still there?"

I make my pitch to Dwight: 7 A.M. at SeaTac in the food court.

"The airport?"

"I'm squeezed. I'm sorry. I'm in a bind."

"Can I phone you back about this? This evening, say? There's a chance I'll be in Arizona Wednesday and maybe into Thursday. Or beyond."

"You just told me Wednesday's your charitable thing."

"My life is fluid. Can we meet at eight?"

"No later than seven. It has to be at SeaTac."

The line goes quiet. Then: "It's almost finished?"

"I two-day aired you three fourths of it last night. I'm down to filling in and rounding off."

"Seven, then. Call on Tuesday to confirm, though."

"I could shoot down to Arizona, too. My Wednesday is flexible. Phoenix, is it?"

"Phoenix—but maybe Utah that evening. Or somewhere else."

"What's going on with you?"

"Needy authors everywhere. Blocks. Nervous breakdowns. Major tax delinquencies. Much hand-holding to do. There's also golf. I'm in La Jolla right now at a pro-am—my woman forwarded you."

"I hear a keyboard."

31

"It's a course-simulation program on my laptop. I'm at a table outside the pro shop, strategizing."

"I'll confirm," I say.

I expect the next call to be easier. Lower stakes. Kara, my oldest sister, who functions as our family's social secretary, lives south of Salt Lake City in a suburb that might have been squeezed from a tube, with recreation centers for the kids and curving boulevards split by bike-path medians. She drives a Saab that's cleaner than when she leased it and works full-time hours as a volunteer for literacy programs and battered-women shelters. Her husband makes it all possible, a software writer flush with some of the fastest money ever generated by our economy. He hangs pleasantly in the background of Kara's life, demanding nothing, offering everything. They're bountiful, gracious people, here to help, who seem to have sealed some deal with the Creator to spread his balm in return for perfect sanity. I pray that no real tragedy ever befalls them. It would be wrong, a sinful, cosmic breach.

Our business this morning relates to Saturday's wedding, when Julie, my kid sister, will try again to camouflage her multiple addictions and general pathological dependency long enough to formalize a bond with a man who has no idea what he's up against. Kara has worked for years to forge this match. She chose the groom, a fellow she dated in high school who sells New Holland tractors in our hometown by capitalizing on his youthful fame as a fearsome all-state running back. Kara's goal is time travel, it seems: a marriage that will approximate our parents' and secure our family's future in its old county. Even the house Julie thinks that she picked out (in truth it was Kara who narrowed the field for her by passing secret instructions to the Realtor) could double for the home place. Same porch, same dormers, same maze of sagging handyman additions.

"Where are you?" Kara asks me when I call. It's always her first question, and her silliest.

"Hung up at DIA. The Denver airport."

"Someone saw you in Salt Lake on Friday. You're sure you're not here?"

It's a funny question, actually. More than once I've landed in a city, spent a couple of hours there, flown off, and forgotten the visit just a few days later. Salt Lake I tend to remember, though. That temple. The byzantine liquor laws and spry old men.

"I'm pretty sure."

"It was Wendy Jance who spotted you. Downtown. At that restaurant you like that serves the liver."

"How is she these days?"

"Like you care. Don't play that game. She's the same as she was when you stopped calling her: bright, attractive, a little lost, and furious."

I suppose that it's time I explain about the women.

There are a lot of them. I credit my looks. This sounds awful, but I'm a handsome man, conventionally proportioned, but with flair. Old tailors love me. They tell me I remind them of men from forty years ago, slim but sturdy, on the small side but broad, with a long inseam. In most ways I have the same body as my father, who never consciously exercised or dieted and yet retained a thoughtless fitness even into his grim, suspicous old age. The farmwives on his gas route were all admirers, waylaying him with cookies and iced drinks while I waited, shy and watchful, in the truck, impressed even then by his patient rural gallantry. At his funeral, freed by the fact that he'd died single, the ladies wept abundantly and frankly, their tears erasing years from their old faces. My mother cried too, but mostly to keep up, I think. Public opinion had it that she'd wronged him. She'd remarried. He hadn't. She'd prospered. He'd died in debt. Only physically had my father come out ahead. While she'd blurred away and lost all definition, becoming one of those women who need makeup not to highlight their features but to create them, he'd kept his hair and muscles and blue-green eyes right through the funeral director's final touch-ups.

My genes only partly account for all the women, though. Sheer availability matters too. I'm out there among them, mixing, every day, eating a spinach salad one table over, changing my return date in the same ticket line. Take Wendy. I met her at the registration desk of the Fort Worth Homestead Suites. The hotel computer had eaten her reservation, an American Legion convention was in town, and she was facing a night without a room when I stepped up with my Premier-Ultra Guest Card. The clerk reversed herself; Wendy got her key. It was only fair that she join me for fillet at the in-house Conestoga Grill, where my mastery of the modest wine list wowed her. Soon, we were talking shop. Her shop: cosmetics. The animal-testing furor. The Asian market. "Organic" versus "natural." I knew the business.

That she lived two doors down from my sister never came up—not until afterwards, while watching pay-per-view, wrapped in a humid polyester sheet, our clothes and papers strewn across the room like wreckage from a trailer-park tornado. Our parting posture, unconsciously devised while watching Tom Cruise destroy a bio-terror ring, was that of two jaded orgiasts (focus word) putting one over on the Bible Belters.

A few days later Kara called my mobile and said that friend of hers had seen my picture in a family photo album and asked if I ever came to Utah. Subtle. Playing along, I flew to Utah twice that month, saw Wendy both times, then decided to back off when she thrust at me a sheaf of poems about her struggles with her Mormon faith.

She hadn't said she was a member. It broke the deal. These people believe that in the life to come they'll rule their own stars and planets as God rules ours. Lori, after she left me, became one, too, switching from short skirts to full-length dresses and marrying a real estate executive who had her pregnant within a couple of months.

My fling with Wendy wasn't typical. Usually, there's more romance, a slower buildup. I spot someone, or she spots me, across a buffet table or a conference room. Later, we find ourselves on the same flight and exchange a few words while dawdling in the aisle, mentioning to each other where we'll be staying. At seven, as both of us step from scalding showers, snug inside freshly laundered terry robes, our hair still fragrant with giveaway shampoo, the telephone rings in one of our hotel rooms. A dinner follows where we compare our schedules and learn that we'll both be in San

Jose on Thursday—or that we can be, if we want to be. The next night, from different hotels, we speak again. For me, no sensation is more intoxicating than lying alone in bed, strange room, strange city, talking to someone I barely know who's also disoriented and on her own. Her voice becomes my chief reality; lacking other landmarks, I cling to it. And she clings to my voice. Each other is all we have. By Thursday, as we park our rented Sables in front of a restaurant that neither of us has eaten at but that both of us have read good things about in Great West's in-flight magazine, *Horizons*, a sense of destiny beckons. Until dessert.

Chance is an erratic matchmaker. Now and then it seats me next to women I wouldn't dream of approaching on my own. On other occasions it dishes up a Wendy, superficially suitable but with a flaw. And a few times, I fear, it has offered me perfection.

"When will you be in Seattle?" Kara asks.

"I get in Wednesday."

"Late?"

"Mid-afternoon. But I might have to go to Arizona instead."

"Here are your instructions. Listening? Go straight to the Pike Street Market—it shuts at six—and order twelve pounds of king salmon, alder-smoked. Send it overnight to Mom's, but make sure you inspect it first. Look for red, firm meat."

"I can't do this over the phone?"

"You have to see it. Make sure it's good fish."

"By the weekend it won't be fresh, though."

"It's smoked. It'll keep. Don't flake out on me this time. Don't pull another Santa Fe."

She wounds me. Santa Fe was a fluke, and not my fault. Our mother had visited a gallery there during one of her winter Winnebago runs with her current husband, the Lovely Man. (So called because he's small, he hardly speaks, and he has no discernible personality.) She fell in love with a Zuni bracelet there and described it to Julie, who mentioned it to Kara, who ordered me, on my next trip to New Mexico, to buy the thing as a gift from the whole family on my mother's sixty-fifth birthday. I did my best, but due to a buildup of errors in the description, the piece my mother ultimately received was Hopi, ill-fitting, overpriced, and, as my mother told the Lovely Man (who then told Kara, proving he's not so lovely), "positively god-awful."

"Unfair," I say.

"Well, this is your chance to redeem yourself."

"Unfair."

"There's one other thing," says Kara. "Tammy Jansen, Julie's maid of honor. She's in St. Louis now. Her car's in the shop, so she's going to have to fly up, except that she can't afford the fare they quoted. Twelve hundred dollars round-trip! I hate these airlines."

"Fine," I say. "We'll both chip in six hundred."

"I already offered. When she tried to book, though, they told her they'd run out of seats."

I know what's coming. Take a hard line, I tell myself. Don't budge. You have a policy, you've stated it often, and now you will have to repeat it for the record.

"Maybe you could cash in some miles," says Kara.

I love my sister. Unfortunately, she's ignorant. She doesn't fly on any regular basis, so she doesn't know what I've been up against out here. For years, Great West has been my boss, my sergeant, dictating where I went and if I went, deciding what I ate and if I ate. My mileage is my one chance to strike back, to snatch satisfaction from humiliation.

"We'll need to find another way," I say.

"This is ridiculous, Ryan. This is sad."

"How's Mom? Have you talked to her?"

"Call her this year, will you? She thinks you've turned into butter, disappeared."

"Those two move around more than I do."

"Be honest: Were you in Salt Lake last week?" she says. "Maybe you have a girl here. I'm concerned. What if you're leading some shameful double life? What if you're in trouble and need help? You're awfully isolated, the way you live."

"Isolated? I'm surrounded," I say.

"We're getting off track now."

"You started this whole subject."

"Let's leave it that Kara's worried. Now let's rewind. Tammy needs to get here from Missouri."

Solving the problem isn't my sister's goal. She rejects any number of reasonable proposals—an Amtrak ticket ("Tammy throws up on trains"); a rental car ("The long drive will exhaust her")—and insists on testing my resistance to giving something away that cost me nothing—or so it seems to her. She calls my mileage rule "this stupid glitch of yours," and though I'm screaming inside, I don't explain myself. The lines we draw that make us who we are are potent by virtue of being non-negotiable, and even, at some level, indefensible. Sally will not wear synthetics. That's who she is. Billy won't touch eggs. That's Billy for you. To apologize for your personal absolutes, for what Sandy Pinter calls your "Core Attachments," means apologizing for your very existence.

The conversation ends here: "My miles are mine."

I put down the phone. I have a plane to catch.

three

i know of no pleasure more reliable than consuming a great American brand against the backdrop featured in its advertising. Driving a Ford pickup down brown dirt roads. Swigging a Coke on the beach in Malibu. Flying Great West over central Colorado. It's a feeling of restfulness and order akin, I suspect, to how the ancient Egyptians felt watching the planets line up above the Pyramids. You're in the right place, you're running with the right forces, and if the wind should howl tomorrow, let it.

Below me, through the milky oval window, I can see a pair of alpine lakes glowing an unnatural chemical blue, the color of pools inside nuclear reactors. Mountains topped by radio towers rise to the south and west. That's Aspen there, the runs cut like bowling alleys between the pines, the metal roofs of the lodges and second homes sending up Morse code glints of morning sunlight. It's a good day in Airworld. I turn on my tape recorder and enjoy a few minutes of Verbal Edge through headphones.

We're flying at half capacity, if that—Desert Air's discounts have been poaching passengers. It's more than a price war, it's opera, this duel. Young Soren Morse, with his B-school line of blarney, against Major Buck Garrett, Korea flying ace. The marketer versus the aviator. Sad. Sad because Garrett, the rugged national treasure, doesn't have a prayer. He does his own TV spots to save money and comes off as a crank. Worse, he refuses to institute a bonus program. Garrett believes that cheap tickets sell themselves, and so they do, for a certain kind of customer—retirees who fly once a year, if that.

Standing on her seat a few rows up, a toddler plays peekaboo with me. The secret involvements children have with strangers behind their parents' backs. I wink, she ducks. "Recognizance: a bond or obligation entered into before a court of law." I study the backs of other passengers' heads. A Dairy Queen spiral of frosty, sprayed gray hair, pinned with a platinum snake. A polished bald spot dented in the center and freckled in the dent.

It's the people I'll never meet who most intrigue me.

"Seditious: given to promoting revolt."

I smile to myself. It all connects up here. Across the aisle from me a famous businessman, a securities analyst with his own TV show and a foundation for troubled urban youth, has fallen asleep with a Sprite in his right hand and the beam from the overhead reading light shining into his slack and gaping mouth. The gold in there is amazing, a savage image that I feel strangely privileged to behold. The flight attendant peeks, too—we share a smirk. That mouth moves markets, and look at it: an ore field!

Celebrities always seem slightly lost on planes. Five years ago, I found myself surrounded by a rock band I'd worshiped as a kid. Two of them sat alone in their own rows and two had girls with them. Their trademark hairstyles—tortured, spiky crests of dull black thatch—looked overdone in such a neutral setting. The drummer, an alleged hotel-room smasher who'd supposedly had his blood replaced at an exclusive clinic in Geneva, thumbed a handheld video game. The singer, the star, sat still and stared ahead as though he'd lost power and was waiting for repairs. His fame seemed to call for a class beyond first, and I couldn't help but think less of him, somehow, for sharing a cabin with the likes of me.

The professional athletes stick out most of all. The moment they were scouted in their teens everything stopped for them. Just stay well and eat. They're served special meals, fat steaks with huge chef's salads, and if they want more salt they hail a trainer, who tells a flight attendant, who hops to it. The players discuss their injuries, their cars, their investments in nightclubs and auto dealerships. It's a sleepy existence, from what I can see, devoted to conserving energy. Parents push sheepish kids to shake their hands and the athletes oblige with a minimum of effort, sometimes without even turning their massive heads. Such inertia, such stillness. I envy it.

This is the place to see America, not down there, where the show is almost over. After college, I crossed the country with a girlfriend, loading a Subaru wagon with beer and sleeping bags and flipping coins to pick that day's state highway. The girl was sheltered, the daughter of two professors who'd consulted with campus colleagues on her upbringing. No TV. A multilingual reading list. She hungered for mini-golf, for roadside farm stands, for wicked stares from old-timers in greasy spoons. She read *On the Road* as we drove, declaimed the thing. I knew I was being used—her native guide—and that she'd drop me once the trip looped back to her parents' cottage on Nantucket, but I wanted to show her something she hadn't seen.

I failed. Nothing there. That America was finished. Too many movies had turned the deserts to sets. The all-night coffee shops served Egg Beaters. And everywhere, from dustiest Nebraska to swampiest Louisiana, folks were expecting us, the road-trip pilgrims. They sold us Route 66 T-shirts, and they took credit cards. The hitchhikers didn't tell stories, they just slept, and the gas stations were self-service, no toothless grease monkeys. In Kansas, my girlfriend threw away the book at a truckstop Dunkin' Donuts stand and called her father for a ticket home. She's a Penn State sociologist now, raising her kids the same way she was raised, and I doubt that she's thought twice in fifteen years about our hoboing. No reason to. The real America had left the ground and we'd spent the summer circling a ruin. Not even that. An imitation ruin.

The TV stock-picker wakes and blows his nose, then inspects the airline hand towel for lost gold. I take off my earphones and open the AirMall catalogue tucked in my seatback to browse for wedding presents. AirMall guarantees next-day delivery on items ordered in-flight, via airphone, and features offbeat products not found in stores: silver space pens whose ink flows upside down, alarm clocks that beam the time onto the ceiling, portable inversion boards for back pain. Sometimes I fall for these gimmicky wonder items, sending them ahead to my hotel so I'll have something waiting with my name on it. I have a weakness for white-noise machines that simulate waterfalls and breaking surf. Lately, I can't sleep without these gadgets. The one I own now is tuned to "summer cloudburst" and I can't wait to turn it on tonight.

I narrow my choices to a robot lawn mower that tracks a grid of buried wires (dyslexic Julie will misread the instructions and send the thing careening across the street) and the safer selection, a six-piece luggage "system" fashioned from heavy nylon with Kevlar inserts. It's not a set I'd ever buy for myself—a light packer, I prefer leather, for its warmth, and because the patterns of scuffs and scratches provide a fossil record of my travels—but for Julie and Keith of the annual jaunt to Florida and the Christmas coach tour of the Holy Land that my mother and the Lovely Man gave them in lieu of a secular honeymoon, these bags should be the ticket. Pockets galore for Julie's personal pharmacy, stain-resistant if she vomits on them.

The girl is past delicate. She frightens me.

Though Kara won't forgive me if I go through with it, I owe Keith a briefing this week, the whole case history, starting with the bogus model search when Julie was fifteen. Like the other local girls caught up in the fraud, she stopped eating. She ran. She gorged on laxatives. When the promoters vanished with her entry fee, she and a few of the other dupes kept dieting. They started shoplifting, formed a little crime club. The school called in social workers from St. Paul.

There was a drug bust, a suicide attempt. Eventually, something turned the girls around, though. They filled out. They got educations. They learned some sense.

Except for my kid sister. So much grief. The teenage marriage. The teenage divorce. The year in massage school. The food fads and the pills. The racist second husband who went to Sandstone for forging savings bonds on a color copier. And only lately, in the last two years, a kind of peace for Julie, a new purpose, rehabilitating injured animals on a Humane Society rescue farm. She even has a degree now—Licensed Vet Tech—and though she's still thin, her eyes go where she points them, which I feel is progress.

Now this wedding. This Keith. I give her two years before she's in a hospital.

"Excuse me."

The stock expert looks.

"One question, sir. I know who you are and I know I shouldn't ask this—"

"Be my guest. I'm used to it by now."

"If you were to buy a single issue tomorrow—a blue chip, as a gift, for the long term, for someone who can't really handle her own affairs—what would it be?"

"The recipient's a minor?"

"Basically. Actually, she's thirty-one."

"But flaky?"

"At a fairly high level. Yes."

"Female, I'm guessing?"

"Extremely female."

"Right." The expert swabs his tongue across his gold

mine. He's thinking, he's taking me seriously. Bless him. There's grace in Airworld. I meet it all the time.

"I'd recommend General Electric, but I can't. Their media holdings offend me morally. A long-term investment should elevate its owner. That puts me in the minority, but so be it. This isn't well known, but I count among my clients the American Lutheran Church. That calls for standards."

I'm inspired. I truly am. The man's a giant. And to think that, just now, I have him to myself.

"I'll tell you what I told the Lutheran bishops: load up on Chase Manhattan under sixty. Chase is your baby. A house upon a rock."

The flight's only stop is Elko, and knowing Elko, no one will get on or off when we set down. A curious city—Basque restaurants on every corner, a few small casinos, miles of trailer parks, and a Main Street boutique that sells candy panties to prostitutes. I once spent an evening there with a billionaire, 104th on the Forbes 400 list, whose family toy firm I'd been called in to downsize. The man was shopping for a hobby ranch and was eager to visit a brothel, but not alone. He had me hold his wallet in case of trouble and I found myself poking through it while he partied. I felt that a billionaire's wallet might teach me something. Inside I found an expired driver's license whose photo convinced me the man had had a face-lift. Also, a credit card. White. Not platinum, white. When I think of Elko I think of that pale card, of what it could buy. Whole states. The desert itself. After the billionaire finished with his girl, we returned to

his jet, which had twin sleeping cabins. I heard him mastur-
bating through the bulkhead, seducing himself in a
made-up female voice that sounded like one of those
singing-chipmunk records.

What you don't want, I remember thinking that night, is
to feature in such a man's dreams. I'm scared of billionaires,
though not for the same reasons my father was. If their goal
was just world domination, we'd all be safer; the problems
arise when they tamper with individuals.

I turn on my tape again, then click it off. Too many
words in one day and I go fuzzy. The flight attendant leans
close. I'm sure I know her.

"Sir?"

"You're Denise. Chicago—Los Angeles."

"Just reassigned last week." She quiets her voice. "We're
having difficulties with a passenger. The man in the golf
shirt"—she points—"beside the lady there?"

"Yes?"

"He's intoxicated. He's bothering her. I know you're
enjoying having your own row here . . ."

"Not at all. Bring her up. I'll move my things."

"She's flying through to Reno."

"Send her up."

I form first impressions more quickly than other people. The woman's sense of space is complicated; her every
movement seems to be a choice between precisely two alternatives, one wholly right, the other completely wrong. She
pauses, and in her pause she weighs decisions, rising halfway
from her seat, then all the way, rotating her shoulders and
then her neck, each action acute and separate, like an in-

sect's. It's not unattractive, the way she stops and starts, but it speaks of a certain painful doubleness, as though she once suffered a paralyzing accident and had to retrain her muscles through therapy. I was in such an accident myself once, though the damage it caused is not for me to judge.

Instead of letting her past me to the window seat, I scoot over one space, my briefcase on my lap. After being trapped beside the drunk, the woman will want an open exit path.

"That jerk," she says.

"They're everywhere these days."

"I'm afraid I attract them. I must send out some signal."

"It's the luck of the draw. We're seated by computer."

So here we are. It's all decided now: in what tone of voice we'll converse, how close we'll sit, how far we'll delve into each other's stories. Such negotiations happen quickly—they're over before you're aware they've even begun, and everything that follows between two strangers just extends this instant contract. We've already faced a common foe, the drunk, and established our superior humanity, but that will be the sum of it, I'll wager. Our vectors are fixed: ever onward, parallel, but fated not to touch or cross. Romance needs conflict, a collision course, but we've been doomed to agreement, to empathy.

She's not the one. The list grows ever shorter. We'll joke and kid, we'll discover odd affinities, but it's over between us, and I'm relieved.

"They shouldn't have served him. He boarded stinking," she says. "I thought the FAA had rules on that."

"They're only enforced in economy and coach. Welcome to the jungle."

"I'm Alex."

"Ryan."

Alex, I'd guess, is an artist of some kind, though not the highbrow type that I dislike. She works on contract. She's learned to sell herself. Her ugly glasses are the giveaway; their dark, chunky frames, which are just this side of dowdy, have an ironic, thrift-shop quality meant to convey independence and eclecticism. Before CTC, when I still did marketing, I worked with graphic designers from time to time; accessories meant everything to them. They'd wear a burlap sack for pants if they could find a cute belt to hold it up.

"Going to Reno for work or for the action?"

She frowns. "The action?"

"The gambling," I say. I can see that Alex doesn't bet, but I sense she regards herself as a free spirit. She'll be flattered that I could mistake her for a player.

"No, but I'd love to learn. I like the craps tables. All the backchat, all the jabbering. I'm here on work—I coordinate events."

"Weddings?"

"Also conventions and benefits. Instant ersatz ambience my specialty."

I contemplate two responses to this comment, which, thanks to Verbal Edge, I understand. One: I'll warn her against maligning her work. It seems adult and witty, yes, but go too far and the joke will be on you. Two: I'll laugh. I'll let her mock herself until she becomes depressed in earnest, and then I'll weigh in with a pep talk and sage advice based on my work with redundant executives who minimized the value of their jobs until the day they lost them and broke down bawling or drove to the river and swallowed a hundred Advils. I'd guess her age as twenty-eight or so, the point when working women first taste success and realize they've been conned. A crucial moment—it's when the ache sets in. Sometimes it leads to marriage and a family. Sometimes it spurs devotion to a cause. Men reach this point, too, of course, but it seldom results in major changes. That's how it happened for me in my late twenties, when it dawned on me that CTC was not just a temporary assignment. I weighed my alternatives, convinced myself I had none, and here I am— subsisting on smoked almonds, chasing miles.

I laugh with her. Run yourself down, go on ahead.

"I'm doing a benefit for an interim senator. The wife of the guy who died water-skiing."

"Nielsen."

"Widowhood with a purpose, that's my theme. Grays and golds for a color scheme. The food? Rare prime rib, I'm thinking. All that blood. Sacrifice and renewal. Martyr-dom."

"Complicated work."

"It's textbook, actually."

This statement offends me; it's subtly disrespectful. Alex doesn't yet know my occupation, but I doubt that she takes me for a neurosurgeon or someone whose work is more challenging than hers. So if she's just a hack, an uninspired grunt, then what does that make me—this man with a stan-dard-issue side-part, wearing a lightweight navy travel suit and synthetic-blend odor-resistant stay-up socks.

"What's textbook about it?"

"It's just so middle-class."

"What's wrong with that?" I ask her.

She touches her glasses, pushing them higher on her bony nose. Her face is handsome, angular, distinguished, the product of generations of prudent mating by people who worked hard and skimped on frills only to give rise to a bohemian.

Her attitude reminds me of my college years. My father should never have sent me to DeWitt. It was the name that impressed him, the slick brochure, the aura of humanistic broad-mindedness. In fact, the place was a haven for bratty pricks—reggae-grooving, seaboard hippie kids in school to refine their contempt for people like me, who'd been raised in the wheaty void between the coasts by mothers who draped plastic on their sofas, which they called davenports. My roommate, a boy from the Washington, D.C., suburbs, smoked dope from a Native American hand-carved pipe, cashed monthly checks from his trust fund that made me gulp, and listened to "world music" on a high-end stereo worth more than one of my father's propane tankers. He called himself a feminist, of all things, and enlisted me in "a self-criticism circle." We met in our opium den of a dorm room, its windows blacked out with Indian batiks that forced me to use an alarm to wake for classes, and when it was my turn to confess my prejudices, I announced that I had none. My roommate kicked me out. I rigged up an "independent concentration" in Comparative Commercial Culture—as close as a kid could get to going square there—and bought a nice glowing Timex and started wearing it.

"I'm sorry to hear you feel that way," I say. "If your

work's beneath you, you should change professions." Maybe we're bound for conflict, after all.

Alex produces, from somewhere, a small inhaler, and mists her lungs with steroids. Her color changes. Not for the better, necessarily.

"I already have. Events are my act two. It's not the job, it's the clients who wear me out. This lady senator. A power bitch. She sent back my sketches of the floral arrangements with big black X's through them and a note: 'More funereal, please.' Can you believe it? Her poor old husband's beheaded by a speedboat and she sees a fund-raising gimmick."

"A Democrat?"

"You've got it. I ought to switch parties."

"They're both corrupt."

"Disempowerment machines," she says.

She's speaking my language now. Maybe she's read Sandy Pinter, or read of him. Maybe there are layers to this Alex.

"So what do you do?" she says.

I leave out my work in CTC and play up my infrequent coaching jobs, using my Reno assignment to illustrate. It's a canned presentation: the Art Krusk story. Retired army tank captain and cancer survivor opens modest Mexican buffet featuring mariachis and wife's recipes. Expands his operation with borrowed money, staying one step ahead of swelling debt load by targeting growing market: young working families. Institutes generous compensation plan to retain top employees but overshoots, breeding widespread resentment when he scales back. Absenteeism follows. An act of sabotage: the suspected contamination of spiced ground meat with human feces. The resulting *E. coli* outbreak sickens dozens and tarnishes Krusk's name. Among my recommendations: a company sports league to raise morale and, on the public relations front, sponsorship of medical "scholarships" for needy local children.

A snack is served: bagel sandwiches of ham or turkey dressed with mayonnaise and lettuce leaves. Alex asks questions, good ones, about Krusk's case, probing the fine points of Brand Reconstruction—a term she actually uses. She's with me, frowning and nodding, synthesizing. It orders her features, draws life into her eyes.

When I'm finished, Alex tells me about herself. She hails from a town in Wyoming, as small as mine, whose claim to fame is the time a local deputy stopped Robert Redford for speeding. I can top this. Back in Polk Center we had a doctor, a friend of my father's through the Shriners lodge, who specialized in medically questionable oversize breast implants. He once performed surgery on a president's mistress. We knew this because the local Western Union handled a White House get-well telegram. The clerk made a copy and tucked it in the files of the county history museum, where my father took me to view it as a teenager, explaining that it was important for young men to see through the saintly posturings of their leaders.

"Wise parent," Alex says.

"I miss him badly."

"When did he pass away?"

"Six years ago."

I feel the syrup well up and stop myself. My memories of my happy youth confuse people—they can't tell if I'm bragging, kidding, or crazy. It's a problem for me, a curious burden: my golden Mark Twain boyhood of State Fair corn dogs and station wagon vacations to Yellowstone. So few shadows, so much, such varied, light. The autumn radiance of sunset boxcars bearing away the grain of Lewis County; the midsummer glare off the fenders of my Schwinn. And my father, the seeming source of all this light, dressed in Red Wing boots and Carhartt coveralls as he strode out at dawn to his truck, a yellow supercab, and woke the town to another day of work. His deliveries fueled the county's furnaces and heated its morning showers. He warmed the world.

But who wants to hear this? No one. I used to try. I tried in the creative writing seminar. A girl half my age said "Show, don't tell." It's pointless.

Alex peels the turkey from her bagel, folds the slice in half, in half again, wraps the whole package in lettuce, and bites down. I admire her willingness to take what's given and improve on it. It's a traveler's trait, and I ask her how much she flies. Her numbers are medium: sixty thousand miles in twelve months, all domestic, on Delta and United. Her preferred lodgings are Courtyard Marriotts, although she agrees that Homestead Suites offers an equal value and better food. She opens her wallet and out falls an accordion of clear vinyl pockets holding her VIP cards.

"You're satisifed with Avis?"

"I am," she says.

"They're stingy with the miles. I like Maestro."

"Maestro keeps its vehicles too long. If a car's over twenty-thousand, I get nervous."

"That new outfit, Colonial, isn't bad."

"No instant checkout. I like to park and go. A question," she says. "Have you ever flown with pets?"

"I don't keep pets, but I wouldn't fly with them. The climate controls in the holds are always wacky."

Alex's face sags. "My new cat's along. I couldn't bear to leave him. An Abyssinian."

"I'm sure he'll be fine. Is he tranquilized?"

"One pill. It's a human prescription. Are animal doses different?"

We descend into Elko through layered sheets of smoke. The Sierras are burning this summer, from Tahoe south, and the sun, which has just ticked over into the west, glows hot pink in my window. Bad news for Alex. Reno is even closer to the fires, though she tells me that smoke doesn't bother her, just chemicals. She used to think her allergies were emotional, a product of childhood tension, she says, but now she blames them on solvents, glues, and dyes. She'd like to remain inside to get her breath back, so she asks if I'll check on her kitten with the ground crew.

"Want anything from the terminal? Milky Way?"

"Have to trim down. Can't risk it."

"Understood."

"I try to go light on the carbs when I'm out traveling."

"It affects the digestion, no doubt about it. Smart. With me it's fats and oils. My scalp breaks out."

"Take chromium tablets."

"I have. I've tried them all."

A ground worker, sportily dressed in shorts and cap and looking content, for once, with his union contract, pushes a wheeled staircase against the exit. Stopping off in transit beats arriving. There's the feeling of visiting an island, of stepping, briefly and sweetly, out of time into a scene you've had absolutely no hand in and have no designs on, no intentions toward. A truly neutral charge is tough to find in life, and that's how Elko feels as I deplane: irrelevant and tranquil. A mirage.

On the tarmac I notice a pet crate being unloaded—to give its occupant water, I assume. I approach, but the baggage handler waves me off. Restricted zone. "The cat okay?" I yell. The handler doesn't answer, too much engine noise, but something in his face concerns me as I watch him crouch, unlatch the crate, and reach one arm inside. He flags down a coworker driving a cart and together they peer through the grating at the kitten.

The second man stands and comes over to me. "Yours?"

"A friend's. Is it okay?"

"Has it been tranquilized?"

"Just one pill."

"It's acting awfully sluggish. Make sure it gets more water first thing in Reno."

I pass through the cinder-block terminal, acknowledging one or two Great West employees whose faces I remember from other trips. By rotating its personnel, who pop up again and again in different cities, the airline creates a sense in flyers like me of running in place. I find this reassuring.

I head for the gift shop. According to my HandStar, Art

Krusk has two young daughters, five and nine. I scan the shelves for souvenirs and pick out two figurines of rearing mustangs. Don't all girls love horses? Sure they do. My sisters were horse-obsessed well into their teens, when my mother cut back on their riding as a way to stimulate interest in boys. They hated her for it. My mother was a scientific parent; she'd taught third grade before she married my father. She believed in stages of development. Under her system, keyed to crucial birthdays, teddy bears disappeared when kids turned eight, replaced by clarinets or swimming lessons. She had us baptized at ten, confirmed at twelve, and bought us subscriptions to *Newsweek* at fourteen. How she settled on *Newsweek* I don't know.

The gift shop lady, a buzzardy old gal with nicotine fingers and casino eyes, slides my credit card through her machine. I can tell she'd rather I pay in cash so she can skim a few bucks to play the slots.

"Refused," she says.

"That's impossible."

She shrugs. "Want to try another one?"

I don't. The card is the only one that pays me miles and enters me in a contest for a new Audi. "Try it over. It'll work this time."

Since my payments are current, there has to be a glitch. But maybe my payments aren't current. I think back. The last load of mail delivered to my old address showed signs of mishandling. Two torn envelopes. Was there a credit card bill? I don't remember. I put through a forwarding order ten days ago listing my office at ISM—I think—but as of last Friday nothing had arrived.

"Refused again," the woman says. She hands back the card as though it's covered in microbes.

I pay with cash, forsaking thirty-three miles. Worse, I left my cell phone on the plane, so I can't call the credit card's customer service line until the young guy at the pay phone by the pop machine wraps up his already-endless conversation about a lost mountain bike.

I make a pleading face.

"What?" the man whispers.

"Emergency."

"Me too."

Elko is not my town. I've never done well here.

Alex looks distressed when I return, her lips clamped down so hard on the inhaler that the tendons in her jaw stand up. I motion for her to stay seated and edge in front of her, eyeing my phone, which I won't have time to use, since the credit card company's voice-mail labyrinth will keep me on hold for fifteen minutes, minimum.

"How's my boy? They taking good care of him?"

"Yes, but he's sluggish."

"You saw him?"

I fib. "I did."

Alex looks unreassured. She tucks the inhaler in her seatback pocket and cinches tight her lap belt. I see now that this is a woman who's made her way in life by playing the spread between modern assertiveness and Victorian fragility.

We take off into the smoke. I'm jumpy too now. Aside from a slim civilian corridor that roughly follows I-80 toward California, the central Nevada skies are Air Force territory, a vast mock battleground for the latest jets, some so highly classified and agile that witnesses take them for otherworldly craft. I thought I glimpsed one once: a silver arrowhead corkscrewing straight up into the sun. Radar dishes stud the scrubby mountaintops, tracking war games and bombing runs and dogfights. America's airspace has its own geography, and this is its no-man's-land, ringed by virtual razor wire. If our plane went down here, they might not tell our relatives.

Alex leafs through an issue of *Cosmopolitan,* which seems beneath her, though I do the same thing: read below my level while in flight. Maybe she's trying not to think about the cat, which I suspect she knows she overdosed. I imagine the creature comatose in the hold, surrounded by Styrofoam coolers of frozen trout, boxes of catalogue sweaters, tennis rackets. A plane is a van whose cargo includes people, but there's nothing special about us, we're just tonnage, less profitable, pound for pound, than first-class mail.

I take out my pencil and paper and try to work, refining my plan for Art Krusk's commercial comeback. I can't say I'm optimistic about his prospects. Healing the wound to Reno's public memory caused by the poison tacos should prove simple, but rehabilitating Art the manager won't be easy. The man's a bitter wreck. Word has it that he's connected to Reno's underworld and that he's placed a bounty on the head of the unknown saboteur. I hope not. Breaking some busboy's arm won't bring his patrons back.

Art may not make it, but he's my only coaching client, my sole relief from the dolors of CTC. Maybe the best I can do is help him fail. There are two kinds of consultants, basically: the accountants and operations specialists who minister to the body of the patient, and those who treat its mind and spirit, approaching the company as a vital being animated by conflicts and desires. Enterprises feel and think and dream, and often when they die, as Art's may die, and as my father's propane business died, they die of loneliness. Businesses may thrive on competition, Sandor Pinter wrote in one of his books, but they need love and understanding, too.

Alex goes off to use the bathroom, leaving me with decisions to make. Every flight is a three-act play—takeoff, cruising, descent; past, present, future—which means that it's time to prepare for how we'll part, on what terms, and with what expectation. She already knows I'm staying at Homestead Suites and I know that she'll be at Harrah's on the Strip, overseeing her benefit, which starts at eight. Maybe she has a local flame, and maybe she thinks I do. She'd be right. Anita deals Pai Gow poker at Circus Circus, a twenty-nine-year-old Sarah Lawrence grad who came west with the Park Service as a stream biologist but fell in with the local color crowd. We got together, chastely, a month ago and took in a traditional Irish dance troupe at the Silver Legacy, but I don't plan to look her up again. Anita had ugly opinions about the Asians who patronize her table, and though I humored her bigotry at first, I hated myself for it afterwards. She's one of those women who take up right-wing views as a substitute for a pistol or can of Mace—in self-defense, as a warning to creeps and stalkers. It's tiresome armor. Time-consuming, too. The Kennedy family this, the World Bank that.

In truth, I don't have much time for Alex, either, assuming that we have prospects, which I doubt. No, the challenge for us will be to separate without so much as a gesture toward this evening. We'll have to use the descent to drift apart and retract any curiosity we've shown. To confirm to ourselves that we worked best as strangers.

It's time to bore each other, if possible.

"California tomorrow," I say when she returns, rosy-cheeked and smelling of moist towelettes. "You know how, in magazine food surveys you read, it rivals New York now? I think that's wrong."

"How so?"

"I just think it's wrong. Where you headed after Reno?"

"Back to Salt Lake City. I just moved there."

"Are you a Mormon?"

"No. They're trying, though. I like having people coming to the door."

"They wear undergarments they claim are bulletproof. I swear it. They'll tell you stories of stopping bullets."

"I haven't heard that one yet."

"Just date a Mormon."

"I thought they didn't date."

"They date like mad. And they're ready with the engagement ring, first night."

I stop. This is getting too interesting, too personal.

"You're sure it was *my* cat you saw, not someone else's? They lose them, I've heard. People's pets wind up in Greece."

"What's that movie called, *Amazing Journey*? The one where

the family relocates to a new town and their dog walks a thousand miles or something to find them? I think it fights a bear along the way."

"There are more than one of those movies. It's a genre."

"I know that word, but I've never quite spit it out. Pronunciation anxiety."

"I know. I'm like that with 'cigarillo.' Hard *l*?"

"For me."

"I don't think that's right, though."

"I'll check sometime."

It's working: we're barely looking at each other and there's the Reno skyline. Ten more minutes. The only threat is our pride; mine smarts a little. Our agreement—the one I drew up for both of us—called for a tender, reluctant edging away, not total detachment. Can't we reassess this? After all, this is Reno we're visiting, a city whose whole economy is founded on errors in judgment and doomed trysts. Can't we at least acknowledge the bitter tang of having grown so prudent with our bodies?

No, because now the drunk is acting up again, heckling the flight attendant for cutting him off. He flicks an ice cube at her, cackles, snorts, his face a chaotic red clown's mask. Alex flinches. Given how much she flies, she should be used to this—these outbursts of entitled rage—but she cowers like a baby rabbit. My chance to put a fatherly arm around her? I'm considering it when the copilot strides up, cinematically handsome in his uniform and cutting such a capable male figure that any protective move on my part would only come off as puny and derivative. He threatens the drunk with arrest when we touch down. He raises one arm. The drunk sputters, then falls silent. The copilot orders the man to fetch the ice cube and stands there, hands on his hips, while he bends down.

The miniature drama has sealed us in our own skins. Alex retrieves her inhaler. She looks spent. She's ready to pick up her kitten, hail a cab, and curl up in bed to the sound of *Headline News*. She'll eat a room service salad with the curtains drawn, then sneak a Snickers from the mini-bar. She'll jam in earplugs, don a blackout mask, and lay down with her clothes on for a dreamless nap.

In no time we're at the gate and on our feet, shuffling out of the plane like day care toddlers holding one of those ropes with all the loops. I walk a step behind her. It's good-bye.

"Good luck with that witch of a senator."

"I'll need it."

"That Colonial checkout procedure? They've stream-lined it. You might want to give them another shot."

"I will."

Where do they go when they leave me? The last I see of her, she's standing by the baggage carousel, fluffing her hair and waiting for the pet crate. I'd be surprised if the kitten arrived alive, and I realize that I've been suppressing real anger at Alex for risking its health just to ease her loneliness. That was my job, her seatmate's, but she let me go. And I let her go. We forgot that in Airworld each other is all we have.

four

i used to try to be interesting. That passed. Now I try to
be pleasant and on time.

That will be impossible today. Behind the rental car
counter a dull trainee labors to slip a key onto a ring and fold
my contract to fit inside its envelope. He should be in college,
judging by his age, but instead he's already failing at his first
job. After he runs my credit card—still frozen; I have to use my
AmEx from ISM, which generates no miles—he manages to
drop it and step on it, scratching and ruining the magnetic
strip. The kid's pathetic excuse is greasy hands; he just finished eating a box of chicken strips. I tell him he'd better eval-
uate his goals and he acts as though I've complimented him,
thanking me and handing me a map.

"Excuse me, what's your job?" I say.

"My job? Filling out rental agreements."

"No it's not. Your job is providing a service that meets a
need."

He stares at me.

"Tell me the need," I say.

"A four-door Nissan."

"Actually, what I want, my basic desire, is to get to a business meeting across town punctually, comfortably, and safely. The Nissan's a means to an end. It's just a detail. Try to think less about isolated tasks and more about the over-arching process. It will serve you, believe me."

"So you're some millionaire?"

"No. Do I have to be rich to give advice?"

"For me to listen to it, you do," he says.

The car, a new model I've never driven before, smells of a fruity industrial deodorant that's worse than any odor it might be masking. The mirrors point off in random directions as though the last driver was a schizophrenic. The radio is tuned to Christian rock. Christian rock is a private vice of mine; it's as well-produced as the real thing, but more melodic, with audible, rhymed lyrics. The artists have real talent, and they're devoted. After the cops led away her second husband, Julie spent a summer as a born-again and worked in a St. Paul religous gift shop whose manager played in a band called Precious Blood. We took in one of their concerts, a spectacle of fog and laser lights and colored scrims. The band released white doves during the encore, and afterwards Julie and others rushed the stage and dropped to their knees before a neon cross next to the drum kit. It shook me to see such need in her, such thirst.

I turn up the station, reorient the mirrors, and drive to the guard's booth, waving my rental papers. The old guy winks and raises the red-striped gate arm and I roll over the angled spikes, away.

On the way to Art's house, where he insists on meeting, I dictate some lines for the preface to *The Garage* into the microrecorder at my chin.

> *For years it has been the same message: Grow or die. But is this necessarily the truth? Too often, growth for its own sake leads to chaos: unsustainable capital expansion, ill-timed acquisitions, a stressful workplace. In* The Garage, *I propose a bold new formula to replace the lurching pursuit of profit: "Sufficient Plenitude." Enough really can be enough, that is. A heresy? Not to students of the human body, who know that optimum health is not achieved by ever-greater consumption and activity, but by functioning within certain dynamic parameters of diet and exercise, work and leisure. So too with the corporation, whose core objective should not be the amassing of good numbers, but the creation and management of abundance. Read on and you will discover in* The Garage: *the Four Plenteous Attitudes, the Six False Missions . . .*

Where these words come from I have no idea. Like the rest of the book, which I wrote over ten months, dictating for two hours before bed in a succession of identical suites whose regulation layouts and amenities allowed me to work undistracted, without thinking, the preface feels like a gift, a transcribed dream. What this means for its value, I don't know. I fear sometimes that the book is just the overflow of a brain so overstuffed with jargon that it's spontaneously sloughing off the excess. I've allowed myself to reread it only once, and some of the ideas felt foreign to me, with no connection to how I actually operate. Is it possible to be wiser on the page than you are in life? I'm hoping so.

Art Krusk's directions guide me through the foothills into the smoke, which smells like burning tires. I know Art moved to a golf course recently, but it's hard to imagine green fairways on these brown mounds. Where does the water come from? It's a sin. The golf culture, which I've had ample chances to join, draws its allure, I'm convinced, from wastefulness, from the lavish imbalance between its massive inputs—acreage, labor, fertilizer, machines—and its nonexistent output. Sad. The few times I've played the game, I've come away feeling like an ecological glutton.

I reach a gatehouse manned by an old woman so flayed by the sun that her skin is like a bat's wing, all pigmentless gray tissue and thready veins. I state my name and she consults her clipboard.

"Art said go on up, the house is open. He had an errand."

"When will he be back?"

"He tore out of here an hour ago. Don't know. Try to drive slowly and watch out for the carts. A lot of our residents won't hear you coming."

The development is unfinished, with heaps of sand along its noodle-shaped streets and cul-de-sacs. With so many tiny lanes and dead-end byways, the developer ran out of normal street names. I take a left on Lassie Drive and curve around right on Paul Newman Avenue. The houses ("Starting in the mid $200s," according to a billboard) ape many styles, the most popular being a sort of Greco-ranch thing combining flat tile roofs with stocky columns. Art's house is among the more elaborate models, with a fresh sod lawn whose seams still show and a faux-marble fountain of dancing cupids. For someone in his predicament, it's offensive. His restaurants send half of Nevada to the ER and the man builds a palace in Mafia Moderne.

I'm tempted to leave a stinging note and return to the airport. Cutting Art adrift would let me build in crucial extra hours to my overloaded schedule. I could buy a thesaurus and touch up *The Garage*. I could get to a gym and tone my flabby lats. ISM would understand—Art's a small client and a chronic late payer—but I have to consider MythTech's feelings, too. If it's true that they're auditioning me from afar, I have to behave impeccably this week. Plus, I like Art. He's crude, but he's a searcher.

I dial the credit card people on my mobile and wander behind the house to the pool, a free-form blue pond with an artificial island and two stray golf balls lying on the bottom, looking like undissolved Alka-Seltzer tablets. My call is passed from computer to computer and then to a person who only sounds like one.

"Where are you presently located?" she asks.

"Nevada. Reno."

"Did you make any large purchases last Friday?"

"That's why I'm calling. You cut my credit off."

"Who am I speaking to?"

I lose my temper. "I'm out here in the middle of a business trip, totally dependent on your card, adhering to our agreement in good faith—"

The woman adjusts her tone and talks me down. She explains that for the past few days someone has been moving from state to state, ringing up major charges on my account: fifteen hundred dollars in a Salt Lake City electronics store, two hundred to a national teleflorist. The purchases didn't quite suit my customer profile, so the bank froze my card. The latest charge appeared last Saturday: four hundred dollars in a Texas western store.

That one was mine. The boots. I tell the woman.

"You're certain you're in Reno now?"

"I'm here."

"And you didn't send flowers last Thursday? By telephone?"

I stand at the edge of the pool, confused and spooked. Ordering flowers for my mother's birthday has been on my to-do list for a week; I even picked out an arrangement from an ad in August's *Horizons*. But did I send them? Nothing.

"Where, to what state, did the flowers go?" I ask.

"Our information isn't that detailed."

"That's one sentimental thief."

"We see it all, sir."

I've read about this: identity theft, it's called. They grab your data, your history, your files. They duplicate your economic self. They scan your signature and forge ID cards and head out into the world under your name to gorge on DVD players, fur coats. The damage can be extensive, requiring months for the victim to clear up and undo. He has to work backwards along the chain of fraud, reclaiming his reputation, his good name. But maybe I'm panicking. Maybe my case is simpler. Maybe some crook just found an old receipt in the trash can of an airport deli.

"There's something I don't understand," the woman says. "You still have the card in your possession?"

"Yes." My life on the defensive has begun. "But I wasn't in Utah last week."

"Where were you?"

I'm thinking. My fast-forward functions, but my reverse is stuck. I can't even remember when I started forgetting things.

"Who else knows your schedule?"

"Assistant. Travel agent."

"Is she trustworthy?"

"He. How would I know? Let's bottom-line this: how soon can you send a replacement card?"

"Immediately. Where should it go?"

"Ontario, California. Send it to Homestead Suites."

"That's a hotel?"

"Where are you, anyway?"

"Grand Forks, North Dakota."

"It's a chain of executive lodging facilities."

I'm still on the line with the woman when Art shows up, dressed for comfort in a black mesh tank top and a pair of clingy runner's shorts that graphically mold his chunky, big man's crotch. He looks like a wilted circus muscleman. His hair is longer than I remember—it must have been tied up when I last saw him. It falls to below his shoulders, a lush gray fan. I've seen such hair on female Christian rockers and always found it intriguing, but not on Art.

He signals me to take my time and busies himself with a

telescopic pool tool, vacuuming bits of debris from the water and dragging the golf balls to the shallow end, where he wades in, bends over, and retrieves them, then tosses them over his fence back onto the course as if he were hurling grenades at the Nazis. He seems to be at odds with his new setup, seeing only its shortcomings and flaws. People in their fifties shouldn't change homes. My parents never recovered from their dream house in a subdivision east of town, where they moved just before my father lost his gas trucks. The Jacuzzi embarrassed them, though they thought they'd like it. The surplus bedrooms made my father blush.

I pocket my phone and join Art at a table shaded by a Pepsi logo umbrella speckled with gray ash. He's been pilfering from his restaurants—a bad sign. A black, volcanic-looking rock holds down a rain-warped fishing magazine and a stack of ads for Reno escort services—the sort of flyers old men hand out on street corners, that get carried a block before they're crumpled and tossed.

"You'll note the lack of a woman's touch," Art says. "Coquilla left Saturday morning. Want a drink?"

"I'm sorry. For good?"

"Well, you can't have a drink. She took all the glasses and stuff. I hope for good."

"Why would you hope that, Art? You love your wife."

"She did it, Ryan. She left a note, confessing. That's where I was just now: at my fancy lawyer's, turning over the evidence. I'm sick. See this spot on my shirt? It's ulcer puke. You believe this crap? I gave her everything. Fiesta Brava was *hers. Her* recipes. Does the rot always come from within, or what? Enlighten me. Is that like some great truth of history? Mixing up bacteria in hamburger and feeding it to kids in paper hats."

"That's a disturbing picture. You must be devastated."

"The shit I took this morning was purple. Purple!"

"What was her motive?"

"You're the expert. Guess."

Art's right: I already know why his dear wife, with her formal, immigrant's English and shy good looks, torpedoed his dream. I know because I've watched Art, studied him. In the kitchen, training bumbling teens to deep-fry tortilla chips in bubbling lard. In the dining room, booming out ethnic folk songs for howling two-year-olds in booster seats. In the office, pep-talking his servers on the importance of honest tip reporting. Every business, at bottom, is a wish, and Art's wish was for the world to rest secure inside his strong embrace. He didn't boss or push people, he fathered them, but the hidden message of his largesse was that the world was a danger to itself, weak and self-defeating and in error. Even the way he pushed his patrons to eat, instructing his servers to refill diners' plates without being asked, was unwittingly belittling. Art's restaurants were fun and affordable but smothering, and though every dining room featured a full-length painting of Coquilla dressed in native regalia and offering steaming bowls of beans and rice, Fiesta Brava was really about him, his heart and potency. His wife's rebellion was inevitable. A man who confuses his business with his family risks losing both, in my experience.

But Art doesn't wait for me to answer his question.

"She did it because she couldn't stand the smell," he says. "The cooking odors. Can you say 'change of life'? The question is: do I prosecute?"

"Of course not. Liquidate and move on. Enjoy your golf course. Sooner or later, you'll get a new idea and then you can call me and we'll hash it out. Don't force things, though. And rule out hospitality."

"Why's that?"

"You give people more than they want. You cut their air off."

Art drums his fingers on the tinny tabletop and little cinders skitter over the edge. I shift my weight to say I'm on my way. I didn't count on a crisis intervention, and Art isn't in the mood to face hard truths, nor should he have to just now. He never liked my ideas much, anyway; he retained me on the advice of his attorney, a celebrity litigator I met in Airworld and now hear has been disbarred for escrow monkeyshines.

"You hungry, Ryan?"

"I ate on the flight in. I'm truly sorry about Coquilla, Art. I'm guessing she has the children."

"They're hers to keep. She's got them thoroughly brainwashed anyhow. They think that because I'm not Baha'i I'm worthless."

"Coquilla is Baha'i? I never knew."

"They're tough to spot. They blend in with all the other groups."

I stand and extend my hand.

"You going somewhere? I thought I owned your time tonight."

"No charge. I'll tell ISM to go light on you. You're broke."

Art folds his thick arms. "So this is how you operate. Guy loses everything, you're out the door. Well, I need company, Ryan. Look at me. Either you're hitting the town with me tonight and matching me drink for drink or I'm going to tell that guy who called last week that Bingham's a dip, he doesn't finish the job."

"Who called you, Art?"

"He was checking references. Whoever it is you're looking to go to work for."

"And what did you tell him?"

"That my wife just left me, but I'll get back to you once I've blown my brains out. Does All-Star Steaks sound good? I booked a table. We can take your car or mine, it doesn't matter."

"Did this caller sound real or did you smell a prank? One of the guys I work with is a kidder."

"What would you say are my chances of reopening under a new name? Not Mexican—something more sanitary. Middle Eastern?"

"That's not as big a difference as you think. If you insist on staying in hospitality, people are having good luck with donuts now. There's a group from down south that's going national, but you have to co-advertise, and the buy-in's steep."

"No presence in Nevada yet?"

"I doubt it."

"I tried donuts back in '69. They petered out in the seventies. What changed?"

"These are the mysteries."

"No one knows? Come on."

"Maybe they know in Omaha. I'll see."

In science, an experiment is meaningless unless its outcome is repeatable. I feel the same way about restaurants and eating out. Unless a dish can be made to taste as good no matter where it's prepared, LA or Little Rock, it doesn't entice me. I like successful formulas. I like a meal that's been tested and perfected, allowing me to order and relax, knowing the chef won't use me as a guinea pig for his new fruit salsa or what have you. In fact, I prefer establishments that don't need chefs because their training programs are so deft that anyone off the street can run the kitchen. That's why I'm glad that Art chose All-Star Steaks. It's one of the five or six chains that I depend on, whose systematic comforts always satisfy. Glass-cased sports memorabilia line the walls and the waitresses flounce around in shorts and jerseys as though they've just risen from bed with athlete boyfriends. They'll have a lawsuit over that, eventually, but until that time, I'm theirs.

We choose a booth of orange textured vinyl stamped with various major league insignias. My challenge is to find a way to ditch Art without endangering my MythTech reference. Three hours from now there's a flight to Ontario, whose local Homestead is granting double miles due to a construction inconvenience. Two nights there will help me recapture some lost momentum.

We order two of All-Star's signature cocktails: jumbo martinis garnished with cherry tomatoes. To slip away, I'll need to get Art tipsy without going sloppy myself. I'm good at this. One technique is to fill my cheek with alcohol, pretend to swallow, then spit into a napkin during a mock sneeze. Also, if the drinks are clear, I can secretly dump them in my water glass, then carelessly knock it over once it's full. I'm slightly ashamed that I'm not man enough to declare my limits as a drinker, but since no one has ever caught me at my tricks, it's a private shame, easy to deny, like the way I sometimes leave pairs of soiled boxer shorts in hotel room trash cans for the maid.

Art gnaws a breadstick. He's breaking my heart today. Men venture everything when they start a business, not just money. Take my father's case. Before he went into propane, he fixed machinery, making field calls for a John Deere dealer. Sometimes, during the harvest, he'd work all night, driving with his tools from farm to farm, rescuing fouled combines and frozen balers. He took caffeine pills to stay awake and lived on chocolate milk. Then one morning he told us he'd had enough and went to bed for a week. My mother sobbed. What finally brought him downstairs was a phone call informing him of a business loan approval. He put on a tie for the first time since his wedding and walked downtown to sign the documents. When he got back, in a new GMC diesel whose doors and tailgate were stenciled with his name, he was a different person, more distinct. The effect lasted years. He walked in his own spotlight.

The steaks are taking longer than they should, considering that we both ordered them rare. While we wait, Art dissects my credit card difficulties, displaying a knowledge of fraud I'm not surprised by. What I'm up against, he theorizes, is not a lone criminal but a far-flung gang.

"The way they work, they steal your info and only have a day or two to use it, so they set up a rolling purchase schedule. Simultaneous charges in different towns would raise red flags, so they space their buys apart, which makes the computers think you're on a trip. People spend more money when they're traveling, so when the charges start to pile up, the software that's supposed to catch the pattern doesn't kick in right away."

"You know all this . . . ?"

Art eats his cherry tomato, blocking his mouth with a napkin to catch the juice spurt. "There's things you never knew about my restaurants. They had a cash side that wasn't on the books. The standard shenanigans. Everybody does them."

"I guess I'm sorry to hear that. Cash corrupts, though."

"I wanted to make it honestly. I tried. I read all those books, the ones by guys like you. *Overcoming No. Get Real, Get Rich.*"

"Don't judge the good stuff by the trash," I say.

"Visualization. Time analysis. Quality Cubes. I tried all kinds of crap. That thing where you get all your workers in one room and sit completely quiet for eight hours, then write down your thoughts and put them in a box that you never open. All those tricks. And still I was losing money. Losing people. Getting certified letters from state commissions saying so-and-so filed a complaint because you fired her for being queer, when the truth was she had her fingers in the till. And all the inspections. Day and night inspections. Your handicapped toilet needs moving—a thousand bucks. That table's blocking an exit, pay this fine. Health cops, fire cops, tax cops. Total hell. Everyone poking you with his little pitchfork."

"In management we call them 'psychic costs.' " I glare at the waitress to hurry her along.

"Ryan, you don't know. I'm sorry, you just don't. Why is our food late, you're wondering? I'll tell you. Because the lowlife overseeing the kitchen ducked out an hour ago to score some dope and got knifed in the arm behind the Stockman's Club, forcing the owner to call in some old wino he fired last week for coughing up green phlegm into the coleslaw. Human Resources? Try human refuse."

To calm Art, I confess to being a bystander who's never actually run a business himself. It's too late, though, Art's off, and even the arrival of a plate-filling T-bone smothered in onion nuggets and floating in au jus can't stem his bitterness. If this mood hangs on, I don't dare leave—he'll be on the line to MythTech first thing tomorrow, slandering me to the skies. My only hope is that he'll collapse in the next half hour or so. The water trick, due to Art's keen gaze, is out, though, and I've already used the napkin trick. I'll pay the bartender to pour a bomb and make mine a tonic water.

"Full bladder," I say.

"Me too."

I'm startled—joint toilet trips just don't happen with men. Art is even lonelier than I thought.

The side-by-side urinals are filled with ice cubes, a touch I've never had properly explained to me. Holding himself with one hand, Art tips his head back and shakes out his Samson locks. I clench. Can't pee.

"Let's hit the Mustang. It's a rip-off joint, but they fly in their girls from the leading beach resorts. My steak's a joke. It's like chewing a catcher's glove."

"Mine's fine. Let's stay for another drink or two."

"Can't now. I've got a picture in my head."

Art covers the meal with two fifties from his money clip. There are money-clip men and there are wallet men. Money-clip men overtip for even poor service, carry only the freshest currency, and they don't end an evening until they've spent their roll. I'm stuck in Reno. The only way to make Ontario would be to fly to LAX and drive, but I don't feel up to freeway traffic.

The lights of the Strip rake our faces with bars of color. A cowboy in the doorway of a pawnshop flicks a lit cigar butt at our feet that skips into the street beneath a limo with vanity license plates: LTHL DOS. I step on a wet wad of chewing gum, remove it, then promptly step on another one that's stickier. A casino barker costumed as a leprechaun but far too stout for the outfit's emerald tights hands us coupons good for two free spins on something called the Wheel O' Dreams. We pass.

"An hour. That's all I have left in me this evening."

"That's fine," Art says. "I'll probably end up in the VIP room, tied to a water pipe with a sequined thong."

I venture a focus word I've had on file. Use them or lose them. "You old sybarite."

The club is set up as a lounge, no stage, no spotlights, just a maze of tables and leather sofas packed in so tight that the dancers and cocktail girls have to step sideways, brushing hips and nipples, when they pass each other on their rounds. Art tunnels ahead of me through the blue smoke to a spot in the back screened off by potted trees with leaves the shape and size of human hands. We sit, and I feel like a hunter in a blind, hidden but with a full view of the field. The women are a cut above, Art's right; they look cool-to-the-touch, both healthy and intelligent. I can see Art growing anxious as one approaches. He thumbs a couple of breath mints off a roll and chews them hard to release the active ingredients.

Me, I'm not tempted. As a younger man I made the mistake of talking to a stripper, in depth and at length, about her finances. Her income shocked me. It was double mine. She claimed to be saving for college, but when I pressed her I learned that she didn't even have a bank account and supported not one but two delinquent boyfriends. I didn't feel sorry for her, I felt insulted. There I was, the sort of clean achiever this beautiful girl should consider marrying, but instead she was shaking me down for twenties to lavish on my Darwinian inferiors.

The girl settles onto Art's lap and starts her act, gripping the back of his chair to brace herself and arching her lovely, articulated spine. On her shoulder a tattooed daisy spreads its petals. I look away, but Art wants to keep on talking.

"I have an idea if I get out of restaurants. It's like a record or book club, but with power tools. April, you get a cordless drill. May, a reciprocal saw. If you don't want it, you have to ship it back. You know how that works. People can't be bothered. The stuff piles up. It's automatic billing, so they're screwed."

"I don't know. Maybe. I'm leaving ISM, Art. I might not be available to help you."

"Just give me hope. —Not so hard there, hon. I'll rupture."

I'm duty-bound to restore Art's optimism, to point him toward new horizons. I have a thought. At GoalQuest on Thursday I'm meeting Tony Marlowe, one of the industry's highest-earning motivators, who I knew through some friends before he got so huge. He'd come up through the speed-reading racket in California, where he played all the planned retirement communities, but left to build team skills in greater Silicon Valley. The man's pure nitro, a self-made high school dropout whose private sessions turn CEOs to jelly. A few hours with Marlowe, on me—that's what I'll offer.

"I'm writing something on a card here, Art. Don't lose it. This is a onetime-only deal."

I wedge the card under an ashtray, and then I spot him: the TV financial advisor from the flight being worked over by a skinny redhead not twenty feet from my table. His hair is different, blow-dried into waves, but I recognize the noble forehead. I swallow and there's a crackling in my ears as the girl wraps one leg around his crooked old back and bends him at the waist into her chest. His head flops like a corpse's. His mouth drops open. There's a flash of gray tongue, of fillings. I shut my eyes. When I open them, its worse. The girl's fingers are buried in his wiry sideburns and she's kissing his glossy bald spot, licking it. One of his hands hangs limp behind her ass, stuffed with enough cash to last the night.

I watch the old man being jostled and wrung dry. The sensation is gyroscopic, with spinning modules. There's shock and disappointment, but that's the least of it. It's my confidence in Airworld that's been undermined, my faith in the ethical bargain between passengers. If I hadn't come to the Mustang Club tonight, my memory of our moment on the plane would have endured unchallenged and ever-golden. His mild, pious eyes. His pinstriped probity as he entertained my humble plea and sermonized on investing with a conscience. What a sham, and how demoralizing. The way I've lived, the way I've moved around, I've not had the luxury of double-checking what I see and hear. I have to trust. If a man who says he's a doctor hears me cough and tells me I should go on antibiotics, I go on antibiotics. Of course I do. In Airworld honesty carries no penalty and deception has no upside. Or so I thought.

Chase Manhattan, solid as Gibraltar. Lutheran bishops. Evil NBC. This from a man who pays teenage runaways to do the watusi on his wizened johnson.

I turn to Art's partner, who's leaving with her money. "That old guy across the way—is he a regular?"

"I've seen him a couple of times. You want a show?"

I shake my head and she jiggles off into the crowd.

"You like that bird's girl?" Art says. His nose is running. He's fiddling with his trousers under the table. "She's taken, it looks like."

"That man she's with," I say. "Famous Wall Street bigwig, Mr. Dow. He gave me a stock idea on the plane today. I phoned it in when I landed. Six thousand bucks."

Art watches him for a moment. "He's hard core. His girl there's a twisted sister. Toilet Terry. She uses guys as fire hydrants."

"Stop."

"She keeps an apartment over by the Hilton. She gets top dollar. Vinyl sheets, the works. If they leave through the side exit, he's going home with her. I'll bet he drinks it. I know a dancer here who'd tell you everything. Pay her enough and she'll get you Polaroids."

Art thinks I crave information about this fellow, but his secret life bores me. I'm not the bloodhound type. That's why detective novels are lost on me. Somebody did it—that's all I need to know. The who, the how, and the why are just details. To my mind, there's nothing drearier than a labyrinth. It's just a structure whose center takes time to find, but if you make an effort, you'll find it. So? The only mysteries that interest me are, Will I land on time? Will the pilots strike? There's enough uncertainty just moving through space.

I glance back at Wall Street, who's sideways in his lounge chair, his head thrown back over one arm as the girl rides him. Soon, he'll be looking right at me, upside down.

"What style of donuts?" Art asks me.

"I haven't tasted them."

"You up for the VIP room?"

"I have to sleep. Come to GoalQuest and meet this Marlowe. You'll thank me, Art. And give me a nice reference if that guy calls."

"I made that one up to get you to come out here. I was going to off myself tonight."

"Sheer fabrication?"

"I've been drunk for days. I think it was."

There—Wall Street sees me now. He seems to frown; it's hard to read his features in reverse, with his lips where his eyebrows ought to be. Our eyes mix it up for a moment. Does he fear blackmail? I could bribe Art's connection for all the dirt, but why? A mystery stated can be more powerful than a mystery solved, and no matter what she might tell me about this fake, he'll never again be this vividly corrupt to me. And Art lied, too. At least he had a need.

I push back my chair and stand to leave, still watching Wall Street hang there like a possum. I used to think there was a code up there. Not true. Well, let them all feast on each other; I'll be out soon. I'll look up at their contrails and I won't miss it. Ever. Though it might be nice if some of them missed me.

five

homestead Suites has three classes of rooms, their specifications the same from Maine to Texas. I like to stay in the mid-range L-shaped rooms. You could fill me with morphine and pluck out both my eyes and I'd still be able to dim the lights, place calls, and locate an outlet for my noise machine.

Not in Reno, though. This room is different. When I go to hang my jacket in the closet, feeling bloated and slow from too much beef and booze, I open the door on a shrunken, substandard bathroom lacking the usual double toilet-roll holder and equipped with a shower but no tub. Even worse, instead of a lamp beside the desk and twin swing-out sconces flanking the king bed, there's a bare, fluorescent ceiling strip bright enough to interrogate a gang lord. And just one bar of soap: deodorant soap. Deodorant soap for the face! They're kidding me.

I call downstairs from bed but no one answers. I'm not so much angry as out of sorts, confused. Even the mattress seems tilted and out of true, while the blanket is one of those foamy nylon jobs that offer a trace of warmth but no security. I consider stripping the curtains off their rods for added insulation, but I need them to block out Reno's all-night glare. It's a madhouse out there, and louder by the minute as America's seniors seek out cheap prime rib and six-figure jackpots on the nickel slots. I turn on the air conditioner to "high fan" and tuck myself in like a bum under a newspaper.

At the end of the bed the TV screen pulses blue. Still hungry for punishment, I click around and manage to catch the last few minutes of Wall Street's daily show. Though he must have taped it in Reno this afternoon, the set features a lit-up New York skyline. It's the little deceptions that no one catches that are going to dissolve it all someday. We'll look at clocks and we won't believe the hands. They'll forecast sun but we'll pack our slickers anyway.

Feeling a need to halt the swirl, to stabilize, I dial Great West's toll-free mileage hotline to check the running tally on my HandStar. I'm wading through the lengthy options menu when my mobile rings on the nightstand.

It's my mother.

"Where am I reaching you, Ryan?"

She feels this matters. My mother has a developed sense of place; her mental map of the country is zoned and shaded according to her ideas about each region's moral tenor and general demographics. If I'm in Arizona, she assumes that I've spent my day among pensioners and ranch hands and driven past the Grand Canyon at least once. If I'm in Iowa, sensible, pleasant Iowa, I'm eating well, thinking clearly, and making friends. Though my mother gets around in her RV and ought to be more sophisticated by now about our American psychedelic rainbow, her talent for turning new experiences into supporting evidence for her prejudices overrides all else. Once, while gassing up in Alabama, a state she considers brutal, poor, and racist, she got to talking with a black attorney driving a convertible Mercedes. The man paid for his gas with a hundred-dollar bill and was forced to accept, in change, a roll of quarters and stacks of ones and fives. Instead of noting the man's prosperity, my mother seized on the pile of coins and bills—an act of humiliation, she decided, by the station's white clerk.

"I'm in Portland," I say. Nevada would worry her. "It's awfully late. Is everything okay?"

If it's not, she won't tell me—not at first. The worse the news, the harder she'll work to counter it with cheerful tidings from the Busy Bee Cafe.

"Did you hear about Burt's medal?" The Lovely Man. "Our congressman finally cut through the red tape and it looks like the Navy sees things our way now. They might do a ceremony at Fort Snelling."

"Great." I cross to the mini-bar for a pick-me-up, set the down the receiver, grab a beer, twist off the cap, and get back on the line, confident that I haven't missed a thing.

"It only took thirty years," my mother is saying. "It all came down to the definition of 'combat.' "

"How's the wedding coming along? Excited?"

Throat clearing, nose blowing. I've hit on it.

"We spent all day stripping thorns off yellow roses. My hands are all scratched. I'll need gloves for the reception. Julie's gone missing. They're cabbage roses—beautiful."

It's out, and she'd hang up now if she could. Now it's my job to press her for details. So she can feel the pain all over again and I can fear I caused it.

"How long's she been gone?"

"Ten, eleven hours."

"Are she and Keith fighting?"

"No."

"You have to talk, Mom. This isn't a cross-examination. Talk."

"Keith is here. Should I put Keith on?"

"Please."

"What time are you getting here Friday? I need a flight number. There's a special line that I can call to find out if you're on time. I need that number, though. Our weather's been crazy, hail and thunderstorms, so there might be delays."

"I'll find it. Give me Keith."

My future brother-in-law's Minnesota accent—the one so many comedians make fun of and which I don't hear in myself, though others do—prevents me from judging his level of concern. "Ryan, I'll get to the point here: she took off. No, we're not arguing. It's about her job. She lost two dogs this morning at the rescue farm. They jumped the fence and ate some gopher poison and pretty much died in her arms, from what we hear. It got ugly, I guess: they coughed up lots of blood. She split in her van and no one's heard from her."

"She hasn't called Kara? She usually calls Kara."

"We think someone saw her in Rochester. A cop."

"Has Julie been eating?"

"Like a horse."

"I doubt that."

"It was the dogs, I swear. They'd been abused. Two Border collies with collars grown into their necks. Should I be worried? She's done this in the past, right? Your mom says this is typical."

She's wrong. Yes, my sister runs when she's unhappy, but there's a novel element in play here: Julie's attachment to the poisoned animals. This is a girl who assumes all bonds are temporary, who's famously well-defended against loss. Her divorces were strangely painless; she skipped away from them, demanding no money, no car keys, nothing. The weekend after our father's funeral, she sang in and won a karaoke contest at a supper club. She took the job at the rescue farm not out of pity or tenderheartedness, but because the vet in charge was a family friend who didn't hold her history against her.

"You call me as soon as you hear from her," I say.

"Kara's flying up from Utah tonight. She thinks Julie's probably crashed at some motel, crying things out."

"This isn't wedding jitters? That farm must lose animals every other day."

"I know what you're saying. Your sister's changing, Ryan. Stuff affects her now. Pray for her, okay?"

"I never stop," I say. "Put Mom back on."

I finish my beer while I wait. It tastes like mucilage, that glue that's used to paste photos into albums.

"Is it raining there?" my mother says.

"It never rains. It's the desert. About this dog story: I don't buy it, Mom."

"Portland's not the desert."

"I'm in Nevada. This wedding is being rammed down Julie's throat. Of course she's AWOL. Can't you people see that? This house Kara picked for her, the whole arrangement, it's like you're hanging Julie in some museum."

"You fibbed to me," she says. "Where are you, Ryan? You're probably not in Nevada, either, are you? You're probably in Des Moines, a hundred miles from here, and you just can't be bothered to come help out."

"You know that's wrong, Mom. Whenever I'm that close to you, I'm there. The force field still works. Do we always have to fight?"

"Kara says you got fired."

"Well, she knows better. You made that up."

"I wanted to be sure."

"I need people not to make things up this week."

"You told me you were in *Oregon*."

"Fight fire with fire. Can we go back to Julie?"

"It's *you* that worries us. She *knows* what she's running away from."

"That's so profound. Someone's been reading a major woman novelist."

"I don't like having to wonder where I'm reaching you. It puts me at a disadvantage, Ryan. For all I know, you're in Japan and it's tomorrow. I'll see you on Friday. We're tying up the line."

"I love you, okay? No matter what you think. Congratulate Burt and keep me posted on Julie."

"How long are you coming for? Just the weekend? Longer?"

"I'm going in segments. I'll get to that one soon. Are you crying?"

"I'm crying a little."

"Me, too."

"I know."

I pour a glass of water to drink in bed but it tastes of chlorine, so I collect some change and step out into the hall to find a soda. Paper menus with early-morning breakfast orders hang from the doors, and I read a few of them. Coffee, juice, and muffins—they're all the same. If the doors were to become transparent suddenly, the people behind them would all be the same, too: asleep with the news on, their bags beside their beds, their next day's outfits hanging on the desk chairs. We travel alone, but together we're an army.

The Coke machine isn't where it ought to be, in a nook by the stairwell. I'm disappointed in Homestead—they've let things slide. The soul of their business is predictability, and if I were consulting for them I'd yank the name off any unit caught screwing with the blueprint.

I walk down a floor and resume my search. I normally avoid caffeine at night, but the news about Julie will keep me up. I'm half rooting for her to stay away, I realize. Wherever you are, my sister, just sit tight. Hug your pillow. Don't answer the door. This Keith's a good man, and Kara wants the best for you, but this is not their life. Just call me, will you? Do you have my number? Call me, Julie.

At last I find a glowing red Coke machine and drop in my quarters. The can thunks into the slot. I heard once that if you immerse a penny in a cola drink the coin will melt. I could use some good strong solvents now.

"You're here," a voice says.

It's Alex, from the plane. My fingers start to button my open dress shirt.

"What a surprise," she says. "Wow." She's in pajamas, a baggy pair of pink flannels that smells of dryer sheets. She's smaller than I remember, slim and kittenish, her hair clipped into a haphazard ball. Primed by the strip club, my nerves swell up with lust, and I take a step back to disengage our auras.

I ask her about her cat.

"He's at a vet. You were right, he shouldn't have come. I overtranquilized. I'm thinking I'll return him to the breeder. I don't have any business owning pets."

"I'm sorry. Hard lesson."

"How'd your meeting go?"

"No casualties. Your thing?"

"They raised a hundred K. The bitch gave a speech about Medicare. Big thrill. I goofed on the food, though. There's half a cow left over."

The light of the Coke machine rouges Alex's face. Down the hall, a door cracks open and a hand reaches out with a menu. We hush our voices. The building slips deeper and deeper into its dreams as my eyes slide down to Alex's bare toes, curling and uncurling as we chat. She polished them once, but the color has chipped away except for a few red flecks around the cuticles. It's a look I remember from high school and I like it.

It seems obvious, suddenly, what's going to happen between us; the only question is how. To move from the hallway straight to one of our rooms would be to forget we're grown-ups, not college kids. We have standards, guidelines, rules of thumb. If we want to maintain our self-respect as wary, wounded, thirtyish survivors, we'll have to go somewhere else and then come back here.

We agree on a plan that only seems spontaneous; in fact, it's as structured as a NASA countdown, designed to land us in bed by one o'clock so we can make our early-morning flights. We'll dress, meet up in the lobby, and cross the street to the Gold Rush Casino. We pad off down the hallway to our rooms for a quick gargle and splash of soapy water. I can almost hear the guests' sedatives kicking in as I pass their doors.

I wear my boots. For once, they're on my side. The angle of the heels and soles aligns my spine and firms my chest and shoulders. The problem is my khakis. They've lost their shape. I'm a hasty packer and hard on clothes; I roll them into tubes instead of folding them.

Alex dresses mannishly and simply in jeans and a V-neck black T-shirt. And a watch. I know the maker—I outcounseled four men there—and I'm sorry she wasted her money. It's ISM's fault. To help the company move its wares upmarket, we urged it to license the prestigious name of a dead European industrial designer. The inferior guts of the timepieces, which are sold alongside Rolexes and Guccis in airport duty-free shops, didn't change, but their prices quadrupled. Poor Alex fell for it.

We link arms. The street is still crowded with hopeful oldies toting buckets of change and plastic drink cups. The important thing is to stay casual, stay light. We're repeating ourselves—we've played this scene with others, and always with the same melancholy outcome—but we don't have to draw attention to the fact, nor do we have to deny it. We'll come through this. We stop on the sidewalk in front of the casino and count out our stake: four hundred dollars in twenties, all of which we agree to put at risk.

The craps tables are packed. We try roulette. A band plays in a corner—a cover combo specializing in stodgy classic rock. I buy two hundred dollars worth of chips for each of us and note our different styles in stacking them. Alex divides hers into four piles, while I build a tower.

"Red?"

"Whatever you like. Just don't bet a single number," I say.

Ten minutes later she's richer, though not by much, and I'm on my way to doubling my buy-in. Make no mistake: good luck is always significant and earning is no substitute for winning. We've made the right choice in coming out tonight; the wheel confirms it. I raise my average wager and hazard a high-odds corner bet, which hits.

A cocktail waitress arrives with our free drinks, two light beers, and I tip her with a chip. This always feels good, for some reason. Mr. Big.

"I have a confession," Alex says.

"You're married."

"I know you. We've met before. I heard you speak."

I look at her, keeping one eye on the wheel. To make the ball go where it needs to I have to coach it.

"Three years ago. At a seminar in Texas. You talked on career development, remember? I think the event was called Prepare for Power."

It's black—I've won again. "I've done a few of those. They keep me upbeat for my real job. Shafting people."

"I went with a girlfriend. She dragged me. You were good. I was a mess at the time, completely drained. I'd just broken up with a famous businessman who'd done a real number on my self-esteem. I sat at the back of the room because I'm shy, but I felt like you were talking to me personally. The line I remember was 'Change before they change you.' Autonomy, right? It's all about autonomy."

I never give the same speech twice, so I don't recall. I'm flattered, though. My fingertips warm as I restack my chips.

"You just dropped into a seminar one day? No reason? Just curious?"

"Total happenstance. We're winning, aren't we?"

"I'm going to double up."

All my good luck has begun to flow together—I've met an admirer and won a bundle—which probably means it's time that I cashed out. The odds are a funny thing. When they run with me, especially after they haven't for a while, I can feel like I'm finally getting what I'm worth and that chance has nothing to do with it. It's justice. The universe is paying up at last. Moralists like my mother and big sister would view this as a dangerous delusion, but I'm part pagan—I believe in breakthroughs, in bursts of astrological beneficence. Things rise and fall, but at times they rise and rise.

"After we got off the plane today," says Alex, "I asked myself why I didn't say I knew you. It's a character weakness. I like to hide and watch. In Texas you came off as pretty cocky, so maybe I was hoping you'd screw up."

"It sounds like you had it out for me."

"Not really. It's just hard to admit that this stranger who gave some talk that struck me as sort of corny at the time and intellectually below my level actually set me straight and helped me grow."

"You're laying it on pretty thick. Fort Worth, you said?"

"You didn't gaze out on the audience and notice me?"

"I keep my face in my notes when I speak publicly. I'd rather not see the assassin's muzzle flash."

"Assassin?"

"I wasn't frank with you today. My main occupation is Career Transitions. You're smart, so you can interpret. Terminations."

"I'm sorry. I didn't know that was a field. How much have you won? Can we stop now?"

"One more spin."

"You're pretty into this, aren't you?"

Should I not be? To prove I can walk away, I slide my chips—all of them—onto red. And red it is. Alex follows me to the cashier's cage, where the casino turns plastic into paper so later it can be turned back into plastic. The clerk counts out ten one-hundred-dollar bills, still stiff from the mint. We're rich. Where now? The bar.

The drinkers, instead of looking at one another, stare down at the video poker monitors whose screens form the resting place for their drinks and coasters. Their eyeglasses flicker as their cards are played. The band plays "Radar Love," stroking its guitars with all the passion of jailbirds shoveling gravel while wearing leg-irons.

"That was incredible," Alex says. "It practically seemed illegal, what you did there."

She's off balance now. That was the point of my big bet, which would have been just as effective had I lost. We're not in control, my sweet. It's all a hunch.

"So how precisely did I help you grow?"

"You convinced me to go into business for myself. Plus, you sort of set me on a path. I had a strange childhood, not traumatic, exactly, but hurtful, uncertain. My father had two families. We knew this. He drove a truck. It happens sometimes. When he was gone, my mother fooled around, spent time in the bars. The arrangement worked for both of them. The problem was me. They had four lives between them, and I was always switching back and forth. A few times my dad even took me to Missouri, where his other kids lived. Their mother was a secretary, so they had more money than I did, and they were Catholic. I had to learn to blend, to mold myself."

"Sounds like it. What a mess."

"I pulled it off, though. I split myself into quarters. I adapted. Then suddenly I'm eighteen and on my own and my special talent isn't relevant. I'm expected to be consistent, and I'm just not."

"Someone usurped my identity," I say.

"Pardon?"

"Usurped. It means 'steal.' "

"I went to college."

"My question is: if they charge things to my credit card, who gets the miles? I'll bet they go to waste."

"I was telling you something. I hadn't finished yet."

"I made an association. Go ahead."

Alex pushes away her beer. "I'm angry now."

"I thought I was amplifying a point you'd made."

"Listen, can we get going? Flight at six."

I'm reluctant to leave the noise and bustle. The casino holds out so many possibilities—my sister might even walk by, you never know—but in Alex's room the script has fewer endings. Because if it's true that she admires me, she won't once we're through. Or is that her plan? To get me undressed and close our stature gap. I don't see much profit in this rendezvous. This Alex is full of schemes, as she's admitted, but I'm happy here, with my winnings in cash, for once.

I let her lead me. Her room is smaller than mine, one price point down, and though she's only been in it a few hours, she's turned it into an atmospheric grotto. She's draped a violet scarf over the desk lamp and set a pair of candles on the bureau, which she lights with wooden matches. Twin flames jump up. A stuffed velour unicorn, worn bare with hugs, lies on the bed beside an open book, and on top of the blanket she's spread a mohair throw. To do this to a hotel room would never occur to me—I take them as they come, the way God made them.

"There's a tape in my little player on the sill. Turn it on if you want. I need to wash my hands."

I do as I'm told and out spills a mystic trickle of formless music—piano, bells, and strings—that sounds like it was recorded underwater. The scene is set for a séance, a tarot reading, and as always when I'm expected to relax, my shoulders seize. I'm not so sure I'm up to this.

Alex emerges in a hotel bathrobe. Her face is different—ruddier, less porcelain. She's a farm girl, just in from watering the stock. Has she put on makeup or removed some?

"You've really made this place your own," I say.

"I always try to warm things up a little. I miss my own bedroom, my stuff. I think we all do."

I don't comment. I let her think I'm human too.

"Take off those silly boots," she says. "Sit down."

The question is always how far to strip, how quickly. There must be books on this, with clever tips. I go down to my T-shirt and boxers, then peel the shirt off. No complaints, no stares.

"Lie down on the bed, on your stomach. I'll massage you. Your body's one big knot."

She kneels and straddles my hips and strokes my neck. She twists the point of one knuckle in a sore spot. "The muscles store memories," she says. She's right. I'm carrying five-year-old Julie on my shoulders so she can see the sights at the State Fair. I head for the tent where the Ice Man is displayed—a wonder my father assures me is a rip-off, an animal hide or a taxidermied monkey. I buy two tickets, mount a few low steps, stand behind a partition, and look down.

The frosty block of ice obscures the details, but it's a body, wrinkled, dark, and hairy, curled on its side like a newborn calf. Convincing. Julie's hands squeeze my skull and I feel a drip. She's weeping. I twist to leave, but she holds me. My neck is wet. "It's a her," she says. "It's a girl. They killed a girl."

"Tender here?" Alex says.

"It is."

"You're shaky. Maybe this isn't our night tonight."

"I'm fine. My little sister trained as a masseuse."

"Don't flinch. I'm on an important pressure point."

"She worked at the Minneapolis Athletic Club. She lasted a week. A man tried to assault her—the CFO of a major retail shoe chain. The cops threw away her complaint."

"Where's all this coming from?"

"My sister gave massages, I'm getting one. Does everything have to come from somewhere?"

"No." She rocks a thumb in the spaces between my vertebrae. No memories there, just pain. A thousand plane seats.

"I followed you, Ryan. You mentioned this hotel. I was about to call your room tonight. Psycho, huh?"

"I've done those things myself."

"Mostly I hoped we'd talk," she says. "Just talk. I feel like your speech in Texas started something—a conversation. You haven't heard my half, though. I took what you said there to heart. I lived it, Ryan. I wanted to tell you what happened, what I learned. I didn't realize how tired we'd be. Too bad."

"Not our evening."

"I'm sorry."

"I understand. I gambled too long."

"A little bit. It's fine. You're running. You're tense. It's natural."

"It's a problem. My ex said I had a problem." I let her rub me. "Where will you be on Thursday?"

"Home. Salt Lake."

Las Vegas—she could fly there in an hour. I'd have to cancel my date for Thursday dinner, but I've been thinking of canceling it anyway. Milla Searle is her name. She's a talent manager; she handles a string of casino magic acts. We were stranded together in Spokane last spring during an all-night blizzard that closed the airport and forced us to sleep on the Compass Club's bare floor beside the big TV. It was a wartime romance—the huddled refugees, the bottled water passed out by the airline, the flashing blue lights of the snowplows through the windows. When our paths crossed again in Phoenix a month later, we reminisced for an hour about the storm, then fell silent. Nothing else in common.

"I want you to meet me in Las Vegas Thursday. I'll fly you in. We'll see a show. No gambling. We'll be rested, we'll talk. I have the whole night free."

Alex lets go of me. I want her back. I reach around and touch her through the robe. She guides my fingers across her hip, no further.

"I saw your itinerary on your HandStar. I already checked on fares," she says. "That scares you."

"You sit next to someone you like, you have to act. People move fast. They'll get away from you."

Alex squeezes my hand and returns it to my side, then bears down on the base of my neck with open palms. "When you terminate someone, does that depress you, Ryan?"

"What's depressing is getting used to it."

"Do you wonder about the people afterwards?"

"You learn to try not to. You learn to trick your mind."

She digs in with her thumbs again. Hurts, but may be good for me.

"You learn to leapfrog. Mentally."

"Relax."

i'm in the back row of the Reno airport chapel, sitting out a forty-minute delay with a fruit-topped frozen yogurt and this morning's *USA Today,* when it happens again for the second time since August: I'm gripped by the feeling that I've just been paged. I missed the name, yet I'm certain it was mine. Someone wants me. Someone needs me. Now.

I fold the paper and put it in my briefcase and listen for the announcement to be repeated. Few people know that most airports have houses of worship: they tend to be white, high-ceilinged, scrubbed, and soundproof, imbued with a spirituality so general that even atheists can find refuge in them. They go unused, for the most part, except in times of emergency and terror—after a crash or when a war breaks out. They're eerie little niches but also restful and perfect for catching up on paperwork. If someone arrives to pray or meditate while I'm using one, which seldom happens, I bow and pretend to be sunk in deep reflection as I fill out an expense report or rejigger my itinerary.

The voice was female, that's all I'm sure of now. Tinny and official—robotic, almost. I examine the speaker recessed in the ceiling and think through the shortlist of the people who know my schedule. My assistant, a temp who claims to be a grad student taking time out from his thesis, but might be anyone, since I doubt ISM checked his background when it hired him. My boss, Ron Boosler, who's fishing in Central America with the ex-CEO of General Mills and a Colorado federal judge he's helping to position for the Supreme Court. And Alex, of course, who was gone when I woke up facedown in a soggy pillow on her bed.

It was MythTech. That's what I thought in Billings, too, when the same thing happened three weeks ago. I was ordering oatmeal in the airport coffee shop, unslept and unshaven after an intensive two-day Career Transitions mini-session that saw the breakdown of one participant who wasn't keen to re-enter the great job hunt and get on the phone to his entire Rolodex with chipper questions about openings while repeating to himself the affirmation: "I'm *motivated*, not desperate." Stark panic often precedes enlightenment, and the former banker left our meeting room purple with hypertension and resentment, getting as far as his parked Buick LeSabre before falling into a catatonic trance that paralyzed his limbs but not his mouth, which belched forth intermittent rasping moans smelling of—they had an odor, these moans—stomach acid mixed with lighter fluid. It was dawn by the time I stabilized the fellow, and my eyes were so dry that when I blinked my lids stuck to my eyeballs with the adhesion factor of Post-it notes on a computer screen. In the cab to the airport I retched into a Baggie I use to store dirty underwear and socks. Then, at breakfast, directly above my head, I heard my name. My last name. I investigated, checking in with the airline and with security. Nothing. I called my voice mail and got a message, truncated and barely audible, leaving a number with a Nebraska area code. I dialed it, expecting Lucius Spack, whose interest in my career I'd been alerted to by a columnist for *Modern Management* who'd interviewed him for a story. Instead, I got an Omaha convenience store whose clerk insisted she'd just arrived at work and that I'd reached a pay phone. She couldn't help me. I spent the flight back to Denver in a muddle, convinced that my ears had deceived me. Then again, Spack and MythTech are covert operators, famed for stealthy head-hunting campaigns. A call from an untraceable public phone wouldn't be out of character for them, and tracking me down at an airport, away from colleagues, where no one could overhear us, would fit their tactics.

When the page doesn't repeat, I leave the chapel, genuflecting by instinct in the aisle even though the room is so stripped bare that I'm not sure if it even contains an altar. At my gate a beeping electric cart cuts past and lets off a swollen old woman on metal crutches who hobbles onto the Jetway, the last to board. The agent rubber-bands her stack of boarding passes and levels a stare at me. "Let's move along, sir."

"I think I just heard someone call me on the PA."

"The aircraft is leaving."

I flash my Compass Club card. "Just try the office. The name is Ryan Bingham."

The agent uses the phone behind the podium. "The last person paged was a Brian Raines," she tells me. "You must have juxtaposed something."

Juxtaposed. It's so easy, but there's a lag before it comes. I'm reaching capacity. No more Verbal Edge. Whatever I don't know already, I'll never learn.

I ask for an extra pillow and a blanket and shift my seat to its fully reclined position. The gentleman behind me groans. He could adjust his own seat for more space, but he prefers to play the martyr, apparently. I didn't look at him closely when I boarded—still preoccupied with the phantom page—but, lying back, I recognize his cologne as one of those aggressive, woodsy scents worn by heavy perspirers. Salesmen, mostly.

I feel a bug coming on. My ears are hot. I twist shut the air nozzle blowing on my forehead and drain a second glass of grapefruit juice to soothe the pulsing rawness in my throat. The superviruses of modern air travel, steeled by exposure to diverse immune systems and virtually injected into the lungs by high-efficiency ventilation systems, can hang on for weeks, bringing on a multitude of symptoms that mimic those of more serious illnesses. Over time, I've grown resistant to most of them, but once in a while one sneaks past my glands. As soon as I land at Ontario today, I'll find a drugstore and gorge on zinc and C. I need to be healthy for my meeting with Pinter.

My seatmate barely interests me for once. His glasses reflect the moonglow of his laptop as he touch-types what looks like a letter or an article. He's chewing gum like a smoker in withdrawal and I'd guess by his mussed, longish hair and casual jacket that he's a working journalist. I'm impressed. Anyone who can reach into the data swarm and pick out what's newsworthy has my respect.

I can't get comfortable in my little nest. My feet have swollen inside the cowboy boots, but I fear the odor if I kick them off. Such a small error, this purchase, yet so disruptive. Traveling, I live from my feet up. Shoes—one more item to shop for in Ontario.

But where's Ontario? I really don't know. A secondary airport outside Los Angeles, a clearing in the suburbs and subdivisions. They call such places faceless, but it's not true. They're bodiless, just signs and streets and lights. In fact, I've flown into Ontario before. I rode the shuttle bus to Homestead Suites, worked for an hour or two on *The Garage*, did some business downstairs in the grill, and returned to the terminal by cab. Memories? None. The smell of road tar, maybe. The trip was no more than a handshake through the ether.

I open one eye to read my seatmate's screen—a breach of Airworld etiquette. Whatever he's writing, he's in the middle of it.

But for residents of this leafy college town, known until now for its world-class Children's Hospital, the tragedy raises deeper, more troubling questions. Questions of media violence, parental neglect, and the aimlessness of the American adolescent. "A few of us worried about boys and guns," says Janet Portis, 31, a part-time den-

tal technician and mother of two, "but girls and guns? That just wasn't on our screens." Local officials echo her shocked confusion. "There was always a feeling of it can't happen here," muses Police Chief Brad McCann, one of the first to reach the gruesome scene. . . .

Something's not right here; I've read this story before. I try to place the source. Was it last week in a club-room *U.S. News* or was it the week before, in flight, in *Time*? The shooting happened in Oregon, I recall, at a softball game, or was it a Wisconsin soccer match? I wait for the reporter to change screens and reveal his dateline but he's stopped writing, hung up on completing this sentence: "Such innocence—"

I can finish it for him from memory: "dies hard." His hands hang over the keyboard as he thinks. Here he goes now: "isn't easily destroyed." Same difference—I was right. I've read this story! Then I place it: *USA Today,* just half an hour ago.

What a make-work universe this is. Judging by the fellow's bunched-up brow, rewriting a story known to all is just as hard as composing one from scratch.

"Got the time?" I ask, pretending to wake. I can't let him know I've been spying.

"What's our zone?"

"Pacific. This is a Tuesday, the third millennium, and breakfast is poppyseed muffins. That's all I know."

"I guess it must be seven then." He clicks back his digital watch but goes too far, clicks it forward, overshoots again, then finally nails it.

"You write for a living?"

"Try."

"For magazines?"

"A Chicago afternoon paper. I'm on deadline. Can you excuse me for a few more minutes? I need to file as soon as we touch down."

He returns to his work, which isn't really his, searching for transitions and adjectives that, when he finds them after much grave frowning, duplicate exactly the other writer's, which probably came from a wire story anyway. I could just give him the paper from my briefcase, but the guy needs to feel important, like all of us.

I shed my boots at last and flex my feet. The odor is inoffensive—warm, damp leather—but the socks, I see, aren't my brand. I only buy Gold Toes. A hotel laundry mix-up? It happens. Still.

I switch on my microrecorder: "Notes for book: hero floats outside of time in *The Garage*. The progress of his projects is all he knows. Self-management means nothing if not this—the task-centered governance of one's very biorhythms. If not for the quarterly financial statements that come to him through the Communications Portal, which he shreds unread, then burns for heat, my hero would not even know what year it is. The man who makes history is a living calendar, his beating heart his only pendulum. When the voice in the Portal says to him "Go faster!" my hero replies with the Fourth Dictum: "Innovation spreads outward from its center, not forward from some arbitrary—"

"Sir?"

I look to the side.

"Your coffee."

Turbulence. Before I can close my hand, the cup leaps sideways, spraying my chin and my collar. I'm wet, but not burned—the coffee was dishwater warm. We jolt again. My recorder hops off the seat onto the floor, and when I pick it up, it's dripping, soaked. I press rewind and the capstans jerk then stop. I pop the tape out and blot it on my shirt. Thirty minutes of lost work not yet transcribed.

I check the window: clear skies, a plane-shaped shadow gliding over a salt flat. Things are calm again. The flight attendant returns, apologizes, then hands me a pen and a voucher from the airline granting me a thousand miles in consideration for my stained clothing. I tell her it's not enough, that I want five, but she says that the best she can do is one. I sign. The miles don't make us even, not even close, but at least I'm not falling any further behind.

The reporter saves his story, shuts his laptop, zips it into a padded black nylon case, and calls for a white rum and diet cola. We're still waiting on our breakfast, but the flight attendant understands that there's no accounting for body clocks.

I quiz the fellow about his job, then mention that I've been doing some writing myself, which seems to alarm him. Another sweaty amateur. I name my publisher to prove my bona fides, but he tells me he's not familiar with the imprint and begins to fidget with his wedding band, sliding it up and down over his knuckle as if to make sure the thing will still come off. I backtrack to my real job and propose that he do a story on CTC men, the smiling undertakers for the still-living. The reporter hasn't a clue about what I'm referring to, but nods nonetheless, then retrieves his cased computer. Inspiration has struck, apparently. Perhaps he'll change "leafy college town" to "shady."

I unlock the airphone from my seatback and steel myself for a call to ISM and the man I like least in the world, Craig Gregory, who came on the same month that I did, way back when. We underwent the same training, same orientation, and we simultaneously requisitioned the same ergonomic desk chairs and keyboard wrist-pads. After that, our paths diverged. Mine traveled flat and away, into the world, while Craig's snaked back into the building and corkscrewed upward. He knew what I didn't—that power in the company lay inside its walls, with his colleagues and superiors, not outside, with the clients. Craig Gregory became a virtuoso lurker in beverage nooks, stairwells, elevators, and men's rooms, emerging from stalls to startle chatting VPs, plunking his tray down across from gossiping temps, getting the dope, remembering the dope, dishing out the dope. He never went home. No matter how early I reached the office, a coffeed-up Craig Gregory was there before me, sparking off with the latest e-mail jokes and showing off curious finds from people's wastebaskets. I suspected he kept a small mattress in an air duct, where he'd also squirreled away chocolate bars and water. And somehow, in time, he gained leverage over me, over all of us. We couldn't shake him, the phantom of headquarters, a pestilent jack-in-the-box with icy Certs breath, and soon quite a few of us were reporting to him, ISM's organizational charts be damned.

I tell him I'm on an airphone when he picks up—it's a way to limit our conversation time. At three bucks a minute I'll have to keep this short.

"How's Krusk? You talk to him about his debts? You're at least coming back with a severed ear, I hope. Hey, I got one of those desk toys—steel ball on strings. The soothing click and clack of basic physics. It fits right in with my teeter-totter monkeys."

"Art's a write-off. He's gutted. There's nothing there, Craig. I won't be submitting my hours on that job."

"Roll the bill over to those HMO guys—they deserve it. Denying cripples crutches. You on your way there?"

The subject of my call. Why even tell him, though; I owe him nothing.

"California today. A little meeting."

"Profiting whom? Not more freelancing, let's pray. Get this: I was in the skybox Sunday aft, grabbing some rented ass that we trucked in for what's-his-face, the mobbed-up solid-waste king, and my guy in Internal Travel lights a Partagas and tells me 'This Bingham of yours is on a spree; he's taking us for a ride, hoss—shut him down.' So I say . . . What do I say?"

"No idea, Craig. We're nearing twenty bucks now, with connection charges."

"Wherever our Bingham goes, the money follows. Let the man plant his seeds. They'll grow to oaks."

"I'm thinking of putting Texas off."

"Unwise. They're laying waste to their whole top floor, those boys. There's gold in that there lake of steaming gore."

"I'll see."

"I just set my shiny balls to swinging. Isaac Newton, I thank you. My man in Travel told me he thinks you're gunning for big round numbers at his and my and the janitor's expense, but I said 'Lay off, he's earned it.' Hey, I crapped today. My first since the operation."

"What operation?"

"A hush-hush female problem. My teenage steroid abuse grew me a uterus. None of your damn beeswax. Important thing: I crapped."

"That's me, applauding."

"That's me, passing blood."

"This is costing us, Craig."

"It's costing all America. It'll show up in next year's productivity figures."

"Are you threatening to cut my travel off?"

"We missed that boat. That boat left port five years ago. We're going to let you sail and sail and sail. Send a postcard if you ever get there."

"I'm hanging up on you."

"Good. I love that sound."

The reporter looks over; he's been spying too, it seems. "Your office?"

"For another couple days."

"You say your profession is dismissing people?"

"That's how it ended up, not how it started. I also give talks on discovering inner riches. I met a fan last night. She bought my shit."

"Maybe you're right and there's a story there. Sorry if I seemed rude before. I'm Pete. Tell me what you were going to tell me."

"Later."

"This is your chance," says Pete. "We're going to land."

"Sorry. Moody. Don't feel much like talking. Another big shooting? I peeked at your computer."

"I can't seem to find the words this morning. Stuck."

I open my case and hand Pete the morning paper. He'll get the same results but get them quicker, and he'll be able to enjoy his cocktail. We all like to think we can add that special touch, and some of us can, perhaps, just not Pete and me. I order my own drink. The flight attendant hustles. For all she knows her morning is my night.

seven

n ot every profession is fortunate enough to have a founding father who's still alive, let alone available to visit and do business with. In management analysis—the good side—that man is Sandor "Sandy" Pinter, a Hungarian who came over in the forties and called upon his training as a philosopher to grapple with the new realities of American business. His first full-length book, *Ideals and Industry,* argued that the modern corporation gains its moral legitimacy from its promise to forge and sustain a global middle class. The book was ignored except by intellectuals, but Pinter's next book, addressed directly to businessmen, created the modern science of management almost by itself. *Making Work Work* earned Pinter fame and riches and formed the basis for the Pinter Institute, a Los Angeles school for mid-career executives where Pinter taught, in person and by satellite, until his retirement three years ago at the age of eighty. From his modest bungalow outside Ontario, he continues to write (an article a year or so, the latest being "Managing for Meaning"), but he rarely travels. You have to go to him.

And that's what I'm doing. I have a small proposal. If Pinter accepts it, MythTech will take notice.

The concept is simple: allow a corporation to endow its physical environment, floor to ceiling, wall to wall, with the philosopher's inspiring presence. Muzak-like recordings of Pinter's lectures will play in the hallways, lavatories, and lobbies. Ticker tapes composed of Pinter's epigrams will run at the bottom of company computer screens. The product-package will be all-encompassing, including "Pinterized'" calendars, coffee mugs, ballpoint pens and other office supplies. Even its carpeting, should the company wish, can be woven with Pinter's trademark "dynograms," from the lightning-struck infinity symbol (Perpetual Discovery) to the star of five crossed swords (Team Solidarity).

Winning Pinter's permission to license such a product should take one afternoon, if all goes well. I happen to know that he's under some financial strain. His thoughtful books stopped selling years ago, bumped from the shelves by his students' shoddy quickies, and his rash investments in fringe enthusiasms such as self-cooling beverage cans and sunless tanning preparations have murdered his net worth. That he's agreed to spend time with me at all shows some desperation, I'm afraid, but I'm not here to take advantage of him. The opposite. I'm here to glorify him.

The problem, just now, is my health. My joints are stiff and I'm coughing up sweet phlegm after a morning of hassles and distractions attributable to the overall decline of American travel services. I was leaving the parking lot in my rental car when its orange oil light flashed on. I circled back to the Maestro garage and was given a choice by the on-duty mechanic of trading down from my Volvo to a Pontiac or changing the oil myself and billing the company. The mechanic recommended a ProntoLube just a block away from Homestead Suites, where he said I could also find a drugstore.

I got back on my way, but formless Ontario, with its poorly marked surface roads and surly pedestrians, swallowed me whole. My gas gauge fell and fell. Three times I passed identical burrito stands before realizing they were the same establishment. Twice I nearly ran over a stray Great Dane trailing a leash that had snagged a plastic tricycle. At unpatrolled traffic lights, sloping muscle cars and jacked-up pickups gunned past me blaring rap. I felt like I was driving in Paraguay. In my idea of Paraguay, at least.

I'm like my mother—I stereotype. It's faster.

Airports are often plunked down in nowhere-lands, and I navigate them by calling on my sense of which sort of businesses go along with which. Find a Red Lobster, you've found the Holiday Inn. But Ontario's layout didn't follow the rules. Its Olive Gardens were next to bleak used-car lots. Its OfficeMaxes abutted adult bookstores. I punched in Homestead's national 800 number and had the operator patch me through to the desk clerk at the local franchise, who talked me, block by block, to the front door. When I entered the lobby, I didn't see him anywhere, though we'd only hung up on each other moments earlier. I pushed the buzzer, waited. Ten minutes passed.

A girl opened a door marked "Pool and Fitness" and asked if she could help me.

"Where's the clerk?"

"I am."

"I was just talking to him."

"Me?"

"A male. The voice was male."

"The pool guy maybe."

I asked if my replacement credit card had arrived that morning as promised, and it had—the girl just couldn't remember where she'd put it. I crossed the street to the drugstore while she searched. Through the locked door I could see the teenage staff conducting inventory. I knocked and knocked. A manager came to the door and waved me off, then pushed a stack of boxes against the glass.

Back at Homestead, the girl presented me with a fax. I asked about the card. "Still gone," she said. The fax, marked "urgent," was almost too light to read, and consisted of copies of copies of telephone messages taken down by my grad-student assistant. Two were from Morris Dwight at Advanta, one was from Linda at the Denver Compass Club, and the fourth read "Please call sister," but didn't say which one.

I went to my room to return the calls, but the phone had no dial tone. I used my mobile. First, I called Kara at home. Her husband answered. She'd already left for Minnesota, he said. Had she heard from Julie? He didn't think so. Did he know that Julie was missing? No, he said, but then he'd only come home an hour ago from a two-day hospital stay. I asked Asif what he'd been in for—a mistake. My brother-in-law's a slow talker, a real enunciator, and it's part of his caring nature to assume that others care equally about him. We do care, but not at his level. He's unique. "They studied my sleep," he said. "I wore electrodes. They taped a little sensor to my thumb to measure the chemical makeup of my blood. It dipped below ninety percent, which isn't good. I snore. I have apnea. It's very common, and not just among the obese. You think you're resting, but actually you're expending as much energy as a marathon runner. Every night."

"I was diagnosed with apnea too, once."

"Which treatment plan did you choose?"

"I haven't yet. Listen, someone's knocking. Have to run."

"We think we know how we're sleeping, but we don't. They filmed me. I was all over the mattress."

"Here's my number in case you hear from Julie."

At Advanta I spoke to someone under Dwight who told me he must have called me from his cell, but refused to give out that number. I pointed out that the number on Dwight's message was the number I was calling now. "I guess this line was supposed to forward then," the underling said. "But it didn't, did it? Shoot." I suggested that he call Dwight on the road and pass on my number at Homestead. Silence. "Wait—I just found a note here. Are you ready? Can't do Thursday SeaTac breakfast. Sorry. Will be in Phoenix on Wednesday. Can you come there? Wednesday is tomorrow."

"Thanks for the tip. I already told him I can get to Phoenix. What's the hotel name?"

"Had it, put it down, and . . . I can get it. It's here. You're the *Garage* guy?"

"Correct. You got the manuscript?"

"I read it. Your man in there, what exactly does he invent? I imagine he's, like, a chemist."

"It's never stated."

"Artistic. Cool. How big is his garage?"

"That's up to you. It's a metaphor. An image."

"So it's smallish, you're saying?"

"Have you been listening? I'm saying its dimensions aren't physical. What's your boss's opinion of the book?"

"He still hasn't read it. He's an editor. I take the first pass and then write up a summary. He decides from my summary whether he'll read it, too."

"You're joking, right?"

"That's the practice."

"I'm stunned," I say.

"Another question: The Second Dictum?"

"Yes?"

"It's a lot like the Sixth. I don't think you need the Sixth."

"Tell Dwight I'll be in Phoenix mid-day tomorrow and that I have some major concerns to share with him. Have you found that hotel name?"

"I had it, I put it down . . ."

"Does Advanta make a profit?"

"It's publishing. Profits are secondary."

"That's what's scaring me."

I decide that my last call, to Linda, can wait awhile. What do you owe them once you've screwed them? Everything.

You've been inside their skins. You've touched their wombs. The only question is whether they'll make you pay, whether they'll call in the note. Most don't, thank goodness. But Linda, I've always feared, will want full value. This doesn't mean I'll have to pay, of course, just that I'll have to live with having defaulted. And I can. I've done it with the others. It's a matter of rolling over one personal debt into the pooled, collective, social debt that's the business of governments and churches. Or I could refinance, amortize over centuries.

I lay down with my boots on for a nap. My sleep was not sleep but a paralytic trance. Asif was wrong: I *know* I get no rest. I dreamed abstractly, of multicolored grids unfurling to the horizon, a giant game board. The game pieces were familiar from Monopoly—the cannon, the shoe, the Scottie dog, the iron—but they floated over the board like space debris. Every few moments, a thin blue laser beam would arc from the board and turn a piece to ash.

Now I'm awake, in the bathroom, gargling Listerine. The membranes inside my cheeks feel ragged, scorched. I touch my forehead. Its neither chilled nor feverish; it's the disturbing no-temperature of paper. I need vitamins. I need certain enzymes. The lack of them is visible on my skin. I tan with the slightest sun, but in the mirror now my face can barely muster a reflection.

The only good news: my credit card is back. They slipped it under the door while I was napping. The identity thief has been cut off, presumably. I'm whole again, with nothing hanging out. My first purchase will be a pair of shoes, and I have a whole hour to buy them—a rarity. According to Pinter's autobiography, he sleeps in two four-hour shifts from 10 to 2, A.M. and P.M., and takes his meals at three. He writes in the book that all humans lived this way before the dawn of agriculture, but he gives no evidence. That's typical. In management, it's the stimulating assertion, not the tested hypothesis, that grabs folks.

I call Pinter's house to confirm and get directions. Margaret answers, his so-called co-domestic. Pinter's contempt for matrimony springs from his belief in male polygamy, which he refrains from practicing himself only because it's currently illegal, but which he doesn't rule out for the future. Maybe when he's a hundred they'll loosen standards.

"He'd like to come pick you up," says Mrs. Pinter. "He bought a new car he's eager to show off."

"That's fine. I can't wait to see your lovely home."

"It's under renovation, I'm afraid. We're down to two inhabitable rooms."

"Maybe you'd like to eat out tonight."

"Of course not. Sandy needs his food prepared just so. He doesn't trust these restaurants. They overheat things and screw up the protein chains."

"When should I expect him?"

"Five, ten minutes."

"I thought he ate at three?"

"This year it's two. Sandy corrected for daylight saving time."

The genius act is beginning to annoy me, and I have a high tolerance for quirkiness, even when it's a calculated put-on. One of the speakers I saw at last year's GoalQuest, a world-renowned alpinist who died on Everest (just for seven minutes; they revived him, but only after he'd received a vision of abiding interest to the business world), wore shearling slippers with an Italian suit and insisted on chewing gum while speaking. His painful, frostbitten feet explained the slippers, but the bubbles he blew were the purest affectation, intended to show that he plays by his own Hoyles. He knows, as all the cleverest ones do, that no human being is so interesting that he can't make himself more interesting still by acting retarded at random intervals.

I put away clothes to prepare for Pinter's visit. How do hotel rooms fall apart so quickly, and even when I've hardly packed a thing? Their surfaces seem to cry out for abuse the way new haircuts cry out for a mussing. Perhaps it's the urge to make the space your own by displacing the aura of the previous occupant. When someone vacates a plane seat or a room, they leave behind a molecular disturbance. This room, I'd guess, was last inhabited by a bickering family on vacation.

Pinter knocks just once. Efficiency. I greet him wearing khakis and a blue shirt and holding a legal pad with writing on it, trying to look like a man who's always occupied.

"We finally meet. A privilege. Excuse the room," I say.

"I need your toilet."

"Of course. It's right in there."

Pinter doesn't close the door completely, exposing me to sounds I'd rather not hear from one of his reputation, whose courses I've audited. The toilet-roll holder rattles as it unspools. Despite his famous abhorrence of waste and excess, Pinter has a lavish way with tissue. I wait for a flush, a running faucet. Nothing. When he reappears I shake his hand, whose absolute dryness confirms that it's unwashed. I understand from studying his books that there isn't a custom, tradition, or rule of hygiene that Pinter hasn't dismissed or tinkered with.

He sits on the end of my bed, not facing me. He's a small man, balding, but hairy in his crevices. His ears and nostrils are densely webbed, and there's fur in the cleft of his jutting, pitted chin. His mouth is a long, lipless crescent, like a drawing.

"I don't see an ashtray. Is this room non-smoking?"

"Don't worry. The alarms aren't sensitive."

"There's an alarm? It's not worth it then."

"I'll join you."

Pinter produces a Baggie of loose tobacco and rolls two lumpy cigarettes. "Why do they have to ruin everything? The California dream was freedom once. Now we're ruled by nags and health fanatics. You're familiar with my definition of health?"

"I am."

"Mediocrity raised to an ideal. Health is why we get sick. Health-consciousness."

But he won't eat in restaurants because they warp the proteins.

Pinter is not a social smoker. He puffs like an Indian, reverent, eyes shut. His free hand opens and closes on his knee like a gasping fish. He flicks his ash on his corduroys and rubs it in with a newborn's soft pink thumb.

"I'm celebrating this afternoon," he says. "I signed a substantial contract yesterday."

Discouraging news—I'd thought he was retired. I'd counted on his poor financial condition to help sell my proposal.

"It's supposed to be confidential, but secrets bore me. An airline out of Phoenix hired me."

"Not Desert Air?"

"You've heard of them?"

I nod. "They compete with the airline I fly."

Pinter coughs. A volume of smoke rolls out and keeps on coming, as if his whole body is filled with it. "Good company?"

"You tell me."

"They have a problem," he says. "They built their business on price and price alone, which is effective but risky. I've written on this. A woman of easy virtue will soon grow popular, but she'll fail when it comes to attracting a loyal mate. Long term, it's better to be good than cheap. Wanton discounting is a downward spiral, so I've urged them to reinterpret their identity. Hauling warm bodies from point A to point B inspires no one. It's a form of trucking. Promoting human togetherness, however, ignites the vital flame in all involved, the worker as well as the customer. Agreed?"

"A marketing angle."

"Much deeper. A first principle. It starts with seating. Like should sit with like. Parents of small children with other parents. Young singles with young singles. No more jumbling. We learn who the passengers are through detailed surveys and task a computer with mixing them appropriately, the way a good hostess would seat a dinner party."

"Manipulation like that can breed resentment."

"People won't know we're doing it," says Pinter. "All they'll know is that they feel more comfortable. Friendlier, closer. We've run some live experiments."

My toes curl in my boots. I feel invaded, as if I've just opened the curtains in my living room and discovered a neighbor with binoculars. Thank heaven I haven't flown Desert Air this month, though if they're doing this, Morse's Great West will follow. I have to admit that, lately, I've felt watched.

"You'd be amazed how well it worked," says Pinter. "We ran a satisfaction survey afterwards and couldn't have been more pleased with the responses."

"What else are you suggesting that they do?"

"Closed-circuit televisions in the gates connected to video cameras in the cabins. To shorten those anxious minutes when people deplane. You're waiting for someone, perhaps you're holding flowers, but it seems to take ages before you see his face. You worry he missed his flight. You don't know what to think. This way you see him the moment he's in range."

He looks to me for a reaction, and I blink. His ideas are pure foolishness, born of arrogance. The man hardly flies, yet he's dashing off prescriptions for a growing regional carrier. This is hubris. This is too much fame. I'm of a mind to pocket my proposal and tailor it for one of Pinter's critics—for Arthur Cargill, maybe, of the Keane Group, the father of Duplicative Skills Reporting.

"Help me," says Pinter. "You're skeptical. Speak up."

"With all due respect, sir—"

"Don't kowtow. It's beneath you. I made a few inquiries after your call and discovered you're very well thought of. An up-and-comer. I agreed to share a meal with you because I expected a peer-to-peer exchange."

I don't dare ask him who spoke so highly of me. Someone at MythTech? I've heard he's close to them. There's a story that he attended the Child's wedding, an exclusive affair in Sun Valley, Idaho, and presented the newlyweds with a silver cheese knife given to him by a Saudi prince in appreciation for his work untangling supply lines in the Gulf War.

"I come to this as a consumer," I say. "A passenger. I appreciate your spirit, but frankly I feel like you're toying with people's lives here. An aircraft is not a glass beaker."

"The world's a beaker. This is axiomatic in our field."

"Churches? Are churches beakers?"

Pinter glares. I've violated the code of our profession by invoking the sacred. I'm out of bounds.

"You're religious?" he says.

"Not conventionally."

"Of course not. No one's conventionally anything anymore. But do you believe in the image of God in man?"

"I see where you're going with this. I slipped. I'm sorry. I've been surrounded by Mormons for a decade."

"It's leaching in. You insulted me," he says. "You implied I'm corrupt. A Faustian. Untrue. Helping this little airline find an edge in an increasingly cutthroat industry offends not a single commandment, that I'm aware of. In truth, it's a moral act *par excellence*."

"I repeat my apology."

Pinter sighs, gets up. The difference in his stature sitting and standing is remarkably slight. He's all torso and no legs, though his long baggy jacket conceals the fact. We face each other. He addresses my chest, as if we're the same height, and in my weakness I play along—I crouch.

"Margaret and I have been cooking. A request: none of your God talk at supper. And no business."

"You do understand why I've come, I hope. My concept?"

"Afterwards. At the table we stay 'on topic.' "

"And what's the topic?"

"That's up to you. The guest."

"I've taken your classes. I want to thank you for them. You were on satellite. You couldn't see me."

"That's an assumption you have no basis for."

"I know how satellites work."

"The old ones, maybe."

Because the street-side entrance to his house is blocked by landscapers and mounds of earth and because the front porch has been removed, leaving the doorway suspended in a wall, Pinter parks his new German sports coupe in an alley. It's been a long ride. Ontario has traffic, uniformly frantic in all directions, like a stepped-on anthill, and Pinter has no business being out in it. His driving style combines inattention to others with a deep absorption in his own car. Even while cruising, he fussed with the controls, tilting the wheel and pumping up the lumbar and adjusting the louvered vents of the AC. He'll die in that car, and I suspect he knows it, which is why he's so eager to enjoy its gimmicks.

Margaret stands on a step by the back door holding an old-style cocktail with a cherry in it. She looks like a girl in her twenties who's been aged by an amateur movie makeup artist using spirit gum for wrinkles and sprinkled baby powder to gray her hair. She greets me too kindly, kissing both my cheeks, yet barely acknowledges her co-domestic, who knifes past her into the kitchen and pours two drinks. The kitchen is one of the two inhabitable rooms, the other being a bedroom whose door is open, through which I can see a massive four-poster bed dressed with paisley sheets and furry blankets like the type you once saw on water beds. Access to the remainder of the house is blocked by thumbtacked sheets of dusty plastic. Behind them, a shadowy carpenter fires off bursts from a pneumatic nail gun. The noise is piercing.

"Sandy tells me you live in Colorado, out on the frontier."

"I used to live there. I had an apartment, that is. I gave it up."

"Where do you live now?"

"Just here and there."

"Literally?"

"People do it. And not a few."

"So this is a trend?"

"Not yet. You'll see it soon, though."

A drink is placed in my hand. It's sweet and strong and

tastes of 1940s Hollywood. Pinter lights another cigarette and resumes his peculiar smoking trance while peppery Margaret continues with the questions, timing her words to avoid the nail gun's volleys. Over the royal bed I glimpse a picture: some mythical scene of a semi-naked virgin being chased through a dappled glade by randy goat-men.

The table is set, but I detect no cooking odors. Pinter wraps an apron around his waist and opens a curvy vintage refrigerator packed solid with convenience food. His cigarette smoke mingles with the frost cloud, a sight I find profoundly unappetizing.

"We're dining alfresco this afternoon," says Margaret. "The construction draws so much current our stove is useless. Did Sandy describe our project to you?"

"No. It looks like it's fairly extensive."

She motions me forward, then peels back the curtain of plastic. I peek through. The living room walls have been stripped back to the studs and a circular hole the size of a small swimming pool has been cut in the hardwood floor.

"Our arena," says Margaret. "Sandy thought it up. See where the ceiling's gone? That's where the lights go. We'll surround it with comfortable seating, pillows, throws. A stage for our debates, out little theatricals. We proportioned it after the Colosseum, actually."

"Your guacamole's skinned over," Pinter says.

"Squeeze lemon juice on it."

"I can't find the chips."

"You ate them in the night. Just use saltines."

Margaret refastens the plastic in the doorway. I have questions, but don't know where to start; the syrupy cocktail has turned my brain to sludge. The puzzle of the arena aside, what happened to Pinter's dietary discipline? The spread he's begun to assemble on the table—plastic tubs of pre-made onion dip, lunchmeat slices rolled and pinned with toothpicks, a dish of canned fried onions, a jar of olives—reminds me of sample day at a small-town supermarket or the grand opening of a Chevy dealer. I wonder if its wealth of additives holds the secret to Margaret's pickled youthfulness.

Pinter refreshes our drinks and we sit down. The china and silver are real, the napkins linen. Pinter, since coming home, has gained in stature, and as we toast—"To the life force," Margaret says—I see that both the table and the counters stand at wheelchair height. I tower beside them. I feel fatherly, monumental. Normal-sized Margaret's the mother and Pinter's our son.

"So," she says, "did you select a topic?" She's poised to start eating, but there are rules, apparently.

"An actual formal topic."

They nod.

"I'm blank. Politics?"

"Anything," Pinter snorts. He's hungry. "Our last guest—"

"Don't lead him," says Margaret. "Let him associate."

My gaze drifts to the bedroom painting. "Pursuit."

They smile and dip their crackers. I'm a hit. I take a rolled slice of bologna as my prize.

"I think it's important to start experientially. Now which of us at this table," Pinter asks, "has actually been pursued?"

"I have," Margaret says.

"Ryan?"

"Romantically? Professionally?"

"You chose the topic. What was on your mind?"

"Omaha."

"Them," he says. "No business talk."

"You know them, though?"

"We've mingled. No business talk."

Margaret dabs guacamole off her lips. "Sandy, you've heard this, so try not to jump in. It happened in London, England, in the sixties. Sandy was there as a guest of British Railways."

"Rationalizing their timetables," he says.

"I'd read about Carnaby Street in all the magazines and wanted to buy an outfit. I took a bus. I rode on the top deck, to see the sights. There were a couple of boys with Beatles haircuts—Sandy had one himself once—"

"Oh go to hell."

"You *did*."

I reach for a black olive. My drink is empty. Why is Pinter staring at my crotch?

"Anyway, two moptops. Drinking beer. Out of those extra large cans the English favor. And I, in what I'd guess you'd call my innocence—"

Pinter's eyebrows arch. His nostrils flare.

"—approach these two lads to ask about their fashions. You know, their 'scene.' Can they point me to a shop, say—some place that's out of the way and not for tourists? They tell me of course, if I'll buy them a beer. A deal. So off we go into the streets, those crooked streets, and before I know it, well, they're groping me. Against a wall. Beside a garbage can. And they take all my money."

"The money that you paid them."

"You're out of rotation, Sandy. You'll have your chance."

"She was shopping for new experiences, not clothes. You weren't around then, Ryan. The LSD years. My Margaret was something of a cosmic voyager. Dragged me out to meet Huxley, Leary, all of them. Hot tubs under the redwoods. Puppet shows. I thought it might break my writer's block. Astrology. And maybe it helped. The visions. The new perspectives. Maybe it helped me turn DuPont around. But what did not help, I solemnly assure you, were Margaret's suspiciously picturesque assaults in all the European capitals."

"I slept with Henry Miller once," says Margaret.

My phone rings in my jacket, a muffled trill. Pinter sneers at me, says "Pff . . ." I reach in and turn off the ringer and apologize, blushing even deeper than I have been.

"Thank you," Pinter says. "I loathe those gadgets. The sins man commits in the name of keeping in touch."

"I normally leave it behind on social occasions. I'm in a fog today."

"The topic," says Margaret.

"Are we ridiculous?" Pinter asks me. "Do we seem ridiculous to you? Our insistence on keeping the dinner hour holy? Our love of discussion? Our odd erotic pasts?"

"No," I say, not audibly.

"If we do, it's because we don't buy it. We just don't buy it. This wireless wired hive of ours. A sinkhole. No one can be everywhere at once, and why should they want to be? We'll come close, of course. We'll come within a hair, then half a hair, then half of a half. But we'll never ring the bell. And that's their plan, you see. Progress without perfection. The endless tease, slowly supplanting the pleasures of the sex act."

"An hour ago you said the world's a beaker."

"Is this still pursuit?" Margaret asks. "Or have we switched?"

"A beaker is a charming antiquity compared to what they've got in store for us. Tiny antennas planted in our follicles. Digital readouts on our fingernails."

"Attached without our permission?"

"We'll *give* permission. They'll promise us free FM radio. Free phone calls."

"They? You don't feel implicated here?"

"Of course I do. I'm in on the ground floor. I'd prefer it if there was another 'they' to join, but this is the 'they' that history offered me. Advice: If you hear there's a 'they,' get in on it, if only to be pro-active and defensive."

"In your seminars you teach accountability. This sounds like passivity."

"It's always a mix—the seminars overstate one element. The seminars are for psychic adolescents, not vigorous whole realized beings with perspective."

"Remind me not to sign up for any more of them."

"Sandy, you were pursued once. By that company."

"That's Omaha again. That's business, Margaret."

"Please," I say. "I'm interested in this."

"They asked me to write down my dreams for them. I did. After three months, they started faxing things back. Predictions. Guesses. What I'd dream of next. At their peak, they reached forty percent accuracy. It's tedious."

"How can you say that? Not at all. Dreams about what?"

"What I'd shop for the next day. Shaving cream dreams. Frozen meat dreams."

"You're joking with me."

"They do some good work. They do some bad work, too. Mostly, they're show-offs. It's all just razzle-dazzle."

"That's not what he thought at the time," says Margaret. "It staggered him. He fell ill for a whole year."

"That was chronic fatigue. That wasn't them. You brought up business, darling. Discussion over."

Margaret deserts us. She carries her drink to the steps by the back door and sits down facing the alley, its peeling palm trees.

"I think MythTech's after me, too."

"You'll know. Now drop it."

"We need to discuss the Pinter Zone," I say. "Don't take this as pressure, but I'm relying on it."

"I'm not sure I want my collected works on coffee mugs. Not that omnipresence isn't appealing. Have to tinkle now. Try those onions there. And why not take off your jacket? You look hot."

With the table as cover, I take out my phone and activate "last caller." A Salt Lake area code. Asif again—he must have news of Julie. Now that he knows there's a crisis, he'll be tireless.

Margaret has turned and seen me from the stoop. "Just make your call. Don't let him rattle you. Do it from outside, if that's more comfortable."

"Thank you."

"My husband would like you to sleep over, but I can see you're not ready. I'll explain to him."

I walk around behind Pinter's car and dial. She answers on the first ring. My sister. Safe.

Her voice is not strong, though I doubt that mine is either. I can hear the road in her voice, the truckstop coffee, as she describes her all-night diagonal journey down through South Dakota and Wyoming in her Plymouth van. She punctured a tire passing Rapid City, repaired it with a can of Fix-A-Flat. She picked up an Indian hitchhiker near Sheridan who gave her a bear-claw pendant for good luck. Crossing the Utah border at Flaming Gorge, she stopped for an hour to examine with her flashlight a hillside bristling with fossil dinosaurs. And no, she insists, it's not the wedding she's fleeing, but the deaths of Miles and TJ, the poisoned dogs, who expired, as Keith reported, at her feet, of unstoppable internal bleeding. Their deaths were her fault. In fact, it's all her fault.

"What else?" I ask.

"Everything." Julie is not right.

"Have you eaten?" I say.

"I'm eating something now."

"What?"

"A licorice rope."

"Licorice isn't food."

She doesn't ask me to come. I'm coming anyway. I can be there, Great West and the flight controllers willing, in under four hours. I'll have to leave immediately.

"I'm pouring a glass of milk now."

"Finish it. Milk is the ticket," I say.

"I've finished it."

Pinter comes out the back door onto the steps and stands with one arm around Margaret's girlish waist. His face has lost its lecherous intensity, and he turns it away to grant me privacy. I tell Julie not to sit up for me, to sleep, and to pass the phone to Asif, which she does. The hum of expensive appliances tells me they're in the kitchen, where they should be.

"Take her car keys."

"I have them."

"Bless you, Asif." The gift of a rich, resourceful brother-in-law who wasn't born in America. We owe him.

Pinter gives me a moment after I'm off the phone. Strange man, but intuitive when he wants to be. "Something's come up, I can see," he says. "You run now." Margaret lowers her head against his shoulder.

"Family."

"Don't explain. We all have troubles. This business between us, perhaps we'll work it out. I'll be at GoalQuest. I need to travel more. You're speaking there?"

"Short talk. To clear the air. Just between us, I'm leaving ISM. They've niched me and it's not a niche I like. Plus, my lower extremities are numb. I'm sorry. It's the same old whine."

"Not really."

"You couldn't drive me back to my hotel so I can grab my luggage and my car?"

"I could, but we might not get there safely. Margaret?"

"Certainly. Just let me find my glasses."

Pinter and I shake hands. His tiny thumb beats with a disconcertingly sharp pulse. I thank him for the meal, his understanding.

"Good topic," he says. "We always enjoy 'pursuit.' "

eight

i was a country boy once. I wore a cap. It promoted Polk Center Gouda, "World's Finest Snack." The girls in town were virgins but didn't know it because they thought having their breasts touched was real sex. The girls were all blonds, except for the exchange students, who came from places like Italy and Egypt and stunned us with their fine manners and silky English. The boys were all blonds, too. Touring polka bands pulled in each summer and people paid two dollars to dance all night and drink keg beer that was mostly tasteless foam. The money went to the volunteer fire department. When we heard about murders in cities, we felt lucky. When we heard about Washington scandals, we felt justified. America was that country all around us, and we knew that we'd go there someday, but we could wait. We were proud of Polk Center. Its farmers fed the world. Our stop signs may have been riddled with bullet holes but our thoughtful drivers still respected them.

It wasn't until the first time I flew, in a medevac helicopter to Minneapolis, that I realized how confined I'd been. I was sixteen. I'd had an accident. Every December, when the lakes froze over, kids piled into cars and hit the ice to race and spin three-sixties. I was driving. I had two passengers, other boys from town, whose fathers delivered propane for my father. I cranked on the wheel and we slammed against the doors. I cranked the wheel back and we hit the other doors. We laughed. We drank vodka. Our parents knew where we were. They'd pulled the same stunts when they were young. Tradition.

Then the hood of the car sloped up and we were sinking. Just like that—slipping backwards through the ice, the coins sliding out of our pockets across the seats. I watched the hood rise up and block the moon and I reached for the door and heaved but couldn't budge it. The water against the windows was black and solid and some of it trickled through a heating vent and splashed me on the chin.

I woke up in the sky, on a stretcher, wearing a mask. The oxygen tasted bitter and dried my throat, and through a window I spotted the North Star. The uniformed man bending over me explained that both of my passengers had escaped the car but that I'd been in the lake for fifteen minutes, which normally would have been long enough to kill me. What had saved me, he said, was the freezing water, which sent my body into hibernation. He asked me if I felt lucky. I thought: Not yet.

They let me sit up as we hovered over the hospital. I could see all the Minneapolis skyscrapers, some of their floors lit up and others dark, as well as the antennas on their roofs that transmitted our radio stations and TV ball games.

I could see the western horizon, where I'd come from, and a dogleg of snowy river crossed by bridges sparkling with late-night traffic. The landscape looked whole in a way it never had before; I could see how it fit together. My parents had lied. They'd taught me we lived in the best place in the world, but I could see now that the world was really one place and that comparing its parts did not make sense or gain our town any advantage over others.

Moments later, we landed. My stretcher jolted. As we waited for the helicopter's blades to slow, the medic said I would be home in a few days, not understanding that this was not the comfort it would have been had I never left the ground. He wheeled me out onto the roof under the moon, which had risen some since I'd seen it from the car. I lifted the oxygen mask so I could speak and asked how long we'd been flying. Just thirty minutes. To reach a city I'd thought of as remote, halfway across the state, a foreign capital.

I told the man I was feeling lucky now.

Tonight, in Salt Lake, I'm feeling lucky again, and not just because I escaped the swinging Pinters. Three hours and thirty-five minutes, door-to-door, across the Great Basin to my sister's mansion in the foothills along the Wasatch Front. I slept, I woke, I hailed a cab, I'm here. Don't tell me this isn't an age of miracles. Don't tell me we can't be everywhere at once.

Getting out of the cab and walking up the driveway, I set off a series of motion-detecting floodlights. The yard goes from dark to a Hollywood premiere. Wheels of mist surround the sprinkler heads buried in the fresh-mown lawn and their droplets splatter a trio of campaign signs for local Republicans. Otherwise, it's quiet. My nephews' mountain bikes lean against a wall of the three-bay, cedar-shake garage. This is Utah, the state of early bedtimes, and Jake and Edward are probably asleep now, dreaming of good grades and science fairs.

The peephole in the front door is faintly blue; someone, deep in the house, is watching TV. That would be Julie. Asif disdains pop culture. He came here from Pakistan to work and save, and the purity of his will is undiminished. Our family felt vaguely shamed by him at first, intimidated by his priestly poise and engineer's exactitude of spirit, but that was our own unworthiness at work. He's tough on himself, but he spoils his sons like princes, for which they're none the worse, amazingly. If anything, they're embarrassed by his lavishness and out to prove that they too can rise unaided, taking on extra science work at school and pitching in on chores like little sailors. I fully expect that by the time I'm old this branch of my family will be a minor dynasty, and I'm flattered that Asif has mixed his blood with ours. Except for my mother, we all are. She's still cautious. She can't believe this wealth is honest, somehow, and hoards savings bonds for her grandkids, just in case.

I open the door and set down my bag and case in the darkened hall. I smell a recent meal—encouraging. As a strict vegetarian in beefy Utah, Asif has had to learn to cook.

"Hello?"

"Down here," Julie whispers. "Everyone's sacked out."

She's dragged a couple of cushions off the couch and is

sitting on them like a yogi, legs crossed, spine straight, watching an old Road Runner cartoon on a children's cable channel. Beside her is a plate of cheese and bread and a tall glass of juice, but this looks staged. She hasn't been eating. Her cheeks are two dirty ashtrays, gray concavities, and her hair, whose fluffiness tells me that it's clean, doesn't reflect the TV glow the way it ought to. The silk pajamas she's wearing must be Kara's. The top is bunched and wrinkled—it's buttoned wrong—and the bottoms, they just look empty.

After I kiss her, I ask her, "Did you rest?"

"I tried," she says. "I'm still buzzing from the drive. My van's so big and shaky. Bad shocks or something. Nice jacket—out of a catalogue? It fits you. Must be nice to be shaped like people in catalogues. The wedding's just going to be suits, no formal wear. Mom's grumpy about it, but men look weird in tuxes—the kind you can rent in Minnesota, anyway. Those bands around the waist, they look like trusses, like something to hold in a hernia. Ryan?"

"Yes?"

"There's a big plate of raisin cookies in the kitchen."

"What were you going to say to me?"

"Stop staring. This is my ideal weight. Just hug me, Ryan."

It's the part I always forget, and women need it. Her body feels old and stony through her PJ top.

"I think your ideals are a problem," I say.

"Yes."

It's always wise, in my experience, to turn off any nearby TVs or radios when trying to dissipate emotional tension; they have a way of blurting out bad thoughts, of lobbing idea grenades into the room. When I settle in on the sofa with the cookies, the Road Runner has changed places with Porky Pig. Is Julie just dying? A cleaver-wielding farmer is chasing Porky, over whose head looms a panicked thought balloon filled with hams and chops and bacon strips. Could it be any worse?

"I'm sorry about those dogs," I say.

"It wasn't them. It's me. I ruin everything. Have you ever looked inside my car? It's all old phone bills and spilled Mc-Donald's Cokes. I can't catch up with myself. I'm underwater. I promise to do something simple, like walk those dogs, but then I remember another promise I made, and another one on top of that, so I make up a list with boxes and little checkmarks, but before I can finish it my pen runs dry, so I run off to find a pen, and then it's quitting time. Pretty soon things have piled up so high I have to call in sick to clear my head, and when I come back they're all angry at me, furious, so instead of buckling down, I run and hide. And it isn't just work I'm talking about. It's everything. It's breathing. It's sleeping. It's feelings. Does this make sense?"

"It's all about managing time."

"It's more than that." She digs a raisin out of a cookie and eats it, the raisin, but leaves the rest untouched. "Anyway, I'm sorry I dragged you up here. You were on business and I screwed you up. Where are you supposed to be tomorrow?"

"Phoenix. I'm meeting my publisher. I hope."

"Kara told me you were writing something. Wow. A mystery?"

"A business parable."

"Is it long?" she says. "I like the long ones. So I can really snuggle in, get cozy."

"Business readers don't curl up with books."

Julie rests her head on my knee. I stroke her hair. I'm ashamed to admit that her thinness has its charms, elongating and defining her throat and neck.

"That was the sweetest wedding present," she says. "Keith opened it by mistake. You really splurged. Who told you we needed one? Mom?"

The gift's not mine; my sister has it confused with someone else's. I picked out the luggage set just yesterday and was waiting for my card to be reactivated before I placed the order. And there's no way for her to know about the stock. Then again, this may be Kara's work. Her standing assumption is that I'm irresponsible when it comes to my sentimental duties; she probably sent something practical in my name, a microwave or upright vacuum cleaner, and forgot to inform me. She covers for me this way, forging my signature on thoughtful gestures.

I probe. "You needed one?"

"Well, no one *needs* one. Our grandparents did without them, obviously."

"What told you it was from me?"

She lifts her head and eyes me at a slant. "Are you okay?"

"A little frazzled. Why?"

"That was such an odd question. Who else would it have been from? Are you still on that medication?"

"That was years ago."

"So no more seizures?"

"I've never had a seizure. That's like calling every lump a tumor."

"Fine, then. 'Fits.' "

"That's even worse," I say.

Julie is misinformed, as usual. She's referring to the beta-blockers prescribed for a funny heartbeat that turned up during an annual corporate physical a few months after our father's funeral. I was tired at the time, surviving on diet cola while shuttling between Denver, LA, and Houston as part of an effort to smooth the troubled merger of two mid-size regional advertising agencies. Worn down by my grief and the gloom of the assignment, which consisted of identifying redundancies and recommending layoffs, I suffered a kind of segmented collapse marked by bouts of irresistible sleepiness during several key meetings and lunch appointments. Because of the politeness of my associates, who declined to mention my little naps after I came to, and because no single individual witnessed more than one of the attacks, weeks passed before I caught on to what was happening. I imagined I'd dozed off for a few seconds, when in fact I'd been falling asleep for a few minutes. I finally learned what was wrong at LAX, where I nodded off at a pay phone in the Compass Club and missed a flight. I was granted a paid leave. I grounded myself for seven weeks (a record), took a few classes to refresh my spirits, and made an adequate recovery. Other than the minor arrhythmia, there was just one lingering complication. It happened that during one of my brief blackouts—at a downtown Denver oyster bar—sneaky Craig Gregory had played a trick on me, slipping my wallet out of my back pocket and inserting a scribbled-on business card for one Melissa Hall at Great West Airlines. "Fantastic meeting you. Call!" the message read. There was also a row of X's and a heart. I found the card while reorganizing my Rolodex, puzzled over it for a day or two, then thought what the hell and gave a ring. Assuming the woman was a flight attendant, I left a sweet, if tentative, voice mail, and received a call back from a mannerly Melissa—Soren Morse's executive assistant and, I found out later, his sometime mistress. Here's what was strange, though: after much embarrassment, and after we'd identified the trickster—Craig Gregory knew Melissa through a cousin—she told me that she'd seen my name while making up invitations to a Christmas party Morse was throwing for Great West's heaviest flyers. We agreed to say hi to each other at the party, which was just a month away, but my invitation never arrived. I called to inquire, but Melissa wouldn't speak to me, and I could only conclude that Morse himself had struck me from the guest list. Jealousy? I tried my theory on Craig Gregory, who laughed it off but no doubt wrote it down for the "This is your life" file he keeps on everyone.

All in all, a murky time for me. But I repeat: there were never any seizures. My sisters spend too much time on the phone together erroneously filling in the blanks of their brother's life.

This matter of having sisters. I've done my best. When Kara was born after years and years of trying—in Minnesota you weren't supposed to have to try; babies were supposed to come like crops—my parents already considered themselves old. My arrival surprised them. My father was as pleased as any man to have a son, but he was busy by then, with a grow-ing gas route to attend to. In helping him I saw my opening. By five I was riding shotgun in the propane truck, learning a business that, if it had survived, I'd still be in today, with no regrets. The secret was providing added value with every refilled tank—carrying the news from farm to farm, adjust-ing and reigniting pilot lights, delivering packages for snow-bound widows. My apprenticeship secured a spot for me in my father's everyday routine and in the larger life of the community.

Everything changed when Julie came along, a month premature but radiant and perfect, with none of that simian newborn homeliness. If I'd been a surprise, she was a shock. Her beauty felt like a judgment on our averageness, and we fell into competition for her favor. My father, who'd grown comfortable by then, cut back on his hours to spend more time at home, while Kara and my mother scrimmaged con-stantly over who would change the baby's diapers and push her in the new stroller through the aisles of the downtown J. C. Penney. I was odd man out again. Whenever I managed to get alone with Julie, I spoiled her with treats and toys and labored to impress her with my manliness. When I was four-teen and she was ten, I knocked down an older boy in front of her. I took her homework when she got home from school and returned it to her in the morning, finished. I was her first crush when she turned twelve, and when I went off to college I sent her letters playing up my successes and achievements and dismissing the girls who supposedly had eyes for me. Our romance crested during a summer vaca-tion when I smuggled her into an R-rated movie and she rested her head on my shoulder during a love scene. A neighbor sitting a couple of rows behind us had a word with my mother. We were finished.

"The wedding present wasn't from me," I say. "Kara must have sent something in my name. What was it anyway?"

"A lawn mower. It follows these wires you bury in the ground and runs by remote control."

My mouth goes dry. I can't swallow my cookie.

"Where was it sent from?"

"Salt Lake City. Here. A store called Vann's Electronics. You signed the card. You're saying you don't remember buying it?"

"I'm not saying anything. I'm going to bed."

I lie in the dark guest room beside a window that frames the spire of the Mormon Temple, as white as aspirin and topped with a gold angel. I've set my sleep machine on blowing leaves and swallowed a sedative. My left hand is tucked under the waistband of my boxers and in my other hand I hold my phone.

"Talk to her. Build her up inside," says Kara. "That's your specialty, isn't it? Be tough, though. Don't tell her she'll be okay no matter what or that she's some infinite bundle of creativity. Don't bullshit her, Ryan. But try to make her feel good. This is a crisis of confidence we're dealing with."

The side of my face with the phone against it aches. I switch to the other ear. "I'm on a business trip."

"Fine. So leave her to run away again. Maybe we'll hear from her at Christmas. Shit."

The air on my chest is heavy, hard to lift. I roll up on my side for easier breathing. "You're saying to keep her with me?"

"In plain sight."

"A question. When Wendy saw me in Salt Lake last week . . ."

"Yes?"

"She's sure it was me?"

My sister sighs. "Out with it. Tell me. You lied to me before."

"I think she was right. I was here. It slipped my mind, though. The cities don't stick in my head the way they used to."

"What?"

"There are credit card records. I made a purchase. Kara, I'm not at my best right now."

A hush. Southerners have an oral tradition, they say. Minnesotans have a silence tradition. Not speaking is our preferred way of communicating.

"You haven't been eating either," she says. "Have you?"

"Poorly."

"Come home. Right now. Come home right now. I know what you're doing. I know what's going on here. This is all about earning free tickets. You need your family."

"My job ends Monday. I'm leaving before they fire me. I have appointments, interviews."

"Come home."

"It's not my home anymore."

"It's where your mother is."

"That's why it's not," I say.

With the earpiece against my cheek I let her rant. One of my nephews opens his bedroom door and I hear him pad down the hallway to the bathroom and tinkle into the bowl. We start so small, and the space we take up as we grow is gone forever. Not everything is recycled. That space is gone.

"I need to sleep," I tell her when she's calmer. "I'll try to talk sense to Julie. I'll bring her with me. I have a meeting tomorrow, but she can come. I don't want her vanishing in that van again."

" 'Take' her with me," she says.

"I think it's 'bring.' "

"I'm coming back there. I'll get her home myself."

"I said I'll do it. I'll bring her down to Phoenix. In the morning I'll put her on a plane back home."

"Why do I have to do everything myself? Why am I always the glue?"

"I'm doing it."

"You're telling me *you're* the glue? You're not the glue! There's a *wedding* on Saturday."

"And you're the glue."

"Die, Ryan. Just get it over with. Goodbye."

I stopped in Salt Lake last week. I wake, remembering. I remember that there was nothing to remember, except for telling a man who'd lost his job that careers nowadays aren't ladders, they're lattices, and then I explained to him what a lattice was and gave him a model résumé to study. I killed time in a store for an hour after the meeting and bought Keith and Julie their gift, which I had shipped. Then I flew off to Boise, I believe, where I gave the same speech to another man. The lattice speech.

There, I remember now. I wasn't robbed. It turns out that we've been together this whole time, all of the Ryans. We just got separated.

This has happened before. I've never told a soul. I've met myself coming and going. It's a secret. It's only because you've been such a patient listener, there in your seat with your drink, your nuts, your napkin, prepared to crash with me, if it comes to that—because isn't that, finally, the contract between us flyers?—that I'm breaking down and telling you.

at seven o'clock on Wednesday morning Asif drives us to the airport in his Mercedes, a long black beauty that ought to have a flag flying from its antenna. The radio plays a conservative talk show whose amped-up host rattles papers into the mike and has mastered the art of speaking without swallowing. Our democracy died in 1960, he says, but he doesn't provide specifics, unlike my father, whose doomsaying always included clear-cut timelines and definite turning points. The sun crawling up behind the Mormon Temple casts a peculiarly weak and filtered light, and a breeze stirs the surface of the Great Salt Lake, which appears to be filled with old bathwater this morning. Even the seagulls windskating its edges seem reluctant to land and wet their bellies.

"When should I pick you up tonight?" says Asif. I can tell he holds my plan in low regard. Not only is he convinced that Julie needs rest, but this notion of visiting a far-off city without spending the night there baffles him.

"We'll get in late," I say. "We'll grab a cab."

"How do I explain all this if Kara calls?"

"Her sister and brother needed some family time."

At the ticket counter I pay full fare for both of us and make my pitch for a pair of first-class upgrades. Julie stands back as I wrangle with the agent, embarrassed by my assertiveness, no doubt. Minnesotans are taught to accept first offers gratefully, but in Airworld you're nowhere if you don't negotiate. Unfortunately, the agent is hanging tough. He grants me a seat because I have a coupon, but insists that I turn over ten thousand miles for Julie's seat—ten thousand miles each way. I roll my eyes.

"Pull up my customer profile. This is crazy."

Julie cringes and turns her head away. The agent runs his fingers over his keyboard, his mind a symphony of codes and acronyms. Though I've never seen him before, I know his story. He's a lifetime employee who lives for strikes and sick-outs and spends his evenings figuring his pension on his home computer. He's an officer in the union, undismissable, who sleeps through his annual performance reviews and savors the frustration of his customers, cheerfully forwarding their written complaints to his impotent superiors. He lives for some strange, consuming, pointless hobby—playing King Arthur in medieval fairs or collecting vintage outboard motors—and has come to believe that if not for certain health problems brought on by his stressful work environment, he might have been a man of influence.

"I have your data in front of me," he says.

"Come on, let's just go," Julie whispers.

I wave her off. "How many miles do you see there?"

He lowers his glasses, which are attached to a cord, like

an old woman's. "Nine hundred ninety-five thousand two hundred and one."

"Drop it," Julie pleads. The agents smiles at her. He's enjoying playing us off against each other.

"And what does that tell you about me? Huh?" I say.

"There's a note in our system," the agent says. He points a stubby finger at the screen. "Did you lose a bag last week, sir?"

"No."

He types some more. "I'm showing we found a bag at SLC and sent it on to a Denver residence per the luggage tag: 1214 Gates Street, Apartment 16B. There was no one home to claim it. Is that your address?"

"It was. I moved out." This isn't making sense. Although it turns out that I did come to Salt Lake last week, I never check bags, so I couldn't have lost it here.

"What's your new address?" the agent says.

"There isn't one. Listen, I didn't lose a bag. I'd know." I look behind me for Julie, but she's gone. "Are you going to upgrade my companion's ticket, or do we have to call your supervisor?"

The agent must feel that he's toyed with me sufficiently; he prints out two boarding passes and hands them over as though all I'd needed to do was ask politely. My platinum customer status leaves him no choice. I ask him if he saw where Julie went and he nods at a newsstand across the terminal, then slips me a card with Great West's lost luggage number.

Julie is browsing the home decor section of the news-stand's magazine rack, mooning over photos of claw-foot tubs and built-in stainless steel refrigerators with ice and water dispensers in their doors. Such publications fascinate me, too, though not because I'm about to enter a marriage whose primary solace will be a line of credit at Ethan Allen, courtesy of Keith's parents, who run an outlet. They intrigue me, these pictures, because the rooms they showcase strike me as buffed-up funeral parlors, basically, designed to display and preserve the upright dead. The flowers, the waxy furniture. It chills me. Lori, my ex, used to drag me to garage sales, convinced that she had a talent for discerning beauty and value beneath the dust and crud. What sorry wastelands. Console TV sets sheathed in chipped veneer. Dressers with sticky drawers and missing handles. The stuff had all been new once, clean and promising, and all I could see in it was depreciation. The depreciation of the owners, too.

I apologize for the confusion at the ticket counter, but Julie goes on reading and won't acknowledge me. Our morning isn't progressing as I'd hoped. My plan was to spend an hour at the airport broadening her horizons and introducing her to America's pumping commerical heart. She's been in Polk Center too long, it shrinks a person, but this is a place of options, of possibilities.

"Let's go to the club. I have to make some calls."

"The club?"

"I'll show you. The magazines are free there."

"Ryan, I need to go home."

"Tomorrow. Thursday."

"I'm letting a lot of people down," says Julie.

"Don't worry. They'll still be there when you get back."

"That's not always true."

"It's true in Minnesota."

The club attendant waves us in with all the graciousness of a royal doorman. I check Julie's face; she's flattered, I can see it. The buffet impresses her too—she pauses, stares. Midwesterners are beguiled by free food, even anorexics, apparently; it speaks to our unconscious, collective longing for a bounteous harvest. I pour myself a glass of orange juice from one of the glass carafes propped up in ice buckets (why do they always offer tomato and prune juice? Does anyone actually drink them anymore?) and watch as Julie reviews the pastry tray and uses a pair of scalloped metal tongs to select a caloric lemon Danish dusted with powdered sugar. And she's not finished. She empties a single-serving box of bran flakes into a paper bowl, tops it with raisins and a glob of yogurt, then breaks off a greenish banana from a bunch of them, peels it, and slices it with a plastic knife.

"Get a table by the big TV there. You can watch your portfolio. CMB."

"What's that?"

"A little global bank you own a piece of. It's up two points. You're richer every minute."

I duck into one of the carrels in the business center and dial my assistant in Denver. He's there, for once. He has a memo on Texas he needs to fax me, but Texas is over, it's obsolete. I punted. He gives me the address of Dwight's hotel in Phoenix and passes on several other routine messages, including another from Linda at DIA. He confirms my Las Vegas hotel reservation, which I ask him to cancel because the Cinema Grand has labor issues, I read in last week's *Jour-*

nal, and part of the new me is not being a scab. I ask for a suite at the Mount Apollo instead, the place with the five-story revolving Pegasus that spreads its great fiberglass wings on the half hour.

"One more little thing," I say. "Contact Great West baggage at DIA and ask if they have a piece of luggage for me. If they do, have it sent to the office and open it."

"You lost a bag?"

"That's what they're telling me."

"I don't know if I should mention this," says Kyle, "but I saw a sort of strange memo on your desk. Craig Gregory's assistant delivered it by mistake; he grabbed it back ten minutes after he brought it. The subject line read 'Faithful Orange.' "

"Interesting."

"Your initials were in the text. 'RB in place,' it said."

"That's all?"

"There was more, but I didn't have time to read it. They snatched it out of my hand, like it was secret."

"Sniff around and tell me what you find."

"What's Faithful Orange?"

"I have no idea."

The air in the club smells of lint and vacuum bags and behind me I hear the cable financial guru predicting a major downturn in corporate bonds. He steered me right on Chase Manhattan, after all. I sit for a while in the tilting, castered chair and watch a light rain gust in out of the west, speckling the runways as it advances and sending the ground workers scrambling for orange slickers. It takes so many people to keep me airborne—night-shift janitors riding rotary waxers, crawl-space plumbers wielding clamps and wrenches, meteorologists, navigators, cooks—and this morning I feel like I'm failing them somehow. My skeleton feels like a ladder of lead pipes.

I recognize Faithful Orange as a project code, but I can only guess what it refers to. ISM's founders came up through the military, a crew-cut cadre of logistics specialists who took what they'd learned supplying Vietnam with freeze-dried beef stew and tents and bayonets and applied it, in their first big contract, to the global distribution of auto parts. The corporate culture they spawned is leakproof, rigid. No shoptalk, no gossip. Dungeons inside of dungeons. For all I know MythTech is our subsidiary, and Great West itself is run by our alumni, with Morse as their strutting puppet. Faithful Orange. Orange is the airline's official color, and considering that it's at war with Desert Air, I wouldn't be surprised if they're our client.

I've never trusted ISM. My position in the firm has never been clear to me, and the path to promotion is winding and obscure. Some people advance by leaving and returning, and the people who don't advance . . . well, they just vanish. Two years later you hear they've opened a bed-and-breakfast or bought out a Kinko's franchise in Keokuk. That's what you hear, but it seems more like they've died.

RB in place. I'm part of something big.

Julie, God bless her, is back at the buffet, spooning more yogurt onto her granola. She looks better already, less sunk inside herself. The rain has picked up and it's sheeting the tall windows, distorting the silhouette of the control tower. I check the departures monitor. Bad news. Our flight, 119, is twenty minutes delayed, and twenty minutes is almost always a lie. It means we'll get back to you. It means buzz off.

"Is that our old friend Ryan Bingham? How's he been?"

There's a hand on my shoulder—I turn in its direction. The face is a jolt, collapsing time and space. Its white pore-less nose hooks almost to its lips and the eyes have a blind and stony quality, like the eyes on Masonic temples and dollar bills. It's the face of my ex-wife's husband, my replacement, with whom she had two children, just like that, proving that I, not Lori, was the barren one. She took his last name after refusing mine, and from everything I know about their life together, the highest councils of heaven have sanctioned the match. I was merely a pit stop, a wrong turn, on the way to their preordained union.

"Mark," I say. I take his extended hand and briefly squeeze it. His other hand grips the handle of a briefcase. Antiqued nickel hardware, natural, top-grain hide. One of Boulder's top real estate salesmen, and still rising.

"How are the girls?"

"They're fabulous. They're dolls. Little Amy is quite the marksman, for her age. That's our family obsession lately: shooting sports."

"Lori, too? I thought she hated guns."

"It must be the country air. We're out of town now. Sixty acres up against the foothills. I subdivided the old Lazy W Ranch and took a nice slice for myself. You have to visit."

"Lori firing a gun. I can't imagine."

"Still renting that one-bedroom?"

"I gave it up."

"You own now?"

"No."

"But you're looking?"

"Not really. No."

Mark's face twists in on itself. He bites his lip. Home-ownership is his church, and he feels sorry for me. He divides the world into two camps, those with equity and those without, and his calling is to unite them. A noble soul.

"There's something I'd like to show you. An opportunity. Do you have a minute to sit and hear me out?"

I do, and he knows it; the airport's at a standstill, pent up under an iron lid of clouds. The soft leather couch is like sitting on a body as we settle in diagonally, knee to knee, and Mark snaps open his case and reaches inside with a smooth and lotioned hand. This is the man who took up where I left off and carried my wife past a biological threshold that I lacked the strength for. His confidence is spellbinding. If I didn't dislike him so, I'd hire him to stand up at hotel banquets and teach his system. I doubt he has one, though. Mark is all instinct and genetic mastery, shot from a cannon at birth. If he had antlers, they'd spread past his shoulders. He's my natural superior.

He opens a folder and lays it flat between us. "These homes will go in the high four hundreds soon, but until the community's finished—and be aware of this, it *is* a community, not just a development—we're slipping people in in the mid-threes." He gives me a moment to absorb the photos; crisp early-morning shots of pillared facades surrounded by spindly staked aspens and split-rail fences. The houses are set at odd angles to one another as though they grew up without a plan, organically, and each has a horse paddock with a lone brown steed that I'd swear is the same animal, duplicated. I detect a computer graphics program at work, but I'm charmed and drawn in despite myself. These happiness professionals know their jobs, and theirs is the sort of art I most admire, because it's effective, because it gets things done.

"The concept is turnkey everything," Mark says. "You buy a maintenance contract with the home. You're traveling five days a week? It doesn't matter. We'll whack your weeds, we'll even change your lightbulbs. Furniture? Buy your own or choose a package. High-speed Internet, too."

"Garages?"

"Hidden. A seamless traditionalism, yet all the perks."

I'm interested, though I'm not sure if it's sincere. Part of me might like to signal Lori through Mark that not only do I qualify financially to own a burnished cube of paradise, but that I'm actually capable of filling it. She knew me just as I was starting to fly and developing my system for compact living, for keeping a portable and tidy camp. She accused me of smallness, of tightness. It wasn't fair. If anything, my spirit was too far-flung. I lived out of a pack because I owned the plains.

"You're concerned about interest rates," Mark says. "Aren't we all? You can't think short term, though. This is an investment. How are your stocks doing?"

"Miserably."

"I'm sorry. Do you have any tangible assets?"

"Not to speak of. A '96 Camry in a long-term parking lot."

I'm trying to sound pathetic on purpose now, to test the depths of Mark's pity. He's always liked me. He met my ex in a supermarket aisle a month before our divorce was finalized, but instead of asking her out immediately, he came to me for permission. Unprecedented.

"Here's what you do if you're interested," he says. "Put down some earnest money, any amount, and I'll hold a unit until you can come see it. I have one in mind. The view-scape's just spectacular."

"I may be relocating soon. To Omaha."

"You hold this house six months, you'll clear a profit. That's guaranteed. If you don't, I'll buy it back. Ryan, we all need a place to call our own. This is America. This is what we're promised." He pushes the folder closer. "Are you all right?"

"Something strange is happening."

Mark leans closer. His breath has the sweetness of a man who jogs, who squeezes his own juice and eats his vegetables. He may be too sane for what I'm going to tell him.

If you fly enough and chat with enough strangers, you hear some crazy things. They stretch your sense of what's possible. Some examples. That a study was done about forty years ago of the chemical makeup of the soil in major American grain-producing regions which found that due to the overuse of fertilizers the soil was bereft of certain key particles and was therefore incapable of yielding even minimally nutritious food. That a science exists by the name of psychotronics which seeks to influence mass human behavior via the beaming of powerful radio waves from a network of secret transmitters located above the Arctic Circle and aimed at Russia during the cold war. That the American Medical Association, soon after issuing warnings about the effects of sodium consumption on high blood pressure, realized that there was no evidence for the warning but declined to retract it out of stubbornness. That contrary to popular belief, cocaine remained an ingredient in cola drinks well into the 1950s. That the odds of winning at blackjack in Las Vegas shift ever so slightly in favor of the player for an average of seven weeks per year and that there exists a high-priced newsletter which alerts well-heeled gamblers to these trends.

Now it's my turn to float a far-fetched theory. Though not as far-fetched as Pinter's dream reports.

"I think someone high up is toying with me."

"Who?"

"It might be the airline. Or ISM. It might be an outfit in Omaha. Or all of them."

Mark's eyes go wide and tender. "Toying how?"

"You know how biologists will tag an elk so they can follow and analyze it's movements? They do this with people, too. Not always openly. One of the Big Three auto companies hired my firm once to follow five new car buyers for their first three months of ownership. How fast did they drive? Did they change their oil on schedule? How many miles did they clock per week? You can do surveys to gather this kind of data, but you'll never be able to guarantee their accuracy. No, what you want is behavior in the raw. That's how you target your ads, create your profiles. Is this making any sense to you?"

Mark nods. "Why you, though? Why would they shadow Ryan Bingham?"

"Because I'm an interesting case to them just now. Uniquely interesting. By Friday night I'll have a million frequent flyer miles, making me one of their most loyal customers. That's the grail in this industry: loyalty. To keep you on board, buying tickets."

"I understand that."

"To them, I'm an optimal outcome," I explain. "If they could create, say, a thousand more of me, just think of the earnings. The market share. I'm gold. There's only one problem: Who am I?"

"I'm losing you."

"How do they re-create me? They need a model. But how do they build this model? They can't. Too complicated. Because what are the crucial variables? My age? My income? Some mysterious psychological quirk? No, the only way to make new mes, new Ryan Binghams, is to track and study, whole, in real time, in my 'native environment,' the actual Ryan Bingham. Right?"

"Okay."

"You look confused. Your face."

"I'm fine. Keep talking."

"I'm everything they dream of in a customer, and that makes whatever I do worth studying, down to how many hours of sleep I get, what sort of rooms I stay in, what I eat. And also worth testing, if possible. They're testing me. They're throwing scenarios at me right and left and seeing how I react. A ticket agent rebuffs some special request—do I get angry or do I accept it? A flight attendant spills coffee on my jacket—do I switch to another airline, or threaten to? These are things they'd pay a lot to know."

"So what are you going to do? If this is true, I mean."

"Nothing."

"Nothing?"

"What can I do? I'm powerless."

"Tell them to stop it."

"Tell who? It's not one person. And it's not like they're trying to control me. The elk, remember? They tag it with a beeper, and let it roam. The data I'm providing is only valuable insofar as I'm acting freely, naturally."

"A beeper. I think that's crazy, Ryan. I'm sorry."

"In my case all they'd probably have to do is put a note in their computer system. It comes up whenever I check in for a flight and tells the agent to ask me this or that and call a certain number afterwards. A researcher answers, asks them certain questions, then forwards the answers to whoever's running this."

"And who do you think that is?"

"Management. Management and whoever's advising management. Assuming that this is happening at all."

"You're admitting you might be dreaming this."

"I might be."

Mark cuts his eyes at the monitor. "My flight."

I've made a mistake. I've chosen the wrong confessor.

"You run along. Forget this stuff," I say. "I'll think about the house. I really will."

"I want you to call me, Ryan. Promise me? Make it a social call, forget the house. I'd like to sit down with you. Just two men. No business. There's a book I read once that really changed my outlook, that pulled me out of a hole I'd stumbled into—maybe we could get together some night and read a few chapters?"

The Bible study come-on. Why won't they ever just come right out and say it?

Mark shuts his briefcase, stands. "You'll call? You promise?"

"Mmm."

"You're in our thoughts, you know."

"Hers too?"

"Constantly. Listen, I'm sorry I'm rushing here. About the house, though—it might be what you need. A house can be a real anchor in this world. Take a good look at that literature."

"Will do."

Mark's handshake leaves a moist spot on my palm that I blot on my trousers as I watch him go. In a couple of hours he'll be home and in her arms, welcomed by jumping dogs and squealing kids, and his decency will forbid a full reporting of what I've told him this morning. Tonight they'll sleep. The stars will wheel forth from their daytime hiding places, crowning their mountainside neighborhood with lights, and one of those lights, slightly brighter than the rest, will be my wingtip, passing over, blessing them.

Sealed in a tube again, but going nowhere. The rain strikes the windows like handfuls of dry rice as a flight attendant stows the wardrobe bags and another who might be her twin takes Julie's drink order: club soda with a wedge of lime, no ice. The engines aren't on yet, so no air conditioning. This is the trick they play that I least appreciate: pushing back from the gate to lock in a departure time, then parking while the cabin steams and swelters.

Julie doesn't seem bothered. She's in heaven, claiming every inch that she's entitled to by gripping both armrests and kicking out her legs and tipping her head back like a sunbather. This trip is already doing wonders for her. She's loosened her shoes, which hang from her bare toes, and spread her knees in acceptance of what's coming: G-forces, liftoff, the future. Poor Keith is screwed. His fiancée has discovered her inner princess.

Me, I'm panicking. I shouldn't be here. This is one flight too many. My hands are gloved in sweat. Until today my momentum was my own, but I'm at the top of the arc now, pitching over, and my seat belt feels thin and flimsy across my middle. I could use a quick blast from the oxygen mask. A beer.

"Unclench your jaw," says Julie. "You'll get a migraine."

"I'm nervous. I'm meeting my publisher today. Assuming we ever take off."

"We will."

"We won't. I've developed an instinct—they're going to cancel us. We'll sit here, they'll string us along, and then they'll cancel. Meanwhile, this man I'm seeing is like the wind. I'll never catch him again. Eternal tag."

Julie refuses to let me bring her down. Her eyes glide around the cabin the way they used to during long driving vacations when we were kids, passing the hours by playing games with license plates. My father was a rigid driver, maddeningly steady on the pedal and unwilling to stop, except for fuel. He'd announce a time of arrival when we set out and do whatever it took to hit his mark—starve us, dehydrate us, torture our bowels and bladders. Everything but speed up. Speed scared my father; delivering flammable liquids had made him timid. There was a bumper sticker on his propane truck: "Don't drive faster than your guardian angel can fly."

I turn on my HandStar and dial up Great West's customer information site, according to which our flight is still on time. How do they keep their lies straight in this business? They must use deception software, some suite of programs that synchronizes their falsehoods system-wide. No wonder I've grown suspicious of them lately—they haven't spoken the truth to me in years. How many times have I gazed up at blue skies and been told that my flight's being held because of weather?

Julie opens *Horizons* to the page where Soren Morse, or whoever does his writing for him, expounds each month on his visionary quest to make Great West "your total travel solution." His photo up top is quasi-presidential, with a soft-focus background of globes and flags and bookshelves. Welcome to my kingdom. I own you here. His face is soap opera handsome. Full lips. Sleek forehead. A scar on his chin to remind you he's a male. His management style, from everything I've heard, is smooth but abusive. Interviewed by *Fortune*, he called himself "process-centered to the core" and a "humanist reengineer," but I've heard tales of tantrums and vendettas, of intimidation campaigns against VPs that left their targets medicated wrecks.

The pilot has an announcement. I was right. Our plane will be returning to the gate. "Please inquire inside for further information."

Julie says, "What does that mean?"

"Nothing good."

Morse is making this personal. He'll pay.

"What do we do? Go back to Utah now?"

"That never works."

"What doesn't?"

"Going back."

t e n

i work quickly, rebooking us to Phoenix through Denver. The only available seats are in economy. The agent
snickers delivering this news; I've dealt with him before, and
he's a pest. He's sickly, always sniffling and coughing, and
handing out infected boarding passes gives him a sadistic
thrill, no doubt. If only Morse knew how poorly his employees, as grudging as nineteenth-century clerks, with no
higher sense of process or brand goodwill, reflect on his
credentials as a leader. Commissioner of baseball? Not a
chance. Commissioner of youth league soccer, maybe.

The agent picks up his phone when I walk off—reporting
to his masters? No way to know.

On our way to the gate we buy mochas and cinnamon
rolls. Twelve dollars. Julie is outraged. She tastes her coffee
and tells me it's not even hot. Mine's not hot either, but I had
no expectations that it would be. That's the secret to satisfaction nowadays. Julie asks me about my book and I say, "Later."
I was supposed to talk with her. I haven't. A rowdy bunch of

uniformed marines shoves past us on the moving walkway, running. A cart glides by with a blind man in the back, his cane sticking over the side and nearly swiping people.

The Denver plane is a 727 with haggard upholstery and discolored wings, black streaks of corrosion trailing from every bolt. It clatters into the air and through the clouds and breaks out into a sunlit turquoise plain riddled with nasty whirlpools of clear-air turbulence. Julie reaches over and grips my wrist while fingering with her free hand a silver cross hanging against her breastbone inside her shirt. When did this strike? She's been born-again again? All around me lately God is claiming people. Am I still on his list, or has he skipped me? We jolt again and Julie bows her head and doesn't look up until the ride is smooth. The fear improves her color.

"I can't go back. I'm going to, of course, but I can't. I'm all confused," she says.

There's a pressure behind her face; she wants to talk now. This isn't the place. There's no room to move, to gesture. Overpopulation has a ceiling: earth's total surface area divided by the dimensions of one economy seat. One more baby is born and hello cannibalism.

"Keith cares too much. It makes me feel . . . responsible. He won't drink the last of the milk. He says it's mine. When we wake up in bed I'm hogging the whole middle and he's falling over the edge."

"A relationship is a closed dynamic system."

"Can I tell you a story? We're shopping for a car. Keith says I need something safe, with lots of airbags, but I'm thinking I'd like a truck, for hauling kennels. I ask the salesman, who's been showing us station wagons, to show us some pick-ups. I fall in love with one. I ask about the pickup's safety rating compared to the wagons. 'Not good,' the salesman says. I turn to Keith and say 'It's your decision, hon,' but he doesn't respond, he just stands there. It gets embarrassing. It's like he's gone catatonic, had a stroke. Finally, I say 'I'll get the wagon, okay?' Nothing. A blank. I literally had to shake him."

She rambles on and I listen without listening. The clouds below have a complicated topography, dimpled and grooved and folded and corrugated, with broad estuarial fans along their edges. (Estuarial—there, I've finally used it.) It's Wednesday down there, but what day is it up here? At times, in the afternoon, when flying east, I can see night bearing down across the continent, and the feeling is one of powerless omniscience. To know what's coming and when it will arrive and see the places it's already been is a counterfeit wisdom. It ought to help, but doesn't.

Julie keeps talking. Though I barely hear her, I manage to be a brother to her merely by sitting nearby and shedding heat. She'll go through with her wedding, I'm certain of it, but only once she's drawn sufficient energy from me, her original hero, her first security. We talk about our father as though we loved him, but that was something we only discovered afterwards; while he was alive, he mostly worried us. He'd taken on so much—the house, the trucks, the loans, our mother—and we could see him sagging. His business was our protection, all we had, but nothing protected his business, and this scared us. We reserved our love for one another, brother and sisters, because everything else seemed borrowed against, at risk.

"Ryan?"

"Yes?"

"Weird question: are you rich? The way you bought my ticket, just like that, not even asking the price."

"I've saved. I'm comfortable."

"Do you date? Do you have a love life?"

"I like to think so. I'm meeting a woman in Vegas tomorrow night."

"A stranger. Disease doesn't worry you?"

"I'm in the soup. If you're in the soup and get wet, then you get wet."

"I don't think you know how proud of you we are. Everything you've accomplished, this book you've written, these meetings you're always flying to. It's awesome. It's like you're out here covering the territory, putting it all together. Our ambassador. We read magazines and expect to see you in them, and even though you aren't, we know you will be. We know you should be."

"Thanks."

"You're done out here. Let's go back to Minnesota," she says.

"I'll get you there tomorrow. I'll be there Friday. I just have a few more stops to make. Appointments. It only seems hectic. Believe me, there's a rhythm. You had to be here when it started to hear it, though."

Julie sleeps.

There are no lights in the garage tonight except for the guttering candle that illuminates the latest quarterly statement from his ac-

countants. According to their figures, the world is his. His products and processes dominate their markets. His name has become synonymous with quality and demand-based value-adding genius. He can quit now and step outside to vast acclaim, assured of permanent wealth and influence. The garage will have served its purpose as an incubator for dreams once widely dismissed and roundly ridiculed, and surely he must preserve it as a museum showcasing in perpetuity the transformational journey of one mind wholly at peace with its core competencies. But as M rises up from his stool to make his exit, something distracts him: a pad of clean white paper lying on the bench beside his instruments. The paper's emptiness cries out for a mark, a sketch, a diagram, a thoughtless doodle. Through the door he can hear his massed admirers calling for him to show himself at last, but while he feels boundless affection for his team, without whose selfless input he'd be lost, he understands also, after a quick gut check, that his work remains incomplete. He lifts his pencil. . . .

The first thing I do in Denver is call Dwight's mobile. He answers on the first ring. It's disillusioning. I'd imagined him hunkered down with a sick author, but apparently he's alone and doing nothing. Behind him I hear splashing, yelling. Pool sounds. His assistant portrayed the trip as an emergency, but it sounds like another golfing getaway.

"I'm on my way," I say. "I'm with my sister. Hard to explain. We got canceled and rerouted, but we should be down there in time for dinner, easily."

"Where are you staying?"

"I'm not sure we are. I have to get her back to Minnesota and I need to be in Las Vegas tomorrow. GoalQuest. I might just shoot over there early."

"The book is just brilliant."

"You got it? You read it? Not just the summary? I don't think it lends itself to being summarized. It's more a gestalt. Is that the word. Gestalt?"

"I have a contract in front of me. An offer. We can work on the figures, the terms, but not a lot. It's close to the best I can do. Just need your signature."

"And I want you to have it."

"Once we've talked. The manuscript has a ragged edge or two. I have a few trims, a few snips."

"It's not too short for that?"

"A lot of our books are read in digest form. You've heard of the journal *Executive Outlines*? They lop the fat off six or seven titles and sell them as a package to subscribers who don't have time for a lot of monkey business."

One of my eyelids twitches. My crownless molar zings and sizzles. I can taste it rotting.

"You'll be here when, exactly?" Dwight says. "Technically, I'm checked out of my room, and my flight to Salt Lake City leaves at seven."

"You're flying to SLC? I don't believe this. That's where I'm coming from. I left an hour ago."

"Too bad. We could have met there. I wish I'd known. Hold on for a minute. The waiter's got my tea."

The tram that I've been waiting for with Julie roars into the loading area, stops. Its doors open and a floodwall of pedestrians surges past us to the escalators.

"Bingham?"

"If I'm going to make it, I have to run," I say. "My flight's two terminals over. This is crazy. What's this last-minute Utah business, anyway?"

"Tennis commitment. I'm sorry. It couldn't be helped. You say you'll be back there tonight? Let's think this through."

"I don't want to think. I want to see your face. There, my tram just left. Terrific. Great." I roll my eyes at Julie, who whispers "What?" and tightens her grip on the bag of fuzzy pet toys she bought for no reason at a stand upstairs. My sister feels ill at ease, I'm learning, if she goes for more than an hour without a purchase. I wish she'd put them away, though—I don't like stuffed things.

"I have a solution," says Dwight. "The Salt Lake Marriott. Tomorrow. For a very early lunch. We'll buckle down and wrestle with this idea of yours and see if we can't get an outline we're both proud of."

"It's down to an outline now? That's all you want?"

"The Marriott at ten. Frankly, I find this hugely preferable. They're practically booting me out of this hotel. This works for both of us?"

It will have to work. Our flight to Phoenix is boarding; we'll never make it. Julie, whose appetite Airworld has revived, bites off a chunk of caramel-coated soft pretzel and eyes me in a childish sugar daze. What's next? I wish I could tell her.

"At ten. Agreed?"

"Fine. I'll see you there. This doesn't thrill me. If this is how your profession operates . . ."

"I don't represent a profession; I've never claimed that. I'm a bookman, Bingham. Just a bookman. If you find our little fraternity too casual, too fallible, too dog-eared—"

"I'm not saying that."

"Good. Because this idea of yours is strong."

"As strong as *Horizoneering*? Morse's book?"

"Odd you should ask."

I listen. Nothing. "Why?"

"Just odd, is all. I'll tell you a little story at lunch tomorrow. And bring an appetite. Their buffet's first rate."

"Where are you—*really*? La Jolla still? New York? Or do you just *pretend* to move around? What's a tennis commitment? That's a *game*."

"Only for those who don't play it well," Dwight says.

"I want you to *guarantee* me you'll be in Utah."

"Guarantee you? Now how would I do that?"

fold certain itineraries in the middle and the halves are
mirrors of each other. I've taken such trips, a yo-yo on
a string, staying in the same places on my way back that I
stayed in, the other day, on my way out. At the outermost
point of such journeys, before the pivot, there's a moment
of stillness, of poised potential energy. To begin the rewind-
ing all I have to do is pick up my change and wallet from the
nightstand, tuck in a shirttail, sign a credit card slip. But
what if I don't? It's always tempting. Rebellion. What if I
step aside and let the string snap back without me? I'll be
free then, won't I?

The next flight back to Salt Lake leaves in an hour, and
there is another two hours after that. Julie wants my decision. She licks a yogurt cone speckled with crystals of red
cinnamon candy and leans on the rail of the rising escalator,
watching her brother sort through his bad options. I've begun to suspect she's pregnant and not telling me. Her face
has that dependent bottomless softness and her appetite for

junk seems driven, hormonal. She's filling out like a moon before my eyes.

"How would you like to see my office?"

"Sure. I thought you'd quit, though."

"That's still in process. We'll rent a car. We'll drive."

I need to get out of the airport. All airports. Now.

My Maestro Diamond card cuts through the formalities and ten minutes later we're buckled up and cruising, watching the Denver skyline climb the windshield and swaying in our seats to Christian rock. Julie has always been up for anything—the source of most of her problems. She rides along. Her beauty arises from her readiness, and Keith, if he's really the lump she's made him out to be, will never drink from its source. That's fine with me. There are parts of her that I'd rather strangers not handle.

I'm a dead man at ISM but they don't know that yet; the parking attendant thumbs-ups me, lifts the gate. We drive down into a catacomb of Cadillacs and take my empty spot, still stained with coolant from my poorly maintained Toyota. When we get out, a man that I know from the hallways and lobby and who I've always assumed is at my level—though how would I know?—stops dead and palely stares. He raises a hand in a lame half wave, then fusses with his tie and turns and goes. There's the flash of a shoeshine, the echo of hasty steps. I lock the car doors remotely, with the smart key, and lead Julie into the elevator and up.

"You're sure we should be here?" she says. "You're not in trouble?"

"Why?"

"Your shoulders. Roll them back. Now exhale. Slowly."

"Massage school," I say.

"It stays with you. It trains your eye. Back there in the airport, the compression of people's spines? It's like they're all six inches shorter than they should be."

"You'd think they'd walk taller there."

"They're munchkins. Crabs."

The point of this errand is still waiting to reveal itself. We walk out onto my floor and nothing's changed except the art. Artemis Bond, the apostle on our board, donated to us a trove of wildlife oils said to be worth millions, though I'd be shocked if that were true. The bugling bull elk and treed pumas and flushing quail rotate through the building, floor by floor; I know it's September now by all the waterfowl. The art is our only connection to natural cycles here. An energy-saving coating on the windows cuts out the heart of the spectrum from the light and turns people's skin the color of old dull nickels. It makes paper explosive, too bright to look at, and assistants have actually left us over eyestrain. One even filed suit, and may have won. Such victories don't pay. The CTC cases I've known who've wrangled judgments for wrongful termination are spacemen now, in orbit, in exile, unwelcome back on earth.

Julie trails me past a gang of cubicles glowing with junior executive ambition to a partitioned warren of larger offices that means we're approaching the operational heart of things. The air swirls and eddies with all the old polarities—fear of the lion's den just down the hall, the hope for an unmolested interlude at the copier or fax machine, the seductions of fresh-brewed decaf in the snack nook. My assistant looks up from his desktop—I've tripped some wire—and reformats his self-presentation appropriately, jerking taut the slack around his eyes.

"It's you," he says.

I point Julie to my office, which has a love seat. A foreshortened sofa, actually. It's never been used for courtship, that I know of.

My assistant rolls back his chair two caster-turns. I'm a sight, it seems.

"Any messages?"

"Just one or two. Your hotel in Las Vegas is covered. The Mount Olympus. They're crowded, so I had to take a suite. They said it has a jukebox and a pool table."

"Nice."

"You think so? It kind of gave me chills. Mr. Bingham alone in some hotel room, practicing his bank shots, playing records."

"Who else. Did a woman named Alex call?"

"Don't think so. Just that airline lady who sounds like Catwoman. She calls every couple of hours. She wants your mobile. I've been guarding your privacy."

"Linda. What does she want?"

"Wouldn't tell me. Is that voice an act?"

"I've never noticed it. Give her my number next time. Nothing about that meeting in Omaha?"

"No, but your briefcase came from Great West baggage. I stood it up next to your chair. Your tie is twisted."

I own just one briefcase, and I'm carrying it. I walk into the office, hip-bang the door closed, and look down at a burgundy case with gold-tone hardware that might have been my style a few years back, but not since I started reading *GQ* magazine. The airline address tag looped around its handle is filled out in my hand, in faded blue ink.

"Is this you in this picture?" Julie is on the love seat, a magazine on her lap. The *Corporate Counselor*.

"That's me. The one they're hoisting on their shoulders."

"Why are your shirts off? What are all those ropes?"

"We were rock climbing in Bryce Canyon. It's a program. Wilderness Accountability. We ate wild grasses. We chiseled arrowheads."

"One of those things where you let yourself fall backwards and everyone catches you?"

"Only they don't catch you. On this one they let you fall. And then they step on you."

I heft the case. It's light, but it feels full. I shake it. Paper. The combination lock reads 4–6–7. I used to carry an expensive pocketknife—a gift from a Waco oil services firm in gratitude for the lawsuit-free excision of eleven second-tier managers, three of them less than a year from being vested in a pension plan that's since gone under—but it was taken from me by airport guards who measured the blade length and said it broke the law. I could use something like it to jimmy the case. I open my top middle desk drawer and stir the junk around, a lot of giveaway convention bric-a-brac, looking for something slim and strong and pointed, but the best I can do is a silver-plated bookmark snagged from KPMG at the last GoalQuest. The thing is hardly metal, a flimsy wafer, and when I wedge it against a hinge, it cracks.

"Back from the vale of sorrows. Ryan B. His mournful dignity marred by coffee stains insufficiently blotted from wrinkled collar."

This man is not worth elevating my vision for, a conclusion I came to long ago, but he might have a knife in his trousers, so I do. It's the same old assault on the senses. Flared canine nostrils snuffling for blood trails near the watercooler. Marx Brothers eyebrows, permanently arched and flaked with dead skin that flies off him when he laughs, which he only does with both hands inside his pockets, as though there's a switch near his scrotum he has to toggle. Craig Gregory, Human Issues Group Team Leader, who came to me years ago in the company weight room, reracked the barbell I was struggling with, gazed down into my clear young eyes, and said, "It's a recession, it's official. Axes are falling. Much stench. Much fear of plague. I know you'll want back into Marketing Group someday but right now the king's army needs some undertakers to sanitize the gore. You say you'd love to? Abracadabra: I grant you better insurance, complete with vision care coverage. Go with God."

Craig smiles at me now, just one hand pocketed. The other will join it the moment I ask for something.

"You stood up our Texas client. And that's okay. Life moves so slowly down in the Lone Star State, beneath those humbling skyscapes, that red sun, that I'll bet you could amble on in a year from now and those lazy cowpokes would still be at their grub. Also, they've written some wobbly checks of late, so I say screw 'em. I say hang 'em high."

I slice a look at Julie, who need not witness this. She stands. The old family telepathy still functions.

"The ladies' room? Do I need a key or something?"

Both pockets now. Craig Gregory locks and loads. It's like him to ignore a stranger's presence until he can actively nullify it. "A password: 'Open sesame, really gotta pee.' "

"Ask my assistant," I tell her. "My sister Julie, Craig. Proof I was born of woman, not spore, like you."

The two of them brush hands and Julie flees. She'll make it a long one, I trust.

"I'm serious, Ryan, you called it right on Texas. Those boys aren't downsizing, they're capsizing. We don't take Monopoly money at ISM. The full faith and credit of Parker Brothers State Bank just ain't gonna butter our bagel. Old policy. No pro bono until Jesus tells us otherwise."

"Is Boosler still back from his trip 9/21?"

"Affirmative. Caught many tuna. Dallied with many maidens. Sucked much synergistic bigwig dick. The question is: when will *you* be back?"

"I'm here."

"Fractionally. I sense brief layover. I'm going to stroll to your love seat over there and sacrifice my commanding height advantage in return for some teammate-to-teammate pillow talk. Walking now. Sitting now. Relating now. What the fuck's up with you, asswipe? They phoned, you know."

"Excuse me if I don't join you in repose. Fresher air up here. Who phoned?"

"Them. The Brain Trust. Operation Gamma Ray. The Seven. Whatever it is they're calling themselves these days to mask the absurdity of their worthless methods. The Omaha Illuminati."

"MythTech?"

"They swiped our big milky nipple this week, Corona-Com. There goes the lap pool we're building up on nine. There goes the Broncos skybox with the wet bar and honor-system humidor."

"Good for them."

"Good for you, if you join them. 'This Bingham?' they ask me. Bold as that, like we're swapping fucking baseball cards. 'What can he do for us? Is he a comer? Rate on a ten scale: Emotional lability. Bilateral orgasmic dexterity. And by the way, since we're speaking frankly now, how does he do taking orders from female Negroes?' "

"Who made this call? This isn't their procedure."

"I am strength and silence. I am Khan."

"Lucius Spack?"

"Is that the quiz-kid pederast? The queer little pink guy with the propeller beanie?"

"You don't have a pocketknife, do you, by any chance?"

Craig Gregory licks his lips. They dry out quickly. "No one called."

I set the briefcase down.

"I'm fishing, Ryan. I'm covering my flanks. They raided Deloitte. They're raiding everyone. I'm going up and down the halls today in search of potential deserters. Don't think you're special. We're an old-line firm, and we take pride in that, but we realize that novelty sings its siren song."

"You're lying. I say they did call."

Again, both pockets. Craig Gregory laughs. "This is fun. It's fun, my job. The Art of the Mind Fuck. You'll be at GoalQuest, surely?"

"I'm speaking there," I remind him. "Please come listen."

"Before or after Tony Robbins? During? Sorry, can't make it. Must touch my guru's robes. Must wash big Tony's feet in thanks and praise for turning wormy me into king cobra."

I cross my arms. "What's Faithful Orange? Tell me."

Craig Gregory cups his knees and slowly rises in lobsterlike, hinged stages from my sofa. "Behind you," he says. "Your sister. Waiting sheepishly. Intimidated by Gregory's musky pheromones."

I turn. We all look so gray in here. Turn back.

"Faithful Orange. A soda pop, I think."

"Is the Marketing Team consulting for Great West Air?"

"I'd like to think we have corporate Denver covered. I certainly hope we are. Listen, you look like hell. Nice boots, but from there on up you're Guatemalan. If I was a fag I'd reach over and fix your hair. And your 'I'm too busy to floss' thing just isn't working. That may go over fine among the Navajo, but this is white America. Colgate country."

"What if I told you I'm taping you right now and sending a transcript to Equal Opportunity? You're going to get ISM sued. You watch your mouth."

"Me? Our first Diversity Training graduate? I'm covered, brother. I have a framed certificate. Sponsor me on my AIDS walk?"

I should quit now. Retrieve the letter from Boosler's desk and read it aloud while standing on my chair. Gather the assistants. The cleaning staff. The letter has several flourishes I'm quite proud of and would benefit from an oral presentation. If I had my million miles, I'd do it, too. But it's ISM's dime that's going to put me over, and I can't afford to lose travel authorization. I recite the letter in my head.

"Until GoalQuest. Anon. Our desert tribal gathering."

Craig Gregory is going. Walking now. Walking and wagging his ass now. He liked me once. He sent me bursting congratulatory food baskets heaped with blue-veined cheeses and vintage vinegars. Once, he even took a dive for me in a company tennis tournament, vaulting me into the finals. These tokens moved me. Maybe my father was not so loving, after all. Maybe there are holes I'm trying to fill.

"Was that your boss?" says Julie.

"That's never been clear. We use the new, confusing titles here."

It must be the briefcase I came for, because I have it now and I'm ready to leave and not come back. I stare at my desk and conduct a mental X-ray of its neglected contents. Family photos? I'm not the type who would bring those to the office—I'd prefer they not know the faces of my loved ones here. Voodoo potential. Somewhere, in some drawer, I stashed a small packet of marijuana once, which I used to use in tandem with my sleep machine during particularly hectic trips. It's a fossil now, surely. No drug dog could even smell it. What else is in there? A stapler. Old Vicks inhalers. Some cream I bought once when I couldn't feel my legs, supposed to promote circulation. It caused a rash. Other than that, though, just business cards and tape and microcassettes and

ISM logo keychains and scads of paper clips that have mysteriously linked themselves together into the sort of puzzle bright children enjoy. Worth holding on to? Anything? Post-it notes?

They give you a lot of stuff when you're first hired and you fully expect you'll use it, but you just don't.

If earning miles were the chief consideration, I would do better driving the rented Volvo at five hundred bonus points per calendar day back to Salt Lake City. In fact, this is the chief consideration, particularly as of 3 P.M. today, with every other seed I've planted lately gone dormant in the clay. Dwight is backpedaling on *The Garage;* the Pinter Zone concept, while still alive, feels vaporous; MythTech hovers obscurely behind a cloud bank; and Alex still hasn't called about our Vegas tryst, which I've begun to regret arranging anyhow. If my chilled, sluggish legs are any indication, I doubt I'll be able to muster the blood flow necessary to cap off our evening in my rec-room suite. My assistant was right; it is a lonely scene, even with a woman in the frame. The jukebox plays Sinatra. The balls go smack. You say to your date, 'Nice shot.' The hot tub bubbles. And meanwhile, in all four directions, above your head, people you've met or may as well have met but at this point will never meet fan out on late-night business that you're not part of and may never be again. Because you had qualms, and you voiced them, and you're tired. Tired, with cold numb toes.

Right now, for the first time in years—the first time

ever?—I'd rather not get on a plane, though. You listening, Morse? Your calf has slipped the lariat. He's driving. He's utilizing the public byways. And still earning chits, still indebting you, through Maestro. Besides the miles I'll give to charity in the hope some sick child will come vigorously of age and knife you in the street for pocket change, I think I'll just hoard the rest. To keep you owing me.

Julie, too, would rather drive than fly now. She covered much the same route just yesterday, but in the dark, and she wonders what she missed. The trip should take us about eight hours, she estimates, and will be like old times in Dad's Chevy, except we'll eat.

Kara looms. Both bells at the New York Stock Exchange have rung, O'Hare has dispatched a dozen flights to Asia and FedEx Memphis has sorted a million legal briefs and tardy birthday presents, and still no status report for our big sister. I'm sure she finds this unpardonable. I find it racking. The longer we avoid her, the louder she speaks. I hear her voice when our tires stray onto the gravel.

The briefcase, still unopened, is in the trunk. Some truckstop along the way will have a screwdriver. My new theory is that the case is mine, that I left it on board a jet some years ago during one of the strobing, amnesiac flutters that follow intensive bouts of CTC work, and that the case has been sailing ever since in the parallel dimension of Great West baggage. I anticipate no epiphanies (Verbal Edge, tape nine, "The Language of Art and Literature") when I crack it. I expect to find socks and boxers and a shirt and perhaps a collection of loose-leaf workbook pages from Sandy Pinter's master-level seminar, the one where participants wore colored hats representing the Six Cognitive Styles and were asked by the trainer to cross a hotel ballroom without letting their feet contact the floor. It was a daunting task for the non-acrobats and the source of much frustration and puzzlement, until the trainer pointed out to us that our feet and the floor were separated by shoes, an obvious fact that all had overlooked and proof of Sandy Pinter's principle that frantic problem-solving is usually evidence that no problem exists.

Either that or the case contains Morse's tracking device and I can go crazy in earnest once I've jimmied and stripped the bug from the lining. To find a bug—how glorious that must be for those who've done it. To have one's fears credentialed, physically. To hold the little gremlin in one's hand and hear it tick or buzz or hum or whatever it does that tells one that it's operating, then to bellow into the ears of living spies! I'd like to sit down with a man who's had this chance. I think he would have a strong spirit as a result. I could offer to agent him as a corporate speaker.

I let Julie drive. I'm accustomed to being piloted. We head north toward Cheyenne, where we'll meet I-80 west and push up over the hump to the Great Basin in the footsteps of the Mormon settlers. They say you can walk in the grooves cut by the wheels of their wagons and handcarts. We'll pass the graves of children, the shady encampments where Brigham spread his bedroll. I've never driven this trail, but I've flown over it, and my sense of its contours and hazards is comprehensive. The West gave people so much trouble once, mostly because they couldn't see over its ridges, but now we can, and it's just another place.

This might be the nicest car Julie's ever driven; she's treating it with inordinate respect. Both hands on the wheel, a stiff, cadet-like posture, much attention to mirrors and turn signals. She's scared. This is world-class imported equipment, and it's intimidating, especially to those who don't rent cars much and believe that the vehicles are theirs illicitly, as part of a scam or a very special favor. Me, I push these cars hard, without remorse, aware that they've been paid for ten times over and will be sold at a profit on top of that. It's sweet, though, to see the meek, more natural atti- tude. May it never die out. It's a cushion for the rest of us.

"What if, when we hit Wyoming," Julie says, "we go right, not left? To Minnesota? It seems pretty easy suddenly. Just swerve. The rest might take care of itself. The wedding. Keith. He's already burying wires for that lawn mower."

"That monster you met in my office made you think. Red wagons and cornfields are sounding pretty good."

"It isn't like that now. We have espresso. Good espresso. Mom's hooked on it. Burt, too."

"The Lovely Man on uppers. What is that like? Just more, faster loveliness, or does he growl at people?"

"Burt's family now. You should get to know him, Ryan. He's full of great stories. He's had a long, full life. He drove an armored truck in Mason City before he started his nurs- ery, and someone, a fellow driver, drugged him once and tied him up with string and drove the truck way out into the woods and tried to rob it, except that he needed Burt's key to open it, but when he reached down to take it, Burt bit his ear off. That wild old movie stuff really used to happen. Burt's been around, you'd be shocked."

"He's good to Mom, that's all I care about. I hear lots of stories. True ones, too."

"Burt doesn't lie. He wouldn't make things up. He made a moral blood pact once, he told me. He opened a little vein along one knuckle and squeezed out a whole teaspoonful and drank it, then said the Ten Commandments with bloody lips while looking into a mirror."

"That's a fancy one."

"It's because he'd told a man a fib that accidentally killed him a day later. That's how Burt made things right with God. He's like that."

"Deranged and ritualistic?"

"He just likes pacts. And he keeps them, it's amazing. He swore off sweets—I was there for this, I witnessed it—and ever since I've never seen him eat one, not even sugar in coffee. It's like sweets vanished. He doesn't see them now. He's trained his mind."

"Enough black magic. How's Mom?"

"You know, she's Mom. She moms it up. You'll see."

"It's good to be down here, isn't it? Old sea level."

"That's not a big change for me. You know I'm pregnant?"

This catches me. "No." I'd guessed it, but it still catches me.

"So what's your job, exactly?"

"You said you're pregnant. Let's go back to that."

"Let's work around to it. I'm always amazed by what people do, you know? How many different businesses there are. That's why that year in Chicago freaked me out. No one I met was doing the same thing. This one guy trades gold—in the future. This woman sues doctors—but only heart doctors. This other guy flies around the country telling zoos how to design the cages for different animals. Does anybody still do anything normal? Who's sewing the shirts? Who's collecting all the eggs?"

"I both do and don't know what you mean," I say.

"Kara and Mom and I, we talk about you, but really we're just guessing, we're making you up. We know you do *something*, you've maybe even told us, but it's so complicated it doesn't stick. Is that what's going to happen to my baby?"

My mobile rings in my jacket, the silent-ring feature that tickles my rib cage just below my heart. I ignore it—ultimate issues are at stake here, at least for one of us.

"Is my baby just going to grow up into some . . . fragment? What happened to cowboys, to *miners*?"

"You'd better marry him. I think you at least have to try it."

"Look who's talking."

"She left me," I say. "She gave her ring back. I'll show you. I carry it. It's in my bag."

"You talk about Burt. You're worse."

"How far along?"

"It's like a plum now. Two weeks ago it was a peanut."

My mobile again. To my father, all phone calls that weren't cries for help ranked as impersonal noise, like the TV, and therefore had no claims on him. Things change.

"Hello?" An uncertain connection. Rolling static.

"It's Linda. Finally. Where are you now?"

Women always ask this question. Men don't. Men find it

sufficient that you're alive and that you're somewhere. They know the rest is detail.

"I'm in a cab leaving SeaTac."

Julie looks at me. Sticklers all. I don't feel I'm lying, though. If this trip had gone the way I'd planned, that's where I'd be now, driving downtown from SeaTac, and frankly I'd rather stick to that. The plan. The plan had beauty, and I wish to honor it. Perhaps, at some level, it's clicking along without me, one of Sandy Pinter's "Artifacts of Consciousness." His example was the lost formulas of the alchemists, which he hints in one book he recovered in a dream.

"That's weird. Someone saw you here," says Linda. "At DIA."

"I flew out of DIA."

"And didn't visit?"

"I'm cutting things close this week. What's going on?"

Linda says something to someone. She's at work, which means her news must be important. She takes work seriously. She considers guarding the Compass Club big stuff.

"It's me again. Don't be angry, just listen, okay? I've been in the computer trying to find you, so I know that you're not in Seattle. Don't explain. Before I tell you why I checked your flights, though, you should know about something I saw in your account."

"Wait," I say. I ask Julie to pull over. I don't want to drive out of range of the connection. And I want to be still when I hear this. "Talk. I'm here."

"You know how you've been gunning for a million? You

talk about it pretty much nonstop, so I know how important it is. It's like a symbol."

I'm disappointed to hear her put it this way. It's insensitive and inaccurate. She demeans me. The Nike "swoosh" is a symbol. This isn't that. This is life, this thing, and this is me, and this woman who claims to care for me should understand.

"I knew this. They're screwing around with me," I say. I've found my bug. I'm angry, exalted, justified. "Linda, hang on. Stay there." I turn to Julie, who's facing out her window, still holding the wheel despite having turned the key off. She's wherever it is that she goes inside herself when some man is calling the shots and not consulting her, or even bothering to make much sense. I suspect it's her soul I'm seeing.

"Julie? Jules? Something's happening. Turn the car around. We need to go back to the airport."

She shakes her head.

"Today's been exhausting, I know. Just turn the car around."

"No."

I give up for now. Back to Linda. To the bug. "What are they doing to me? Lay it out."

"Redemptions. It could just be clerical, some mix-up, but someone's been redeeming miles for tickets. I know how you are, so I knew it wasn't you."

"Hell no, it's not me."

"Hawaii. Alaska. Orlando. All first class. Three in three days, all last week."

"For future dates? I hope you're not saying someone *used* these tickets. You're saying they're gone? The points are gone?"

"Relax."

"I find this sick. I find this worse than sick. This is diseased, what they're doing. This is *dogshit*."

Julie opens her door a crack. For air?

"They haven't been used. You can cancel them. Calm down. You'll just have to change your ID numbers or something. Maybe someone hacked them. Those hacker people."

"This comes from the top. This is dogshit from the top. Make no mistake, Linda. These are sad, sick people. These people are losing a proud, established, major American transportation company to their own short-term lusts and half-baked theories, and in consequence they are sick and sad and desperate. You work there. I know. You can't afford to hear this. I pity your dilemma. But this is truth. Rock-hard cold impregnable truth."

"There, I'm in the system now. I'm canceling."

"You're canceling the mischievous effects, not the intentions behind them. Those persist."

"What was strange were the dates. The trips were for a year—a year to the day, almost—from the reservations. Someone expected to go to all those places on three consecutive days? It just looked wacky. Or maybe they were keeping their options open."

"Don't second-guess the pathological mind. That's a trap. It's bottomless. Don't start."

The driver's-side door slams and Julie is out and walking, straight on up the highway, heel to toe, treating the shoulder stripe like a balance beam. Trucks blast past and lift her pretty hair.

"Should I tell you why I was poking through your bookings?"

"Does Morse ever do that walk-among-the-peasants bit, strolling through the airport, shaking hands, patting workers' backs? Is that a thing of his? The Pope-in-disguise-among-his-children stunt?"

"You mean have I met Soren Morse? I've met him. Why?"

"The touchy-touchy type, or more reserved? This is called casing the joint for unlocked windows. Does he ever eat lunch in the food court? The humble act? My guess is he'd go for that California pizza place, the one where they don't use red sauce, just so-called pesto. That's more his trip. The pine nuts. The thin, charred crust. Not pizza as you and I know it. Power pizza. Or does he just hang loose at Burger King?"

"You sound bad, Ryan. Are you on stay-awake pills? I used to take those when I worked the red-eyes. They made me like you're being now."

My sister is dwindling. It's flat and vast here and it takes time to dwindle, but she's managing to and soon I'll have to catch her. There are rules for when women desert your car and walk. The man should allow them to dwindle, as is their right, but not beyond the point where if they turn the car is just a speck to them. That angers them.

"Listen, I'm at my desk here," Linda says. "Guests are flashing passes and I'm not seeing them. They might be expired. What I wanted to tell you was that you mentioned Las Vegas the other day and it happens the airline is sending me there tomorrow. I wanted to check if we'd cross. Looks like we will. Which place are you staying? I'm at Treasure Island. I guess it's a suite."

"Las Vegas is mostly suites. Underpromise and overdeliver. Like catalogue companies. They say it will come in five days, it's there in two, and you feel like the Prince of Morocco. It's a trick."

"That was uncalled for."

Julie is tiny now. Is that her thumb out? We're past the speck point, into the unknown. This will go down as the time I cast her off in northern Colorado or southern Wyoming and will pass to Kara as part of her moral arsenal. In the story it will be over a hundred degrees out or well below freezing, with Julie wearing just socks, and as the years go by and I forget things Kara will remove the socks as well and I will fail to correct her and myths will petrify. She'll bring out the story at Christmas, with all the others. A house full of women. My father suffered too.

"Ryan?"

"Still here. Just reflecting. I should go."

"You'll call me at Treasure Island? Let's say five?"

"Why would the airline send you to Las Vegas?"

"Some seminar. Career enhancement stuff."

"I'm going now. I'm really going now."

I slide over behind the wheel and drive to catch her, two wheels on the shoulder to signal that others should pass. She's walking normally now, no balance beam, and at a clip. I roll up next to her with the window down and tell her I'm sorry, I must have sounded bizarre there, but I'm recovering now, so please get in. We'll be in Salt Lake City before dawn. We'll drive the Mormon Trail, those hard old wagon tracks. We'll commune with the grizzled ghosts of the frontier.

She starts to walk again. Heel to toe again.

"Think about your baby."

But nothing works.

t w e l v e

as long as you're aimed at a city with an airport, you can get anywhere from anywhere and there's no such thing as a wrong turn. That's why I didn't consider myself off course last night while driving north in accordance with Julie's request to get her as close as I could to Minnesota before I flew back to Utah and then Nevada. It seemed to surprise her when I agreed to this, perhaps because she holds fundamentalist attitudes toward time and space and motion. I'm also convinced she believed that sheer inertia would carry me right on through to Minnesota, where, as she put it to me over crab legs in the Casper Red Lobster, "at least it's safe." (Her lips emphasized the word "safe"; my ears heard "least.") She failed to take into account my mental map. In Billings, Montana, I'd find a portal to Airworld, and I could be back in Salt Lake by 9 A.M. then off to Vegas by noon.

This is how the country is structured now, in spokes, not lines. Just find a hub.

I worked on my speech to GoalQuest as we drove and tried not to think about whether there's a heaven, what was inside the briefcase in the trunk, and what Soren Morse expected to accomplish by waging petty psychological warfare on his, statistically speaking, best customer. These were Airworld concerns and we were earthbound—doubly so because we were in Wyoming. When viewed from above, some state boundaries make sense—they follow rivers, declivities, chains of hills—but the straight lines defining Wyoming are purely notional and basically delimit a mammoth sandbox. Wyoming is just the land no other state wanted endowed with a capitol building to make it feel good. But such a pretty name. The prettiest.

Before my sister could critique my speech, I had to explain CTC to her in depth. This is never easy—with anyone. Most people assume we're brought in to do the firing or that we find the fired new jobs. It's neither. Our role is to make limbo tolerable, to ferry wounded souls across the river of dread and humiliation and self-doubt to the point at which hope's bright shore is dimly visible, and then to stop the boat and make them swim while we row back to the palace of their banishment to present the nobles with our bills. We offer the swimmers no guarantees, no promises, just shouts of encouragement. "Keep it up! That's great!" We reach our dock before they reach theirs and we don't look back over our shoulders to check on them, though they look back at us repeatedly.

That's the parable version of what we do. In practical terms, we give our "cases" "skills sets." We coach them in how to make employment inquiries without sounding scarily hungry or submissive. We urge them to be patient, patient, patient. There's a rule of thumb that for every ten thousand dollars of desired annual salary, a job seeker should expect to spend a month calling still-working friends and headhunters and Xeroxing hundreds of letters and résumés while waiting for them to call back. Since a lot of our cases have solid six-figure income histories, their searches can eat up years and far outstrip the duration of their severance benefits. Finding a job is itself a job, we teach, and not working is work, too, so don't get blue. If you do get blue, forgive yourself. You're only human. But also superhuman. Because you have untapped potential, and it's infinite.

"So in other words you talk baloney," Julie said, pushing us up through Wyoming. "I'm surprised at you. I'm surprised you'd do a job like that."

"I'm telling you what I learned, not what I hoped. You're getting the panoramic hindsight view."

As first portrayed to me by ISM, CTC was nothing like I've described, but represented an ethical revolution in American business practices. Yes, it served the downsizing employer by minimizing potential legal blowback from the parties dismissed, and yes, one could view it as a half-assed penance that chiefly consoled the client corporation, but was it wrong? Did it hurt people? It helped some. It helped quite a few. And there were studies to prove it.

My first big assignment took me to Davenport, Iowa, the blighted Grain Belt home city of Osceola Corp., a manufacturer of heavy machinery. Their backhoes and tractors were piling up at dealers, deeply discounted yet still not moving. Their corporate bonds had been downgraded to scrap paper. Cuts were inevitable, and so they came.

I was given a small beige office in the rear of the company's crumbling brick waterfront headquarters and tasked with the care of seven executives who were let go in sequence, one per day, and sent to me before their tears could dry. All were middle-aged men with families, and all but two of them asked me what they'd done wrong, to which I answered, "Nothing. Blame interest rates. Blame low commodity prices. This problem's global." One heavyset fellow, a face like a potpie, his suit full of strange custom seams to hide his girth, mistook me for a priest and made me kneel with him while he prayed from a card he carried inside his wallet. Another asked me if I would call his wife and repeat my interest rates remark.

I counseled these men for two weeks. The company gave them offices next to mine where they could make phone calls and draft their pleas for help and fill out the numerous tests and work sheets that sought to identify their strengths and weaknesses, goals and longings, habits of thought and feeling. I scored these surveys, interpreted their results, and provided each man with a "master self-inventory" of five double-spaced typed pages, his to keep. One man set his aflame before my eyes, but most of them clung to and studied these documents with the devotion of Egyptologists poring over tomb writings.

For three of the men it seemed to work. They passed through guilt to anger to despair to something approaching acceptance, if not hope. My bright-eyed graduates. My little soldiers. A fourth man dropped out at anger and, months later, was arrested by Secret Service agents for driving an Osceola diesel tractor into a crowd at a presidential campaign stop. The other three men were unreadable. They clammed up. Oddly, these three were the first to find new jobs, while two of the success stories still hadn't when I stopped tracking them one year later.

In time, I learned not to track my former subjects, just as the elders in our field advise. Unfortunately, it was not by force of will that I accomplished this necessary forgetting but through reflexive, progressive memory loss. I learned to live from the present forward only, and I don't regret it. One must these days if one is to stay in business, and it's all business now. Try selling stock to last year's buyers. Impossible. Try marketing tractors to your customers' ancestors.

All in all, by the time my plane left Davenport (my first trip in a spacious seat up front) I was fairly sure I'd done some good and certainly no real harm. A solid beginning, and one that set my course for years to come. There were bleak spots, naturally, but ISM threw me enough upbeat executive coaching jobs—Art Krusk, some others—that I muddled through them. The mounting memory problems weren't really an issue because there was nothing particularly worth remembering in my life just then and also because I'd developed regular habits. Pack one bag well, with the necessities, launch yourself into Airworld, with all its services, and the higher mental functions become irrelevant. That's the merciful nature of the place, and the part I'll miss.

"This is your speech?" said Julie. We'd reached Gillette by then, a natural gas boomtown where flames burn on tall stacks and deer cross the freeway in lines of six and seven.

"It's just the setup. The lead."

"It's awfully long. Just give them the finger and be done with it."

"These are hardened professionals I'm speaking to. I have to crack their armor plate by plate."

I intend to crack it by talking about Vigorade. A few of my listeners will have similar stories from their own practices, but this is mine, and I hope to tell it well, without too many Verbal Edge curlicues and a minimum of M.B.A. abstractions. I don't require that they cry, though. Let them laugh. I'm the one resigning. I don't need followers. I just need to bleed a little, publicly. Preferably all over Craig Gregory's shirt.

Vigorade was based in San Diego and sold a line of secret-formula sports drinks that acquired, over time, a curious reputation on college campuses and other youth spots for mild, euphoric, narcotic-like effects when drunk in large quantities or mixed with alcohol. The company was small, its products specialized, but the fanaticism of its young customers yielded crazy margins. For a period. Disaster struck when an anti-drunk-driving parents group obtained a memo from corporate marketing outlining strategies for targeting teens with the myth of the Vigorade-vodka cocktail. Petitions went out. Class-action suits were filed. Sales spiked at first due to the furor, but soon they stalled, then slid. Executives who'd been living extremely well by veiling a humdrum beverage in urban legend were summoned upstairs and told to empty their desks even as guards, directed to search for documents that might play into the hands of legal foes, were emptying them for them.

I counseled three senior people in sales and marketing. One woman, two men. All were furious. They wailed. This time, though, I didn't sympathize. Vigorade's troubles were purely of its own making, and these were the folks who'd hatched the basic plot. With court battles already raging and tempers raw, my job was to neutralize the threat from three insiders who might well retaliate, and possibly scuttle the whole enterprise. There was no sentimental fuzziness around the true identity of my client. I was working for management. Private Bingham.

And they armed me well. Along with my usual inspirational literature, Craig Gregory fed me a package of psychological tests formulated somewhere in the depths of ISM Research. The tests were unfamiliar to me. Strange. And some of the questions seemed out of line, and haunted me. "You're an astronaut on a three-man mission to Mars and you discover, privately, in flight, that only enough air remains for two of you. Would you: (A) inform your crewmates and participate in a negotiated solution? (B) conspire with a second crewmate to murder the third? (C) say nothing and leave your survival up to fate? (D) spare your team by committing suicide?"

As instructed, I administered the tests, scored them using the relevant keys, and consulted several manuals to ascertain the meaning of the results. The findings shocked me. All three subjects, it seemed, suffered from deep personality disorders predictive of poor—the poorest—career performance.

These people were freaks. Deficients. Messed-up specimens. Had I made some mistake? Were the manuals at fault? I sent the documents to ISM, who double-checked them and vouched for my conclusions, which they ordered me to keep a secret so as not to arouse or embitter the ex-executives. Frankly, I was relieved. I went on counseling them, focusing on the bright side of unemployment, then packed up my kit and flew off to my next job. Just one thing nagged me. If the subjects truly were as disturbed as the tests suggested, wasn't someone obliged to offer them expert help?

Like I've said, I'd stopped checking on former cases by then, but these three intrigued me. They were special. Unique. I inquired about them at three months, six months, one year. By three months, one was dead. The woman. Suicide by blocked tailpipe in sealed garage. Her note singled out her abusive husband for blame and it emerged in a search of old police files that he'd been battering her steadily for years, had been arrested over and over, but was always released when she declined to press charges and took him back.

At six months, one of the men was facing trial for possession of a Class Three substance—heroin and stolen Percodan—with intent to distribute. I followed his trial and it came out in court that the man had been using heavily since college and selling the stuff to his son and his son's friends. They convicted him.

At a year, the third subject, who'd struck me as the dull one, was America's latest paper billionaire, having taken public a tech firm whose leading product none of the business journals could clearly describe, noting only that it involved microscopic lasers and the man-made element seaborgium.

What to make of all this? I'm not smart enough to know. And that's what still floors me: how little I knew these folks and how far they must have already progressed toward their ultimate, outrageous fates by the time I started seeing them. Would the expert help I sensed we owed them have done any good? For the suicide perhaps. Not the billionaire. And junkies are junkies. And how revealing, really, were those test results? Could any of what happened been foretold? Not by me and not by ISM. And anyway, the counseling is the same whether the subjects are upstanding citizens or masochists, drug fiends, and scientific geniuses.

Career Transition Counseling is not just bad because it peddles false hope—most products and services do that, more or less, including a lot of the ones my fired subjects made big money providing, temporarily—it's bad because it's uniform. Steady state. People are going to prison and making fortunes and bailing out violent lovers and duping teenagers and CTC just sits there and sucks its thumb. In every kind of weather. All day, all year. It's divided against itself and numb and circular and feels, to someone who does it for a living, like some ingenious suspended-animation scheme designed to inject you with embalming fluid while still allowing you to breathe and speak.

Vigorade, the beverage, still exists. They added herbs, reconceptualized the packaging, and repositioned it as an endurance aid for aging jocks and outdoor enthusiasts. But

I won't drink it. It's ever so slightly salty, just faintly sweet, and it tastes the way I imagine tears would taste if you could collect enough to fill a jug.

"It drags," Julie said as we put Gillette behind us and pressed on toward Billings and its many spokes. "Some twists at the end there, but otherwise it drags."

"Does it cohere, though?"

"Not sure I know that word."

"Cohere? Coherent? They're pretty basic, Julie."

It was early morning Thursday by then, and time that we dropped each other off. Time to get Maestro its car back, to buy our tickets, and for me to get back in the sky and her to marry.

the first leg is Billings east to Bozeman on a Bombardier prop jet, a flying soda can that barely clears the weather as it cruises and sets down cockeyed and skipping on the runway, sounding like it's lost at least one tire and prompting a cabin-wide exchange of looks that said I don't know you, stranger, but I love you, so just hold on, we're going to paradise. In the terminal I phone Alex from my mobile and get a machine that plays the theme from *Brian's Song* but doesn't include a voice, a message style I've always found conceited—it strikes me as a subtle power play, leaving callers wondering if they've found you. I give my Las Vegas hotel information and hang up half-hoping that Alex won't show, which would leave only Pinter, Art Krusk, and Linda to deal with and allow me to rest my brain before my speech. If Alex does come, I'll have to shake off Linda in some casino, though the nice thing about ditching women on the Strip is that the odds of them finding you again are worse than a single-number roulette wager. It's the capital of lost dance partners, that town, and some never even make it home at all, like the former Desert Air flight attendant who won ninety grand on three quarters during a layover and rushed out and bought a condo and a Lexus and a picture-window-size tank of tropical fish, which were the only possessions she hadn't pawned four months later. She gave them to a fish shelter. Such facilities actually exist, and it's just this sort of oddball knowledge that makes Airworld not only fun but educational and sets one up for a lifetime of winning bar bets.

BZN to SLC departs on time and locks in another five-hundred-mile increment that I trust will be safe from Morse and the identity thieves. I've met a couple of goldbugs in my travels, surprisingly young men with buried footlockers whose existence they felt compelled to share in the way of most people who cache things in the ground—serial killers, gun nuts, toxic waste disposers—and then can't stop thinking about them day and night. I'm beginning to understand the mind-set, though. An icy electronic wind will blow some-day, and no amount of backup or duplication will save the numbers we think of as our wealth. The dispossessed who've kept thorough written records will wander the land waving sweaty scraps of paper that may or may not win recognition from the precious-metals power elite. It's not a wipeout I'm likely to survive or that I'd want to. My miles would be gone, and with them, I suspect, my drive, my spirit.

To throw off my trackers I order tea with milk, a new drink for me. From now on I will act randomly while air-borne, rendering myself useless as a research subject. My seatmate has on the classic sneakers and windbreaker that undercover men think make them invisible but stick out to anyone vaguely in the know like a British admiral's uniform. He's reading Dean Koontz with a squinting intensity that Koontz just doesn't call for and must be fake.

"Is Salt Lake City home?" he finally ventures, much too casually.

I nod my lie. Though maybe it's not a lie. Maybe it's all my home, the entire route map.

"I'm Allen."

"Dirk."

"That's not a name you hear much anymore."

"You never did. It never had a following."

The agent closes his Koontz on his thumb, but not at the place he stopped reading. An amateur. I ask him his business and wait for a real lulu.

"Memorabilia. Class rings," he says.

"Not for Heston's?"

"The only player left." He's authentic, it seems, he just dresses like a spook.

"You'd know my old buddy Danny Sorenson, then."

"I'm sorry," he says. "Or maybe you haven't heard yet. Danny passed."

There's always a lag for me with such euphemisms, a few seconds before I realize they mean death.

"I saw him last Sunday night," I say. "My god."

"He was in Denver at some suite hotel and when he still hadn't checked out at three P.M. a clerk went in and tried to shout him awake, then left when he couldn't and didn't follow up, just charged him for a new night and let him lie there. Our hospitality industry today."

"Is his wife okay? Do you have a number for her?"

"Danny was gay."

"He talked about a wife."

"I'm sure he did. It's a conservative company. How did you know him?"

"Planes. Like I know you."

"So a passing acquaintance, basically."

"Not quite. I don't know. Maybe so. *Completely* gay?"

Allen looks put off and opens his paperback to the first page of underlined Koontz I've ever seen.

"That came out wrong," I say. "I'm just surprised by this. Usually I can tell. That sounds wrong, too. I'm all off balance now. I adored that man."

"On what basis?" says Allen. "Occasional proximity?"

As if that's tiny. As if there's anything else. The impossible standards these non-flyers set! What were we supposed to do, make love in an exit row? Hand-feed each other peanuts?

"I don't think I have to justify my grief," I say. There are open seats across the aisle.

"Completely," says Allen. "Unlike me. I'm semi. Fridays and Saturdays, major cities only. No anal. Strictly oral. Not Danny, though. He ordered off the whole menu. Completely."

I move.

Every great corporation does one thing well, and in Marriott's case it's to help guests disappear. The indistinct architecture, the average service, the room-temperature everything. You're gone, blended away by the stain-disguising carpet patterns, the art that soothes you even when your back's turned. And you don't even miss yourself, that's Marriott's great discovery. Invisibility, the ideal vacation. No more anxiety about your role, your place. Rest here, under our cloak. Don't fidget, its just your face that we're removing. You won't be needing it until you leave, and here's a claim check. Don't worry if you lose it.

Still, I'm surprised that Dwight is staying here. He seems like the type who cherishes his vividness. I arrive fifteen minutes early for our lunch, my bags stowed back at the Compass Club for my Vegas flight, and sit in an armchair facing the elevators browsing a gratis *USA Today* and trying not to imagine Danny's night as a paying corpse at Homestead Suites, the charges still accruing to his dead soul the way they say dead people's fingernails keep growing. Had he left his TV on? How many blankets covered him? The paper is written such that I can think these things yet still get the gist of the articles. It's genius, almost on a par with Marriott's. How many times did his phone ring? Rest in peace, sir. For all I know, I'm the best friend you ever had.

I consider my strategy for my lunch with Dwight. No more Cub Scout, no more bottom dog. Like we say in CTC, value yourself as you hope the market will and if the bids come in low, discount accordingly but think of it as a one-time-only sale, not a final re-evaluation. At ten I put down the paper and watch the elevators out of an old conviction that there's an edge in seeing the man you're negotiating with before he sees you. Business is folk wisdom, cave-born, dark, Masonic, and the best consultants are outright shamans who sprinkle on the science like so much fairy dust. Use a customer's first name three times in your first five minutes together. Three, not four. They don't have to notice your shoeshine to feel its presence.

Each parting of the elevator doors discloses another person who's of no use to me, and after ten minutes of predatory staring, I turn my head toward the registration desk, wondering if Dwight's indeed a guest here, which of course is the moment when he slips in and taps my shoulder, the better sorcerer.

"Here we finally are," he says. He's caught me sitting and I rise to my feet in humiliating freeze-frames and take a hand that's all aura and no flesh and leaves not the slightest sensation when it's withdrawn.

"I thought we'd try the Carvery," he says, "unless you're stuck on waitresses and tablecoths." His field, his ball. Resist now or be subsumed.

"No, but I'd like to think our meeting warrants them."

"The Carvery's better lit. World-class iced tea."

"Fine."

"Your call. There's McNally's Bistro, too. They mix their iced tea from a powder. A so-so burger, but that can be remedied at the fixings bar."

"The Carvery." I'm a shame to my own name.

Dwight leads the way. What at first looks like a limp reveals itself as a fundamental mismatch between the hemispheres of his egg-shaped body. Dwight's mass and vitality all come from his left; his right side is just a hitchhiker, an add-on, as if he's absorbed and digested his Siamese twin. His hair has a complicated, unnatural grain that's suggestive of camouflaged transplant work, and yet the general effect is masculine, harking back to a time when men fell apart at thirty and could only fight back through tricks of dress and grooming. I thought he was my age once, but I'm unsure now. Too much reconstruction, too much work, to tell.

The Carvery has a pub theme, Utah style. Much brass and wood and bric-a-brac, but beerless. Behind a long slanted shield of milky Plexiglas three fiftyish men whose career paths are enigmas—shouldn't they at least be chefs by now, or have they been flash frozen by a benefits plan that fosters loyalty but kills ambition?—draw knives with scalloped blades through hams and roasts whose crusts show the charred cross-hatchings of butcher's string. Dwight holds his plate out and gets three cuttings of well-done pork loin too thick to be called slices, too thin for slabs. Portion control is a Marriott obsession. Dwight nods at the carver to request a fourth piece and the fellow's reaction shows he's been well-schooled and qualifies as a professional after all; he delivers up a mere wafer on his broad knife blade, but with a flourish. To get his own back Dwight loads his plate with side dishes, just as Marriott expects him to. At pennies per pound for the cheesy potato medleys and oily pasta salads, the joke's on him, though he struts away like he's looted a royal tomb. There: a weakness to file for later on. The man doesn't know when he's being nickel-and-dimed.

But where's the contract? No bulges in his blazer.

He chooses a two-setting table on a platform and takes

the wall seat. From his perspective, I'll blend with the lunch crowd behind me, but from mine he's all there is, a looming individual. Fine, I'll play jujitsu. I angle my chair so as to show him the slimmest, one-eyed profile. The look in my other eye he'll have to guess at.

What I want most now, besides a deal, is the story about Morse Dwight promised me, but I can't predict the emotions it may stir so I'd better leave it for dessert.

"Your book kept me awake last night," Dwight says. "Can we bypass the small talk about our food, our meat?"

"By all means."

"The Garage is . . . It's a prism, isn't it? It's multidimensional, not just some flat tract."

A prism. This sounds to me like boilerplate.

"Or a palimpsest, maybe that's more accurate."

Tape two—I've come armed. My one eye shows comprehension and Dwight looks stunned.

"The garret. The studio. Now the garage. It's an all-American updating. And the book itself was conceived in a garage, because isn't that where art comes from, so to speak?"

"That's true," I say. "What part kept you awake?"

"The whole. The sum. This sense that your concept predates both of us. That it wasn't so much authored as channeled. Eat."

"I like to get it all cut up in squares first."

"I've had this feeling before with certain manuscripts, that I'd seen them before, in some other life perhaps. Frankly, I smelled plagiarism."

I laugh from a place in myself that doesn't often laugh. A place I associate more with rippling sobs.

"That happens," Dwight says. "Naked copying. Sheer fraud. It's not always a crime, though; sometimes it's an illness. The writer knows the book appeared before, but he feels the original author was the plagiarist and stole from him telepathically. But not in this case. This was daylight larceny. The writer—a midwesterner like you, from one of those states like Missouri, but not Missouri, the one just like it—"

"Arkansas?" I say.

"I think of that as the South. A former slave state."

"Missouri was too. Read *Huckleberry Finn*."

"Please. Do I look like a man who hasn't? Please."

"People read and then forget. That's all I meant."

"You're speaking of yourself here?"

"No, everyone."

"Anyway, I dug up the original, showed it to him side by side with his book, and even then he had a fancy story. Very different from your case."

"My book's not stolen."

"You've yet to end it. How could it be?"

"I'm close, though."

"Does he leave the Garage? I don't see how he can. We think of garages as places men put behind them once they're successful. Lincoln's log cabin. But that's your twist, of course—for you, the garage is holy and sufficient."

"Interesting. Until now my idea was that he'd leave eventually, but only once he realized that the whole world . . . Interesting."

"I'm looking at you. You're sincere. You're puzzling through this. I'm glad. This heartens me. You're not a thief. What's happened here is pure Huck Finn."

"Excuse me?"

"Reading and forgetting. And by the way, you were right, I've never touched Twain."

"Are you saying this isn't my concept?"

"Or title or character or theme or anything. It's a first-class subconscious memory you have. Photographic. Yet lost to you. Amazing."

I lay down my fork. What's eerie about Dwight's hunch is just how close it might be to the truth given what I've been learning about my brain. If I didn't know otherwise, I might share his doubts, but in fact I remember clearly how, when, and where the idea first arose. His name was Paul Ricks and I'd just helped fire him from Crownmark Greeting Cards in Minneapolis. When I showed him his master self-inventory, which rated high for artistic talent and enterprise, he tore the thing into strips and said "You're kidding, right? You really believe I can leave two decades of copywriting, roll up my sleeves, hide out in my garage, and hatch a whole new existence?" To which I said: "If I didn't, I couldn't do this." And Paul said: "Prove it." And I said, "Tell me how."

"You're innocent, but you're guilty, too," Dwight says. "I'm deeply sorry, Ryan." He salts his pork.

"Suspicion is not conviction. You're way off base. My book seemed too good for a novice and so you dreamed this."

"I had a tip," Dwight says. "You mentioned one of my authors yesterday. Soren Morse, the aviator."

"Aviator?"

"I'm doing his sophomore book. We talk quite frequently."

I'm dumbfounded. There are layers to this thing . . .

"So I mention your book to him, because I'm proud of it, and Morse said that's like *The Basement*, isn't it? I searched the Net and came up with a synopsis, the best I could do since the book is out of print. Coincidence after shocking coincidence. I called the publisher, hunted down the editor, and got a fuller description. One example: the protagonist of the basement is unnamed."

"Two characters without names is not the same name."

"Over my head, that. Try this: a phrase from your book that appears nineteen times and also occurs in the subtitle to *The Basement.* 'Perpetual innovation.' "

"No one owns 'perpetual innovation.' That's like saying someone owns, I don't know, 'Get well.' Morse put you onto this scavenger hunt?"

"Someone would have."

"He's my someone. Every single time."

"How exactly do you know each other?"

"Distantly but intimately," I say. "I'm tired of explaining how well I know people—no one respects my answers. I just know people. Hundreds. Thousands. From sea to shining sea. And no, I don't think I coined that. See this napkin?"

"In detail."

"I'm seeing the same napkin. You and me, both sane. The here and now."

"Let me finish," Dwight says. "I hadn't quite lost faith

yet. There's a collective mind, it's very real. I can't name one, but I'm aware of major inventions that appeared only days apart on different continents. This was like that, I hoped. I knew you traveled, so you're exposed to the ether more than most of us, the cultural cyclotron, the particles. Bombarded by particles. Then I called the author. At nine. This morning."

"Pause, pause, pause. Cheap drama. Spit it out."

"He knows you. You had a run-in once, he claims. He also distinctly recalls the conversation in which he announced his intention to write *The Basement*. Name of Ricks? A Minnesotan? You're all midwesterners."

I push back my plate and look over at a wall of injection-molded coats of arms. Made-up legacies, random heraldry. My father bought one once off the TV, the genuine Bingham family crest, authenticated. Stags and lions and eagles and battle-axes; we were dragon slayers from way, way back, and my father bought it all, poor man. He was living alone by then, stalked by private Rockefellers, but the crest put a bounce in his step, aligned his spine. He stowed his TV tray and started eating downtown. He detailed his Monte Carlo. All the crest. Two weeks of nobility that I'm glad he had, but then he went for a haircut with old Ike Schmidt and there it was, over the comb jar of blue Barbicide. A gentle being—he let Schmidt go on dreaming of Round Table banquets, ale from hollow horns. He kept his peace and let himself be shaved.

I'm not up to his level. I have to fuss and struggle. "The concept was both of ours. It was simultaneous."

"Weak. Two objects can't occupy one space."

"Ideas aren't objects. He went out and really wrote it? He left the strong impression that was my job."

"What are they, then?"

"Ideas? Do we have to play these games right now? I just spent a year investing in my future, dictating notes from here to Amarillo and all points in between, and now you tell me this Ricks, this jobless loser, who scored in the lousy twentieth percentile for follow-through and reliability—facts I concealed from him because I'm decent—strolled back to his sad little house and scooped me blind. When was this rip-off published, anyway?"

"Four years ago."

"He worked fast. Did this thing sell?"

"Hardly at all, but it wasn't pushed correctly. Scattershot marketing. Hangdog author's photo. A golf publisher that went out on a cute limb."

"That's good news, at least."

"I'll do much better. This is Advanta's sweet spot. We'll swat this ball."

"Incredible. You're one nervy little fatso. Is that a weave or plugs? Dyed beaver? Orlon?"

"Ricks says you had him fired."

"Ricks distorts."

"You fire people for a living. Now that's a book. You'd have to strike the somber, reflective pose—the old recovery gambit—but that's a memoir. Advanta has crack ghostwriters, real mind readers. You'll think every comma is yours. Your natural hair."

"Such thick skin on you reptiles. I'm gone. Cover this check. That iced tea was powdered, too."

On my way out of the Carvery I sweep the crests off the wall, a dozen of them, and no one stops me because they know I'm serious, Bingham the dragon slayer. We go way back.

fourteen

a VIP commotion at the gate complicates and prolongs the boarding process. A convoy of electric carts sweeps in loaded with uniformed security and a couple of bison-shouldered civilian toughs talking like princesses on cute red radios. The pedestrian flow through the concourse snags and eddies and at the heart of the turbulence I spot him: the retired Supreme Commander of Allied Forces, General Norman Schwarzkopf, signing autographs for full-grown men who are lying if they say they want them for their kids. I've seen these mementos, and I know where they go: under plate glass on desktops, front and center, for a quick-hit morale boost during high-stakes conference calls. They'd pluck the last hairs from the general's rhino head, but he's probably already selling them through an untraceable chain of sub-sub-agents, encased in clear acrylic, as paperweights. The relics that come off these supermen—astonishing. I've seen every stick of gum Mantle ever chewed in some corner office or another, every last Zippo Patton ever lit.

Schwarzkopf is a motivational mainstay, right up there with Tarkenton, Robbins, Ditka, the pre-trial O. J. Simpson, and Famous Amos, so it's no surprise to see him here, mobilizing for GoalQuest with us ants. I've heard him four times in six years, and he delivers. B vitamins straight to the heart muscle itself. You stand up afterwards ready to thump someone, just name the cause, and though this wears off and leaves a startling thirst that not even gallons of Vigorade could quench, a virtuous residue has been deposited that kicks back into the veins when you grow weak and jolts you straight when you nod off at the wheel. The magic works, almost all of it, to some degree, and that's what the skeptics find so intolerable. Just peek at the gurus' pay stubs. The market knows.

Because I'm off to Omaha at eleven, I'll miss the Supreme Commander, and I could use him. He finally boards behind his human wedge but the spot where he stood remains vacant for a minute; step on it, you'll break your mother's back. Even people just now dismounting from the walkway who don't know he was here avoid the patch. Well, let me be the first, with both boots. Shazam! I feel it.

No joke. It's real. Forty grand for forty minutes and no one ever wants his money back. I wrote a book that someone else wrote first and I feel like Tom Swift on his tin-can rocket ship beating Neil Armstrong to the moon.

El Supremo sits to my front and to my right and the distraction he causes among the crew lifts my sense of being scrutinized. My voice mail yields Julie, safe in Minnesota, and Kara double-checking on that salmon I was instructed to feel and taste and eyeball. Another reason to fear reincarnation, which, if it's all about unfinished business as my Hindu seatmates keep telling me, will consist for me of rounding up and stamping many hundred unmailed birthday cards and overnighting endless coastal delicacies to the eastern edge of the Great Plains. If God or Shiva or whoever's on duty that day is a Minnesotan, as I was taught, CTC will be deemed the most pardonable of my sins—the boy did what they told him, he had to *eat*—compared to the unFedExed coolers of tiger prawns my mother died in her driveway waiting for.

I leaf through the GoalQuest program. "Break Down, Break Through, Break Out: Third-Generation Dot-com Retailing. Guided Informal Group Discussion. Snack." "Is There Life After Gold? A Journey Through Depression with former Team USA hockey coach Brett Maynard, cofounder of Camp Quality for Kids." "Prayerful Pragmatism by Charles 'Chuck' Colson." "The Buck Starts There: Making Customers Your Boss." "Pinter on Pinter." Elegant, that one. And this, of course, head to head at 9 A.M. with "You Plus Me Equals ??? by major CEO to be announced": "One New Beginning Fits All by Ryan M. Bingham. Light Continental Breakfast."

Aren't they all light? Isn't that what "Continental" means?

There's a flutter of emotional cabin pressure as El Supremo slinks into the aisle and meekly heads to the bathroom. We understand, sir; we're all God's children here. Still, as his visit lengthens, I feel a shift as all of us stop thinking about ourselves and wonder why that closed door is staying so closed. A hand-washer? Normal travelers' diarrhea? It's painful to picture the Big Guy so confined. The cold steel john. The little tampon slot. Like most frequent flyers I've talked to, I sometimes thrill myself with hyper-detailed crash scenarios, and in my favorite I'm right where he is now when the death plunge comes. I balance myself in my new sideways world and squeak out a note with a soap bar on the mirror: "I loved you, every one. I'm sorry, Mom." It's a variable fantasy; my testaments change. Once I just drew a heart. How sweet of me. Lately, it's been six zeros and a one. What would El Supremo write? "See you in hell, Saddam"? Or "Grrr"? I like that. In an actual crash, of course, the Christians among us would likely just draw a cross. Saves time, it's manageable from every angle, and it well might open a few doors.

Mount Olympus reminds me how poorly I know my gods. The young redhead at check-in wears a light suede toga cut to resemble a deer or antelope hide and over one shoulder hangs a bow and arrows. As she hunts for my reservation on her screen a bellhop in a winged helmet scurries over and offers to carry my briefcases, the one still locked, and my strangely deflated carry-on. (Have my clothes shrunk?) I give him all of it and request a screwdriver, which he doesn't find odd, apparently. Wings on his shoes as well. Mercury? Who's Mercury? Evil? Good? Or were those old gods both?

"It looks like your companion checked in already. Alex Brophy. Keep this on her MasterCard?"

"Are you still in that cross-promotion with Great West?"

Nods.

"On mine," I say. "Who are you, anyway? Your character?"

"The huntress."

"Your name. Your powers."

"Laurie. I water-ski. You have two messages."

"Read them."

"Art Krusk: 'I'm at the Hard Rock. Nab some dinner? This Marlowe's a pisser. Glad you hooked us up.' A Mr. Pinter next: 'Quite busy tonight but will see you at your talk.' He's staying here."

"No Linda?"

"Sorry."

"It's good. It simplifies. Is my companion in the room already? You wouldn't know, I guess. You're Circe maybe?"

"It's just a theme. It's not a college course. Go ask at Excalibur which of you is Lancelot? This really isn't the city for history."

"That's why it grows and grows and grows and grows."

Pinter's interest in my little speech renders me weightless in the elevator and puts a pair of wings on my feet, too. And Krusk likes Marlowe. I've brokered a great match. The idea of Alex, a jukebox, and a pool table suddenly blossoms with sexy possibilities. Good riddance, *The Garage*. It's a world of flesh, not inky paper, and from this moment forward I only take huge bites.

A suite, as I understand it, is two or more rooms, but as part of the erosion of all fixed standards and the upgrading of the subpar, a single room with an alcove or an angle or any hint of partitioning at all now qualifies for the title. Here, the suite feature is a modest nook showcasing a scaled-down pool table but still too small, at first glance, to wield a cue in. The jukebox is the real thing, though: a vintage Wurlitzer featuring curved glass tubes of backlit jellies that generate long, sluggish bubbles as they're warmed. The buttons are within reach of the king bed on top of whose satiny spread stand two black shoes next to a crossed pair of blowsy red roses.

I find other tableaux as I pace around the room, still waiting for my baggage and the screwdriver. Alex has been fussing like an elf. There are clusters of white votives on the nightstands and on the desk two slim black tapers standing aslant in hotel water glasses. The silk scarf lamp trick. Cones of incense on a plate. I sniff them. Jasmine? What does jasmine smell like? So much lost sensual knowledge with men like me.

Incense to me means drugs, a mask for pot smoke. Will we get high tonight? Might be nice. Or horrible. My last few drug experiences hurt. A line of coke with the cackling Vice President of Human Resources at Pine Ridge Gas sniffed in a Houston TGI Friday's. My heart beat lumpily for hours. I cried. And just last month a pellet of red hash shared with a deadheading flight attendant in Portland. We partook while sitting up to our bare chests in a volcanic Homestead Suites hot tub, and when the stuff hit the chlorine fumes from the water whooshed up my nostrils and filled my vision with glowworms that fattened and brightened and wriggled when

I blinked. I fled to the locker room for a cold compress, and when I tottered back out to the tub how many minutes later I couldn't tell, my date and a bare-assed, crew-cut college kid were pressing their privates against the bubbling jets and toasting each other with pink wine.

I go to wash my face and on the sink board is a muslin bag of potpourri and a zipped-up leather toilet kit. I dare not look, but I do, and I find: pills. Ten or twelve brown bottles, most of them with that telltale orange warning sticker familiar from my high school days as a burglar of medicine cabinets. The sticker meant narcotics, pills worth stealing, so what do we have here? Xanax. Darvocet. Vicodin. Wellbutrin. All from different doctors in different cities. At one time or another I've taken all of them, but separately. Ambien. Dexedrine. Lorazepam. Names that are all connotation and assonance, Z's and X's for ups and M's for downs. Is that where the poets have gone? To Merck and Pfizer?

The bellhop interrupts my inventory. He puts the bags in the closet, then produces one of those multi-function pocket tools that will rebuild our civilization if the bomb drops.

"My supervisor needs this back," he says. "I'll wait here while you use it, if that's okay."

"Did you help the woman who's staying in this room?"

"Sure."

"How was she? Her demeanor. Her vibe."

The bellhop's face cools and stiffens. He doesn't rat. She made illicit requests of him, I know it.

"She was fine," he says.

"Didn't ask for special services?"

Standoff. Two male primates, taking stock. I take out my wallet, engorged with business cards I never look at and should probably paste in an album eventually.

"I don't want to spoil anything," he says. "Any surprises."

"I don't like surprises. I get enough of them just walking around."

He takes my twenty and vanishes it, a petty-cash Houdini. "It's not your birthday, is it?"

"I've lost track."

"Well, lots more candles, for starters, and lots more flowers. And other sentimental stuff. Just cute stuff. The names of some stores. I think she's planning a party. Nothing bad, though. And a shoulder rub."

"You do that for your guests? Not a topless shoulder rub, I hope."

He smirks.

"She's not my wife. It's fine to tell me."

"I need that tool back. It's like my boss's right hand."

I shut myself in the bathroom with the locked case, lay it on the sink, and start to pry, first at the lock and then, for better leverage, along the hinges. Something splinters, pops. I put the case on the floor and wedge a boot toe into the crack and grip the lid, both hands. I yank. It gives.

I leave the case lying open, its contents exposed, dismiss the bellhop, shut my eyes to think, then raid the mini-bar for three wee bottles of Johnny Walker Black that I empty into a cling-film-covered glass back at the sink. Gingerly, with my toe again, I prod the thing out of the case onto the floor and flip it over, fuzzy tummy up. It's Mr. Hugs.

I threw the bear away years ago. He's back. His forehead is punctured and over one soft ear white cotton puffs out where the bullet must have exited. Assassinated.

In CTC work they're known as grieving aids, but the slang term is better: "squashables." As in "The poor lady was hysterical, ripping out drawers from her filing cabinet, screaming, so I gave her a squashable and she calmed down." They aren't always teddy bears, or even soft. Brock Stoddard at Intersource who out-counsels high-finance types uses a baseball-size chunk of chalky rock that he challenges emotional ex-brokers to squeeze and squeeze and crumble into dust. Becky Gursak at K. K. Carrera offers modeling clay. Some counselors don't use squashables at all, but those that do tend to favor stuffed animals—a plump brown puppy that sits there on the sofa, just part of the office scenery until one morning when some menopausal former manager who gave up on kids so she could pledge her all to International Hexbolt's holy war for the South American market share suddenly—and I've seen it happen myself, it's like a slasher movie—begins to spout red gore from her left nostril before the brave smile has even left her face. Stress is the killer, they say, and I believe it. I've seen the eruptions. I've Kleenexed up the fluids. It progresses nine tenths of the way in stealth and silence, until the tenth tenth, when it wails. It roars.

I remember the day the bear entered my life and I remember the client: Deschamps Cosmetics, which was almost entirely female—aging female. I was off to the airport in a company Lincoln when Craig Gregory leaned through the window and said, "For this job, Ryan, you'll want to take along a squashable. Meet Mr. Hugs and his darling button nose."

I demurred—too gimmicky, I thought—but Craig Gregory pushed, and he was right to. The Deschamps ladies crushed the toy shapeless. They mangled it. Mr. Hugs became a fixture in my practice. He burst now and then, but I always stitched him up. The more use he showed, the more willingly they embraced him, and the less likely they were to hurl him back at me. Then I couldn't look at him anymore. Two years of rough handling had given him a soul, an expressive face and figure all his own. "Sad" doesn't capture it. Help me, Verbal Edge. Martyred. Forlorn. Unconsolable. Woebegone. Baby Jesus left out in the rain.

I'd rather not touch him now. I withdraw my boot. I pick up the shattered briefcase and look around for somewhere to dispose of it. I stuff it between the jukebox and the wall, then realize I should search it for a note, drag it back out, and find nothing. I examine the tag again. My writing? The block capitals could be anyone's. Likely suspects? Practically nothing but.

The scotch isn't cutting it. I eye the toilet bag. How would one medicate this particular fright? I line up the pill bottles and play mad scientist. Xanax and Vicodin for drifty pain relief countered by the peppy Wellbutrin? Too nuanced. I need a blunter instrument. Some Ambien, that quick-absorption knockout drop favored by intercontinental flyers? The heavyweight gut punch of Lorazepam? I don't want to put my feelings in a coma, I want to vanquish them. Blast the vampire with sunlight.

Dexedrine. I took it for a few months after my narcolepsy diagnosis; it's as potent as street speed but without the lockjaw and much easier to calibrate. In low doses it gave me confidence, pizzazz. At higher doses I was fairly sure that the King James Bible could be improved upon and that I was just the fellow to do it. Then my tolerance grew and I felt nothing. If I damp the high notes with Xanax and Johnny Walker, I'll be in the flow, the center of the chute, not suppressing my horror at *Mr. Hugs: The Sequel* but sledding its leading edge. The feelings exist, as we say in CTC, and you can either ride them or let them flatten you. I believe it's only fitting, little bear, that I take my own advice today.

The bottle overflows with orange tablets and a drawdown of twenty percent shouldn't be noticeable. If Alex is such a junkie that she counts them, I won't respect her opinion of me anyway. I gulp three tabs, stash seven in my pocket, and lay in a gorilla dose of Ambien for a sound night's sleep before my talk. Two Vicodin in case I fall and break something and have to haul myself to the ER.

I douse Mr. Hugs in sterilizing scotch—why am I suddenly certain he has fleas?—and kick him behind the waste can under the sink, then pick up the phone that's mounted beside the toilet. You never see this placement in private homes but it's become de rigueur in nice hotels. I associate it with invalids' cries for help, but I know that's not why they do it. It's a puzzle right up there with ice cubes in the urinal.

"Art Krusk's room, please." I need time with a man's man. Someone who's been slapped around a little.

"Bingham?"

"I'm going downstairs to play some cards."

"I just went to bed from yesterday," Art says.

"I've got stuff to fix that. I'm at Mount O."

"That Marlowe kicked my everlasting butt. You didn't tell me there'd be role playing. Thanks, though. I feel sharp. I've got my fangs back. He gave me this first one as a favor to you, but what's it going to cost when he starts charging me?"

"All depends on how deep you want to go."

"It's exciting the way you say that. Things in store for me."

"You've entered the dragon, Art. Blackjack pit in ten. Wear your medallions. Pour on the Vitalis."

"You have a girl for tonight?"

"A teddy bear."

"Right. Me, too. That dancer we saw in Reno doing the old guy. I flew her down, but I think she's gone out free-lancing. I guess she's just part of the general hoo-ha now. She carries a beeper, but I can't get through. Marlowe says let it go. I'm like his zombie now."

Art's a moron, pathetic, but we click. I should slip him a ticket to Schwarzkopf. He'd be wowed and the favor might win me some leeway in my next life. Don't you think so, Mr. Hugs? He does. Whatever you feel, your squashable feels too.

There is so much they want from us here besides our money. Art disagrees. He thinks their greed is pure. I direct his attention to our dealer's eyes, her flat black tiddlywink pupils, the scaly lids, then ask Art if he's ever visited Disneyland, because if he has, then he knows we have before us an animatronic biomorphic puppet whose battery cells—they're sewn into her scalp, and if we shaved her head we'd find round ridges—have been charging themselves off our body heat for an hour now, robbing us of the strength to leave a game in which we're losing four of every five hands and try our luck at the flashing-dollar slots arranged in a horseshoe around that red Dodge Viper, which is actually an elaborate chocolate cake formed around earth's most perfect natural emerald.

"Sorry, can't keep up with you," Art says. "Pills haven't hit yet."

"Just swing."

"I need a six, Shawn."

Art reads all their name tags, not realizing that they're aliases, although the hometowns engraved on them are accurate. Whoever she is, this latex-sheathed destroyer, she was really built in Troy, New York, where they also make rototillers and small gas engines that I'm told are the best on the market. One hears this everywhere.

"You keep looking around," Art says, "like you're expecting someone."

It must be Alex. I left her a note that was legible but cramped—there was so much information to squeeze in. My allergies, both proven and suspected. My turn-ons and turn-offs. My feelings about war. Oh, that first rush of Dexedrine on an empty stomach.

"Over there, Art. Check it out," I say. "Hillary Clinton,

trying for the Viper. It's nothing but gods and legends in this place."

"You know who actually is in town," Art says. "Thatcher."

"Former leader of the British Tories? She lives here, Art. This is her home now."

"For a speech. I met a busboy smoking behind the Hard Rock who says he can get me in for fifty bucks. Might be worth it. I'm kicking it around."

"You know what I want, Art? My family in one place. A place even farther away than they are now but where they won't miss me, because they'll have the ocean. Tomorrow night I'll have a million miles, and though I've assumed I'd want most of them myself, they're all, as of now, one-way tickets to coastal Ireland for anyone who can prove that they're my kin."

"You shouldn't kid around about blood relatives."

"For those twenty seconds, just those, I wasn't kidding. I was daring myself to be a better man. Three hundred thousand, that's all I'm going to keep."

"You're not a bad man. You're just run ragged."

"Alex!"

She turns. From the back she was Alex—from the front she's what's her face from TV. Who sleeps with senators. She says she wants loads of children, but it won't happen. My ex talked that way too but didn't get pregnant until she shut up and started screwing Mormons with no expectations whatsoever. None. Except that the men would worship her perfect toes.

"I'm feeling them now," Art says. "You really sat with him?"

My Schwarzkopf fib; I knew he'd call me on it. "We discussed my future. Man's an empath. Total empath. St. Francis with a side arm."

"Ryan!"

It's her. Not Alex—Linda. Morse's operative. She has on an airline-issued orange turtleneck that she seems to believe can double as swank casino wear if it's accessorized with a rhinestone pin.

Anyway, we kiss. So now that's over with.

On to the next thing, whatever she suggests.

"Hi, I'm Art Krusk," Art Krusk says. Know thyself. He offers Linda his broad right hand that's as tanned on the palm as it is across the back.

"Nice to meet you," Linda says.

"Same here."

Boy, are these two on their game tonight.

"I'm so glad I found you, Ryan. This city's a zoo. Guess who I'm pretty sure I saw at Bally's stepping out of a roped-off elevator?"

One, two, three, four, five. A, B, C, D. She'll crack eventually, and I can wait.

"Brando. He's giving a speech, I guess."

"They all are."

"Could we maybe talk for a minute? Over there. Excuse us, Art."

"Excuse us, Art," I say. It's a technique: Neurolinguistic Mirroring, they call it. Do as the greats do and you can be great, too. Copy their walk, their inflections, everything. Big in the seventies, came back in the nineties, faded some, but will surely rise again.

We move "over there," which feels like the same place and wasn't, to my mind, worth the whole upheaval, emotional and physical, of getting to. Linda seems happier, though, and I'm happy for her. I count the pills in my pocket between two fingers and am disappointed with the tally.

"I was right about those hackers, Ryan. We're not supposed to tell customers, so don't spread this, but someone in Spain got into our computers—just some young kid, the FBI is saying—and scooped up account information, credit card numbers—"

"Anonymous Spanish teenager. Strangely plausible."

"He e-mailed the data to friends who e-mailed their friends and now it's all over the world and it's still going. We're getting calls from China. I'm serious."

"Our global globe."

"I'm not kidding. Cancel *everything*."

"I've been working up to it all week."

"Ryan?"

"Yes, ma'am?"

"You're loaded. It hurts to look at you. Can I get something off your forehead that's been bugging me?"

She goes right ahead. I'll never know what it was.

"I was going to say we should eat. You probably need to. This isn't you, though. This is not my friend. I'm going to my room to study my materials for tomorrow's seminar."

"Don't do it. Be kind, it's that easy. Burn all workbooks. Erase all cassette tapes and dub them over with song."

She kisses my cheek and it burns like the hot match heads my mother would use to make ticks release her children. "Goodbye, Ryan. I don't think we'll have more dates. This seminar has me thinking I'll try nursing school, so I might not be at the club much longer, either. I think I always meant to be a nurse but veered a few degrees. Like you've said you did."

"What did I tell you I set out to be?"

"A folk guitarist."

I'm baffled. It's so specific. "When was this, anyway?"

"June. Three months ago."

"Wait here a minute, Linda. I'm coming down. Some ice water to dilute this and I'll be me again. I want to reconstruct this folk guitar talk. Were we at your condo? Come back. Don't wave. You know how we think we don't have feelings for someone, but maybe it's because they're just too powerful? I love you. I have always loved you, Linda."

Oh well, she had her chance. We're all free agents now. Remember, it's a lattice, a continuum, so it's not like anything's final. Nothing's final. To the contrary. It's win-win. It's synergistic. Read Pinter on Quantum Granular Non-Hierarchies. Or hell, read between the lines of *Winnie-the-Pooh,* that cuddly avatar of Taoism. Milne knew it, he just couldn't say it plainly then—the shadow of Victorianism or something. This is twenty-first-century Nevada, though. Scream it, feel free. Nothing's final. It's all a loop. We've been re-engineered. Like PepsiCo.

Back to Art and the tables. He's behaving like I was, razzing a new dealer from Lima, Ohio, about the healed-over piercings in his eyebrows, discerning the face of the Virgin in his cards. He either lost everything while I was gone and bought back in with a mad five thousand bucks or he's in the statistical slipstream, he's supersonic. If you come in at the end of someone's streak, the two conditions appear identical. If anything, it's the big winners who look depressed, because grins are jinxes and it just can't last, and the losers who smile, because they can go home soon.

I wander off into the crowd. GoalQuesters dominate. I get a fat wink from Dick Geertz at Andersen, who hit his United miles mark a year ago, but only because he commutes to Tokyo, so really there's no comparison between us. I notice a drink in several colleagues' hands of layered purples and violets and toothpicked melon chunks, so I flag down a waitress and order one by pointing. I ask what its name is and she says no one knows, that everybody else just pointed, too. When I tell her that *someone* had to start this thing, she flat doesn't buy it. She's a creationist. She's also, I sense, much happier than I am.

"Hey, Bingham, I need you to meet someone. Get over here."

It's Craig Gregory calling. I hustle toward my punishment. The waitress will hunt me down. She'll use her network.

"Bingham, this is Lisa Jeffries Kimmel. Lisa, Ryan."
"Hi."
"I've heard your name."
"I've heard yours." What satanic liars we are.

242

"Lisa is coming to ISM next month after an interesting stint in Omaha. I know you think they're pursuing you, that bunch, so I'm guessing you'll want to pick her pretty brain."

Lisa looks down. She's small and dark and beautiful and bizarrely shapely in the way of a bonsai tree compared to a full-size tree.

"Not that Omaha's called him," Craig Gregory tells her, "or written or faxed or anything like that. It's just something he thinks. It gets him through the night."

Someone squealed on me. My assistant, no doubt. Some agency sends them, you think they're harmless drifters, be gone by winter, but really they're your minders, briefed at a central location and later debriefed. It's a business model, even if it's not true.

"I'll leave you two here. Full evening ahead of me at the convention center, followed by Streisand's annual farewell gig at the MGM."

I snag his elbow and step back from Lisa. "Someone sent me that bear you gave me, Craig. Mutilated. I'm pinning it on you. You're who I gave him back to when he retired."

Craig Gregory rubs his chin and opens a shaving cut that smears blood on his thumb tip, which he kisses dry. Tough little Lisa torches a cigarillo and hungers over the craps action all around us.

"That toy had two consecutive huge Christmases. I doubt you're in possession of the original. By the way, your corporate AmEx? Confiscated. No more charging Hong Kong custom suits."

"Computer crime. It wasn't me," I say. "If it goes in my file, I'll sue."

"Did you overhear that one, Lisa? Any thoughts?"

"Blameless. It's happened twice this year to me."

Craig Gregory folds his hands. He bows, comes back to me. "I'll be there for your breakfast sermon tomorrow. The title has people concerned. I'm not one of them. I know how you pussy out. I'll sit up front. Lisa, this is a man on his last legs, so give him much succor. We hear you give great succor."

"Die in hell, you gonorrheal prick."

"Hear that, Bingham? What this bitch just said? That's how healthy people respond to me. Take note. You're not too old to get it right."

The purple drink is still out there looking for me when I sit at the bar with Lisa and order another by pointing at one just like it two spots down. The bartender, leaves in his hair, a loose white robe, asks Lisa if she'd like one, too—a mere formality—and she says no. It's a startling negation, and it's infectious. I cancel my order as though I never meant it. The craze will be extinct within ten minutes.

I want this Lisa. I excuse myself, swivel on my stool, sneak two more pills, and phone my room on the mobile. I have a plan. If she's there, I'll hang up. If she's not, I'll dare to hope that she's joined Art's girl out there in the cyclone. No answer. Will it be safe to go back up, though? What I should do is book another room and abandon my personal effects, which, by design, are not that personal but standard items available anywhere. I'll miss my sleep machine, whose "prairie wind" track is unique as far as I can tell, but nothing else. The tapes of *The Garage* are best mislaid. That way there's at least a possibility that in ten years or twenty, at a rummage sale, an intern at *Business Week* will pay a nickel for them, listen to them on a whim, and call his boss. The authorship of the scrolls will be disputed—Tarkenton? Salinger? Billy Graham the Younger?—and a stream of pretenders will come forward waving bogus polygraph results. Me, I'll hang back in my Idaho retreat, content with my dogs, my Mormon faith, my wives.

Or, if this works with Lisa, my one true love.

"What's MythTech like?" There's no other way to start. "I thought no one quit there. I heard that if you're fired they buy you out for life, or pretty close."

She pinches the filter off a Marlboro. She's out of little cigars and needs particulates.

"Of course people leave. They just don't blab about it."

"Scared?"

"I'd say cautious. Maybe still perplexed. It's not like a regular consultancy. Take what I did: Market Ecology. The study of non-obvious interactions among diverse commercial entities."

"Beautiful. And no CTC department, am I right?"

"No departments at all. The model's plasma. Nuclear plasma fields. Pretentious."

"Gorgeous. At play in the fields of the Lord. Just think, just float. And no travel, I hear, and just a bare-bones headquarters. You can work from home. From anywhere. It's all electronic, humanistic, fractal."

"What are you on? I want some. I'm fading here."

Somehow I produce three pills for each of us. It's like the loaves and fishes, my right front pocket. Or did I lie to myself about how many I stole?

"Anyway, Lisa. Me. The market ecologist. A project comes down one day from Spack and Sarrazin. It isn't true that they're lovers, by the way. Sarrazin is crazy for his wife and Spack is a neuter. Born that way. He'll tell you."

"Haven't heard one breath of any of this. A friend of mine who said he had a wife died this week and I hear now he was gay, so basically I've written off these topics. The people themselves don't understand their leanings—that's my conclusion. I'm growing wise by leaps."

"The problem was tripartite," Lisa says. "Fiber optics, red meat, and propane gas."

I clutch her gesturing hand in mid-air. "My dad sold propane."

"I started with the easy ones. Gas plus red meat equals grills and patios and heart problems and the insurance that covers them and all those ramifications. But fiber optics? Maybe a gas grill that's somehow data-linked to a repair center whose low-wage workers only lunch at Wendy's or McDonald's not just because it's a grunt job and they're broke but because they're on call to diagnose malfunctions and can't leave their screens for more than fifteen minutes?"

"You're asking a question?"

"Or maybe it's like automated cattle ranches fed with real-time commodities reports that lead to higher profits per animal and thus increased contributions to co-op ad campaigns promoting beef versus chicken? I couldn't think!"

"Who was the client? A supermarket chain?"

"I'm not even sure there was a client, Ray."

"Ryan. That's okay. It's dark in here."

"That's a non sequitur," Lisa says. "I know what you mean, though. I'm high myself, from earlier. What's 'blue bottle'? That's what the kid kept calling it."

"I'm not down on the street a lot. Don't know."

"It felt like pure R&D to me," she says. "No timelines, no meetings, just live with this strange problem and send us your thoughts as you think them until they've stopped or you feel satisfied. Casual directives, and yet you feel this incredibly formidable potential wrath just waiting to sweep down and smash your life the moment you slack off or add some numbers wrong or make some other mistake you're bound to miss because no one's told you how to measure progress, they've only said something like 'Give it your best shot' or 'We know you have this in you, Lisa. Just try it.' "

"Compensation?"

"You honestly stop caring. It seems terrific at first, but then the costs of just maintaining yourself so you can work— the therapy, the stationary bike, the weekend antiquing so you can clear your head, the soundproofing for your home office so no one hears you throwing your stapler or yodeling for the hell of it—"

"Mounts. I needed to say that so I could breathe. I still have one question: What's the product? The service?"

"I was heading there. You've heard of that genome project? The human gene map? That's what they're after at MythTech, except with commerce. All the angles. All the combinations. And they know it won't be a 'eureka.' It won't just pop someday. It's going to take piecework and steady crunching away on every front. It won't take forever, but it won't be quick. That's why they don't worry about profits. Let someone else chase money in the short term; long term it's all MythTech's, anyway. Because the second MythTech gets this map, the second they lock those files in the vault, everyone else is a plowboy on their farm. Fact is, the money we think we're making now, the money we think IBM makes, Ford, Purina, KFC, Ben & Jerry's, the *LA Times,* it's actually just a loan from MythTech's future paid backwards to us in the present so we can eat until they've got things nailed down and they eat us. We're all Thanksgiving turkeys in their barnyard and tomorrow is November first."

"They still need operating funds. Who'd invest in this?"

"Who wouldn't, Ryan? Any investor who feels this thing might work knows he'll have nothing unless he's on its good side."

"I don't see how you could leave a place like that."

"Look at me, listen to me. Feel my hands. Do I seem like I've left? Sure, you can go to work for someone else—hell, they want you to; they *need* you to—but who are you really working for? Get with it."

"And if you leak their secrets they don't pursue it?"

"You still don't get what their product is, I'm seeing."

"The code. This perfect comprehensive map."

Lisa snaps off another filter and lights up. She leans back on her stool, cross-legged. Regards me. Sighs. "I'm selling it to you right now. You buying, boy? No, you already bought. It's in your eyes."

"I was thinking we should get a room. We're pretty far gone and it's only six o'clock."

"It's *fear* of the code. The fear there *is* a code and that someone else is going to crack it, so you'd better just cough up your energy right now, either to us or one of our subsidiaries. Or, if you're rich, send a check. It's all a racket. It's extortion, Ryan. Sheer extortion. The code is a bluff. It's all Beware of Dog. It's Daddy's deep, loud voice."

"Can I trust you with something?"

"No. But go ahead."

"I'm flying there tomorrow."

"Why fly? You're there."

"Craig was right. It's a hunch. There's no offer on the table. It's hints. It's signs. It's smoke signals. I know that. I have to see, though. What's my downside? None."

"After all I've just said you still want them to want you. You still want to shine in some interview," she says. "Not sexy, Ryan. Very not sexy, Ryan."

"What you've said makes me think it's the same whatever I do. If I go or don't go."

"What's the same?" she says. "Then I'm going back to my hotel."

"The result."

"That's all you care about? Results? Man, have they ever got their claws in your brain."

She swings down off her stool and picks up her little bag and fishes out some lipstick and does a touch-up. She looks into my face like it's her mirror and fills in a corner, puckers. There. She's done. She puts away the lipstick, zips the bag, steadies herself in her tippy heels, and goes. Definitely the one, and there she goes. And yet I still have a date tonight, so screw her. Screw Linda, too. Ryan Bingham thinks ahead.

fifteen

a lex says she wants to "do" Las Vegas. She's been hitting the guidebooks, apparently. How dreary. Or maybe she's thinking I'm so in-the-know, so seasoned and so locally plugged in, that while she's at the vanity getting up her getup and I'm out here sinking trick shots on the pool table, I'm already scrolling through the top five menus and mentally ranking in order of their significance in the great junk-culture scheme of things the biggest ten magic acts, lion extravaganzas, artsy European circuses, and toned-down, export editions of three-year-old New York performance art one-woman shows.

"Where were you all day?" I shout into the bathroom while sighting down my crooked, wavy cue. I'll skip the white over the orange and hit the red and the red will cause a scale-model Big Bang of symmetrically diverging suns.

"People-watching. The faces here. Amazing."

"You plan events for a living and huge festivities but you've never been to Las Vegas? Are you successful?"

"What?"

"That wasn't to you. I'm mumbling."

"Can you just give me some time here? Five more minutes?"

"What?"

"Can you just—"

"Kidding, Alex. Kidding. I wish you were in here to see what I just did."

She shoulders the door closed and I welcome this because I can stop looking through it at the floor where Mr. Hugs' legs can be seen behind the trash basket. I hang up my stick and leave the rec room. That was my all-time high point, that last shot, a miracle on felt that won't come twice. I lie on my back on the bed and I replay it on the expanded field of a beige ceiling so heavily textured and spackled and swirled and pebbled that I expect it to crumble or start dripping. Tomorrow's the day, tonight is just survival, and knowing that should make everything a bonus. If I eat one good shrimp. If I snatch another Dexedrine. If I glimpse Lisa's back in a crowd and flip her off or see Craig Gregory lose just one quarter. I can treat these next hours as one long jubilee and Alex as Bathsheba come back to life, and if I don't I'm just stealing from myself. This is why a man must set clear goals, because in the final countdown to their fulfillment, especially if that fulfillment feels inevitable, he can be as playful as he wishes, because all but the riskiest risks are now risk-free.

I'm ordering a limousine tonight. I'd like to see an impressionist. I shall. I'm raiding Alex's pharmacy in broad daylight and if she catches me I'm going to grin the naughty disarming grin I just now practiced, before I'd even imag-ined a context for it. I want to find whoever's dealing "blue bottle" and buy a six-pack, if that's how it comes, and dose Alex's drink without her knowledge and carry her back here giggling and fizzing and primed to act out the back pages of *Hustler* slathered in mentholated shaving cream.

Still, I worry that she's not successful. Because that will come out at some point and could be hard for someone as madcap and effervescent as the new me. She's already men-tioned that she did public relations once—she noticed on the jukebox a band she'd represented—but she didn't explain how she got out of it, which means her departure was prob-ably not voluntary. We'll need to avoid that particular episode and any stretch of either of our lives that words such as episode can be applied to. That will be easy for me, since I'm a master, but could be tough for her as she gets drunker and starts to confuse my radiance with warmth.

Judging by how long she's been in wardrobe, she's going to thrill me when next that door swings open, so there had better be some music playing. I logroll across the mattress and sit up and stare down into the jukebox's bright innards. I'm looking for something light and old and tuneful with no strong associations for either of us. Just a song for two generic flatlanders who've known the sprawling opportunity cities but still remember cold drumsticks at the swimming hole and that jig Poppa danced when he drank too much schnapps, even if things didn't happen just that way. Is there a song like that? Evocative but not stirring? That takes you back without taking you over? If there is, it's my theme. I'll make it my new sleep machine.

But it's not here on this old Wurlitzer. I'm stumped. No Sinatra, no Broadway, no Motown, no bubblegum, just tons of glum college-radio alt rock and overproduced AM country and—it's so wrong—much melancholy yet strident sixties protest crap. I may as well just punch stuff up at random; a dangerous thought, since that's what I'm now doing, as though my ideas are now starting in my fingers and traveling upstream to my cerebrum. Out slides the arm and the record from its rack and up comes, at a volume I can't lower because I see no knobs or dials anywhere, "If I Had a Hammer" by Peter, Paul and Mary. It's just the tune I didn't want to hear and of course it's also Alex's cue to open the door, spread her arms, and say "You like?"

She takes the catwalk. She's dipped herself in black lacquer that still looks wet and tied her straight hair back in a whiplash ponytail that she swings around in a slashing full rotation while bowing her head, and I'm really not sure why. Her shoes are the kind you don't notice, you just see legs, and the whole effect is pure campy female cutout, like those busty silhouettes on truckers' mud flaps.

"Rate me," she says. "Be vicious and be cold."

"Ten is inhuman and never sounds sincere, so I'll say nine point seven. Nine point eight."

An abrupt Bond Girl pivot, hand on hip. Reverses it.

"This music's awful."

"Do something about it. There's not much there."

"I don't make decisions tonight. I'm full-on Barbie. Just pretend they never burned the bra and you've never heard the word 'empowerment.' That's hard in your line of work, but just pretend."

"Last time you wanted to talk. Now this," I say.

Cocks a hip, trails her fingers up her sides. Ooh, that tickles. Oh, but it feels good. Pouts and half closes those lashes and strokes her cheeks. "Now this. One request only: a very long black car. Like something you'd see at a Playboy Mansion funeral."

"The phone book's already open to that page."

We're riding around and still talking destinations when it strikes me that what would ruin things forever would be for Ryan to get flashy with his credit card—the one that earns miles and the only one not hacked, because it already was and he replaced it—and prematurely hurtle over the goal line down here on Las Vegas Boulevard with a woman dressed as a Bahraini sex slave and him so zonked on prescription everything that he won't remember his big finish. That's never been the picture and mustn't happen. The picture is specific and very dear to me. One, I'm alone or with a total stranger, which represents my customary mode. Two, there are fields below, even if I can't see them. There's more, a score of picky stipulations that have barnacled onto my skull over the years, but lately I've been rationing the previews so as not to pre-empt the real hit show.

"Driver," I say, and not because I like it but because the old guy insisted on being addressed this way, perhaps from some creepy role-playing addiction, "I need a bank. I need a cash machine. I'm only spending fresh green bills to-night."

"All the casinos have several ATMs, sir."

"I can't explain why but I'd like it from a bank."

The gentleman already knows we're freaks back here. The pills are out and a bunch rolled under the seat and it probably looks to him in his rearview mirror like we've been bobbing for apples these past few minutes. In the limo's doors are insulated wells stocked with pop and beer and crescent-shaped ice cubes, and we've made a mess of these as well. We sip once from a can and decide it's not our flavor and thrust it back into the ice pile and it spills and we crack another and fancy it even less and it tips and gushes, too, and we're all sticky, so out come thick wads of multicolored napkins that we're just too lazy to use singly, and plus we're paying for them, so who cares?

"You up for a good mimic, Alex?"

"As always."

"So why did you quit PR?" I feared this subject, but as is my habit I'm rushing right in toward it because I don't want it crawling up behind me.

"I got let go."

"For cause? I'm sorry."

"Shrinkage. Not enough desk chairs to go around one day, but they tried to be sweet about it. You know. Help us."

"Why did you say 'you know' like that to me?"

"Because you know."

I swing around to Driver like I've been kicked and do what he told me earlier I should do: ask him anything. What arises from this are two tickets and a firm price—we just have to give the box office a note that Driver's now scribbling on a pad beside him while Alex watches the road because he isn't and I can see she thinks this actually helps—for one Danny

Jansen at some casino showroom. It's ninety bucks per head. We find that bank. The machine is on an outside wall and hungry drifters lurk on every corner as I make the withdrawal, but vanish once I've made it.

In line for the act I say, "I *don't* know. Tell me." Right straight at it again.

She doesn't answer me until we're seated and Danny swaggers on as Schwarzkopf—topical—and there's no way out. Just fire exits.

"You honestly don't remember me? Our sessions? It wasn't a seminar, Ryan. You outplaced me. I was waiting for you to confess," she says. "I thought you were playing with me by holding back. Then I realized you weren't and didn't know what to think. But you've really forgotten me, haven't you? That hurts."

"This started in Reno?"

"It started on the plane. I assumed you were playing chicken with this gal."

Danny proves to be one rare monster, stout as a hog but nimble as a lemur yet something else as an itty-bitty kitten flung down a basement staircase by its tail. Three minutes into his leaping, bucking, slithering, A-to-Z, pansexual imitation of everyone from Stalin to Shirley Temple—and he can do them simultaneously, too, sitting on a park bench licking sugar cones or with their heads stuck through adjacent guillotines—I've so horrifically received my money's worth that I'm about to pee my pants with glee. And indeed I feel a tiny trickle, which I suck back up or at least prevent from soaking me. I ask Alex if she'll excuse me for a moment. She won't, though. She refuses to excuse me. She grabs my hand and crushes ligament as Danny dipsy-doodles through the Louvre as both the Mona Lisa and Picasso, and after about thirty seconds of tense resistance I decide that there's another, better way: I'll just go limp and take whatever's coming and hope some skilled clinician can save me later.

"Stop that," she whispers. "Don't squirm. It's almost over."

I resolved to go limp, but I didn't manage it. This time I will. I imagine soft old rope rotting on a Lake Superior dock.

For the show's last ten minutes I picture various deaths at Alex's slender hands. Yet I don't feel her anger. This troubles me even more. I was going to run into one of them, eventually, but I figured it would be a swift, short blow. I'm sick of waiting for it. I want it now.

Driver is in position when we're reborn from Danny's seething necropolis and straggle out into the light of late-night Vegas. Move toward the light, it's all a soul must know, even if it comes streaming from the red eyes of a mammoth re-created sphinx with two front paws the size of super-tankers.

"Well, I guess it's all out in the open now," says Alex, re-clining against the molded leatherette of our American-made black mass on wheels. Driver is taking us somewhere he thinks we'll like but he wants it to be a surprise. He's being Driver.

"I'm so, so sorry," I say. But just so-so. Why bother with guilt when she's about to hang me? It'll be her turn to feel guilty soon.

"Slide over here and make it up to me. Kiss my legs or something. Right on up."

I obey her, both in letter and in spirit. The alcohol in her perfume stings my tongue. She must have bathed in it.

"Came early, stayed late," she says. "Worked weekends. Holidays. I had a sick kid brother with no health plan, a mom who shared a dad with someone else and liked the nice girly things he couldn't give her. Mostly, it was for me, though. I drove Miatas. One-year leases so I could try new colors. You know who I represented once? Barbara Bush. Pretty fabulous. I got some hand-me-downs. When she'd built up to five copies of one necklace that she couldn't risk wearing the original of, guess who got the sixth, with a sweet card? That's how they became the Texas Kennedys: cards for everyone, wrote them day and night." She leans back further. "You're doing good. Go, Fido."

"Ma'am?" The voice of Driver.

"I'm still a miss. A junior miss."

"We're there."

"Just circle, please."

I cast up my eyes at the giantess. She pats me. If this is the sum of my obligations to her, I'll gladly go till dawn. Till dawn of spring. Or could it be that I payed my spiritual debt by watching Danny mutate for an hour and now I'm into the extra-credit zone.

"I slept with the boss man. I didn't feel exploited. I felt like he was offering me insurance. He wouldn't just hump any of the young things, and the ones that he did hump had major blackmail power, all seventeen of us. God, I loved PR. The privilege of it. Showing the world that Texaco and

Exxon only drilled and brokered and refined as a way to support their truer passions: saving the porpoise and promoting opera in the inner city, which they'll rebuild someday and not even take the write-off—it's a gift. Being entrusted with tall tales that vast just swoops you up onto your silver princess throne. More, give me more. Give me harder ones, you shout. Let me position private penitentiaries as walled Montessoris for late-blooming unfortunates. Your appetite for deception spreads and grows, and just when you think it can't gape any wider, someone hands you a folder tabbed 'Pesticide Spill: Monsanto.' It's like bliss. You don't have to chew so hard, Ryan. Focus. Focus."

"I apologize, miss, but my left rear tire feels flat. There's broken glass all over the road tonight. I'll need to stop up ahead and use the jack."

"Can you just lock us in?"

"Of course I can."

"Then it's not a problem."

"Yes, miss. Thank you."

I hear a door slam muffled by so much skin.

"But then we lost some big clients," Alex says, "and one of our rainmakers died and . . . dominoes. I truly think they drew lots to choose who went. You still don't remember me? Those suits I wore? I'm up to our first meeting."

The harder she bangs on this lid, the tighter it seals. A moment ago I felt it opening—a vision of Dallas office-tower blue glass, an artsy reception area with seats resembling children's wood alphabet blocks, extreme-angle views of parking garages with painted helipad markings on the roofs—but now it's all black again, and shut; Chernobyl entombed in its smooth concrete sarcophagus. The barricades are up on memory lane.

My seat seems to tilt. Is this the jack at work?

"You don't remember the exercise?" she says. "That workshop hour where you were some big headhunter and I was supposed to sell you on my skills without using words like 'need' or 'want' or 'hope'? You cracked pistachios to show uninterest, which you said I'd have to be prepared for, and I unbuttoned my cashmere cardigan, the top two buttons, and you said, 'That looks desperate; you want a new job, not a sugar daddy.' Nothing?" She lifts my chin with two hands and makes me see her.

I apologize and apologize. The seats tilt. I'm afraid if I move I'll shift the limo's balance point and crush Driver under an axle.

"You cared," says Alex. She closes her legs with her dress tucked in the V. I'm off-duty now; I uncramp my neck. "You didn't want to be there, either, did you? We had that in common. We both wanted to scream. You fidgeted, your nails were bitten raw. I should be consoling *him*, I thought. I knew my job couldn't last. It wasn't meant to. Exxon. The Bushes. Festivals must end. But you thought *you* were responsible. So earnest. I wanted to cook you a great big hot peach cobbler."

And then all is level and we're on the road again. The limo founders in a swarming crosswalk and long-haired rowdies slap the windows, holler. A can of something thunks the roof and skitters and Driver accelerates and through the floor I feel the wheels lump over a large soft object that I'll always remember as a body, even if it was a mail sack or a garbage bag. I want those Ambien. I find strange capsules, ones I haven't seen yet, shining in an upholstery crack. I gobble them. Alex is still reminiscing. "You cared," she says. It's the mantra in this monologue.

And then we're dancing somewhere. We're back indoors. Or is this the new outdoors? The purple drinks are back—they'd just gone dormant—except that now they're made of frozen slush that you can scoop up off the dance floor if you spill one and pack back into your cup like a wet snowball and pierce with the long straw and keep on sucking. Other dancers keep shoving me. A cubist Alex, all planar overlap and sextuple foreheads, surrounds and eludes me simultaneously, omnidirectionally dancing with all of us. She grinds on my hip, she whispers in my ears—both ears at once. She loves me, loves me, loves me. Her ponytail slices a Z in the green fog, smoke, the Mark of Zorro. She's hanging on my neck.

I squirt through a crack in her cycloramic presence and make it to the bar and ask for milk. In a corner Art Krusk consults with Tony Marlowe, still plotting his comeback as an ethnic food king. Marlowe will cost Art. The newsletter. The videos. In CTC, all I wanted was a clean getaway, but Marlowe's game is different. He sticks around, angling to be your Pope, your spouse, and soon you're paying him to certify you as a trainer in his franchised cult. Goodbye, Art Krusk. The grating is off the storm drain. You're underground now, blowing through the mains. The two of them rise from their table with their snow cones and stroll away like president and premier talking peace on some Camp

David bunny trail. Tomorrow Marlowe will give Art his new name.

"You little shit. You ditched me," Alex says. Her heat-rashed throat is like an oriole's and her high birdy voice weaves through the DJ's drumtrack, which is all he's spinning tonight. Percussion.

"I needed cool dairy. Where are we? Where is this club?"

"Under Mount O." She index-fingers my temples. A current crackles between the diodes. "It's me."

If this could just conclude, please. I guzzle milk. It's not the taste, it's the texture. It's how it coats.

"You knew it would have to happen, didn't you? Someone was going to see under your black hood and realize the Grim Reaper was just a kid. This is our chance to heal each other, Ryan."

Where is all this eloquence coming from? She's mixed her pills better than I have. "You have a mustache." She licks the two percent off my upper lip and I lick off the wetness of her licking.

"Did you rehearse these things you've said to me?"

"Day and night since Reno. Certain lines I wrote down. The Barbara Bush part."

"You're good," I say. "You're scary good, in fact."

"I want us to go upstairs," she says. "Just give me half an hour. To set the mood." She hands me her violet frosty to hold and kisses me and does the Bond Girl turn and activates her jetpack and whooshes off, right through the ceiling. Her contrails smell of propane.

But has anyone paid Driver? I fix on this in lieu of the big questions, such as how frightened to be of a young woman who aches to redeem her for-hire persecutor. I count my bills on the bar and recognize that I never coughed up for the Danny tickets, either. The harder I try to close out my accounts, the more people I owe. But I'll never find that limo. People who don't insist you pay them up front do you no favors. They're spiritual Shylocks.

I decide to consider my cash the house's money and find a quiet table and let it ride.

The winning streaks you're obliged to leave midway continue indefinitely in your dreams, until the sum you might have won if you'd only hung around dwarfs the stack you walked away with. I leave the blackjack pit after thirty minutes up around eight hundred bucks, but I cede my sunny Bahamian retirement and golden years of anonymous philanthropy to an old desert rat who's in my stool before its vinyl cushion can replump. It may be the greatest favor I've ever done anyone, but he can't acknowledge it and I can't take credit.

The elevator halts on every floor, it seems, but only twice do passengers get off. We glare at one another as we rise, wondering who's the prankster or the moron. Most Las Vegas rides from the casino back to the rooms breed comity, compassion—everyone's been fleeced by the same con—but this crew stews and accuses. The four people I leave behind when I step out are poised for a bloody cage match.

I insert my card key. The light blinks red. I flip the card over. Still red. I'd knock or call, but I don't want to spoil Alex's set design by forcing her to leave her mark. She lives for stagecraft. It's really all I know about her. So what's in store? Gothic dungeon? Bridal chamber? LAPD interrogation cell?

I was right not to knock, I see; this isn't my room. The number beckoned because it's also the PIN for my Wells Fargo cash card. I look both ways. The rows of doors look phony, as if they conceal brick walls or dusty air shafts. I walk along but no digits jump out at me. Then I smell incense. I slot my card in. Green.

Inside, a moment of night-blind blackout yields to imprinted ghostlights from the dance club and then to a Russian Orthodox cathedralscape of shadows and candleglow. The room's mock-suite shape, its notional entryway, blocks a full-Broadway beholding of the king bed and whatever pose my date has chosen there—champagne flapper, minky Marilyn, Cleopatra with serpents. I see the flowers, though. Carnivorous white lilies on the pool table and more of them on the dresser-credenza thing. No music, though. No beatnik minstrelsy. That Wurlitzer let us both down. Three steps, a turn.

Home to fulfill the obsession I deserved.

It's like a fairy tale. The bed stripped down to its sheets. The banks of roses. The powdered skin and many, many lit tapers. All gauzy and medieval and surely calculated to address the ancient child in me even as it rebukes the infant grown-up. That seems to have been her intention, at least. To enchant and correct at the same time. But her thrashings and half-conscious gropings have mangled things. She's on her side in a kind of frozen crouch, fouled in the linens. The roses are a mess. Only the chess-set lineup of pill bottles on the nightstand beside my sonic sleep machine—tuned to the "rain forest" track; I hear the dripping now—memorializes my girl's perfectionism.

I receive it all as a kindness. She could have hung herself.

To grab the phone I have to reach through flames, and I suffer a burn I won't feel till hours later. The receiver is off the hook—evidence of second thoughts? I'm shaking her with one hand, but I'm also listening for a dial tone. Then I see the cord yanked from the wall jack. I frisk myself for my mobile. 911? Or patch through to the desk for the in-house team of medics that any hotel this size must have on standby? The decision hangs. I shouldn't have to make one. I've outsmarted myself by imagining the medics.

The emergency operator wants my room number, which I never noted; I followed the jasmine. The lady drawls. Her westernness offends me. I run to the hall, read the number off the door, then hustle back to list the names of the poisons, the medications. I arrive at the wrong side of the broad mattress and instead of circling around I climb across. I brush her skin, traversing. It might be colder. Still time to pump her stomach, to give the shots. The small print on the bottles' labels is faded, low contrast. I squint and report. I'm asked to speak more clearly.

Instructions next. Check the airway for obstructions; the victim may have aspirated vomit. I don't understand. "With your fingers," drawls the operator. I'm surprised she didn't call me "hon." I ask her for specifics, mechanical drawings. Which fingers? How many? In the throat? Somehow I fumble the handset in my scramble and lose it in all the roses and knotted laundry. It rings seconds later, an automated callback, but I perform the more critical mission first. I roll her on her back—I'm sure I'm wrong here; the victim *belongs* on its side, so it can drool; so its gullet can eject the foreign material—and I spread her wet chin and jaw and make my probe, index and middle, it's coming back to me.

Jaws dully close and gum me—wakefulness. Then her head makes a ripping, canine shake. She bites.

"The fucking hell . . . ?" Huge eyes she has. Like Lazarus.

"Alex, oh fucking god."

"You choked me. Shit!" She jerks back her knees and goes fetal against the headboard. Cornered, curled, as if I had a knife. Extremely wakeful, though. My phone still ringing.

"You never came," she says. "I fell asleep. Where were you?"

"Are you okay? You said to wait."

"Not two hours," she says. The phone is by her hand, I see. She slaps it and it goes quiet.

"I," I say. "I," I continue. "I," I offer. I pause.

"Playing cards? Just one more hand?" she says. She gathers the sheets and covers all her good parts. Again the phone rings. She answers it and listens and says, "I'm fine," and repeats it until even I'm convinced, her face showing comprehension of my mistake, of everyone's mistakes, and then disgust.

"Thank you. I know, but it wasn't that," she says. "He's self-important, so he thought it was. He knew I used sedatives, but apparently . . . I know, I know." They're hitting it off, these gals. "He got himself all hung up in the casino and tiptoed in here with a guilty conscience and saw what he wanted to or hoped or something. His poor, poor Juliet. If you want to send someone over to confirm, be my guest . . . Right. Okay. She wants to talk to you."

I explain that there's no emergency after all and turn the mobile off and face my date. If she lit all these candles when she first came in and they were new then and now they're this burned down I'm surprised it was only two hours I wasted down there.

"You got the bear, I noticed," she says. "From Paula. My friend. Who you don't remember, either. Tall. Wore flannel slacks. She worked that mannish thing."

"A Paula. Statuesque," I say. "A Paula."

"When I told her I saw you on the Reno flight, she said 'Oh goody,' and asked me for your info. You ticked her off. She's touchy, but she's a gas. She said she was going to do something, but not what, though it must have been her because she gave those bears for Christmas once, the year we were fired, when those bears were big. She's back in PR, in Miami. Fashion stuff."

"I should probably get my own room tonight, you feel."

"Get me one. This one's trashed. I want fresh blankets. I spent a lot of money on all this gear."

"Or maybe we can both get a new room."

"You must think I'm a pretty lonely lady. Pretty twisted, too. Just say it."

"No."

"That was your moment of grandeur, wasn't it? Your slain despondent virgin," Alex says. "I know your big atonement's set for nine, but I'd just call and cancel if I were you. You haven't really earned the cross, you know? You flatter yourself and it's sort of getting old. Try to book me another suite. Or anything. It doesn't even have to be Mount O."

I take down the cue when I'm alone again and venture a few four-bumper extravaganzas, but I'm out of my groove and not much sinks. Pool balls not sinking, just knocking around, are sad. Some entertainment? I should love this Wurlitzer. These are my people. Haggard. Baez. Hank. Country-Western Music as Literature. I'm told I had ambitions as a folk singer, and I don't doubt it, but it's too late to learn an instrument. I click my sleep machine to "prairie wind" and gobble a pill I found under the sink and an Ambien from my pocket, to hedge my bets.

I call Alex in her new room three floors above me to see if she's comfortable and to make sure she won't be down to murder me in my sleep. She answers from the bathroom, from the john, whose whirlpooling I can hear when she picks up. I'm calling from the same spot—we've found a wavelength?—though I've already flushed. I flush again, a kind of mating call, and Alex says she's preparing to go out again and I say, competitively, that I am, too. "As what?" she says. It's the question I should have asked her; she's the one who's always going out as things. "As Danny," I say, and at last I get a laugh from her. Why didn't we begin things in this fashion, toilet to toilet, at a modest remove, the way the balanced Mormons do their courting?

I ask her why she takes so many pills, my concern for her seeming genuine, even to me, and she says she doesn't—the pills are a collection, a way of adapting to the flying life and self-employment, which she's never grown used to. Consulting with a doctor in each new city is like redesigning the lighting in her hotel rooms; it helps her to feel connected and at ease; and she only asks the physicians for prescriptions because she's from Wyoming and grew up poor and believes in value for her money. She broke them out tonight because she saw I'd stolen a fair number and she concluded that drugs were my passion or maybe just my pastime and she wanted to swing along, not be a spoilsport. I tell her I buy all this, although few others would, because I know what she's up against out here, having to set up anew each time she lands—I do it, too, by rooting for local teams, and I tell her the story about the Bulls and Timberwolves. "So: Poseidon's Grotto in fifteen minutes? Come as whoever," I say. And then I add: "I finally remembered you," because it's true. A minute ago, when I realized there'd be no penalty, I flashed on the morning I played headhunter to Alex's kittenish job seeker in cashmere, though the nuts were peanuts, not pistachios.

"We had chemistry, didn't we?" she says.

"I wouldn't go that far. I enjoyed the outfits. I wasn't capable then of having chemistry."

"You think our limo's still out front?"

"I'm certain."

"We could drive to that secret air base in the desert where they supposedly autopsy the aliens and sit on a rock with a carton of cold milk and watch the skies for experimental craft."

Now, that's my idea of doing Las Vegas. "Yes."

"Why weren't you like this before?"

Can't answer that.

"Or maybe," she says, "we should wait a week or two and see if we're still interested?"

"Oh."

"That would be wiser, I think."

In bed, alone, I recall that tonight was about survival only, so I've succeeded. The rest was all a bonus. And I may just have met my soul mate tonight, though I'm still not sure which one she was.

this business of hassled travelers waking up not knowing where they are has always seemed false to me, a form of bragging, as when someone tells me at a business lunch that it's been years since he really tasted his food. The more I've traveled, the better I've become at orienting myself with a few clues, and the harder it's gotten to lose myself. I'm perpetually mapping and triangulating, alert to accents, hairstyles, cloud formations, the chemical bouquets of drinking water. Nomadism means vigilance, and to wake up bewildered and drifting and unmoored is a privilege of the settled, it seems to me—of the farmer who's spent his whole life in one white house, rising to the same roosters.

The light in my room is Las Vegas morning light, there's none other like it in all America—a stun gun to the soul. It picks out the pistils and stamens in the lilies and the ashes of the spent incense cones. My mobile is halfway through its second ring, and because I'm now down to unwelcome callers only, I hesitate before answering. I'd give anything for a moment of dislocation, a blessed buffer zone.

"I'm downstairs with a car on the way," Craig Gregory says. "I thought you might like a ride to the convention center. You'll want to check the acoustics, the power spots. You going to use a lectern and sermonize or do the walkabout talk-show act? We're curious."

"I haven't showered."

"Use it for effect. Too conscience-stricken to bathe. I'll wait out front, next to the big pink granite Dionysus."

I do my best with razor, soap, and toothbrush, but it's like polishing a wormy apple. Motivation is low. Virtue's bugle call is silent. I rehearse a few brave phrases from my talk but the face in the steamy mirror seems unmoved. The point of the speech was to hear myself deliver it, but I already have, a hundred times, and clearly my best performance is behind me. The true act of courage this morning would be to cancel and live with the knowledge of Craig Gregory's office-wide "I told you so's." It's the sole penance left to me, and I must snatch it.

I pack up my carry-on but it won't zip. I leave it on the bed. My briefcase, too. Luggage, for me, was an affectation anyway, a way to reassure strangers and hotel clerks that I hadn't just been released from prison and that I'd make good on my bills. I ditch the white-noise generator as well. The thing enfeebled me. If a person can't lose consciousness on his own, if thinking his thoughts is that important to him, then let him lie on his bed of nails. He'll cope.

Only the HandStar is indispensable, if only for nine more

hours or so. Its flight schedules, mileage charts, and activity logs will tell me when I've passed over my meridian. After that, the trash. My credit cards, too. The fewer numerical portals into my affairs, the fewer intruders. I may keep one Visa so I can pump my gas without having to face a human clerk, but I'll toss the rest on the unloved-numbers dump. 787 59643 85732, you may no longer act as my agent. Permission denied. My phone I'll retain in case I witness a car wreck and can be of aid. The boots stay, too. To help me walk the surface of the earth and look silly doing it, which is how I'll feel. Not forever, I hope, but certainly at first.

I check out by remote, via the TV, and ride the elevator to the casino, where I notice a few of the players from last night still humped up over the tables and machines, though not the fellow who copped my lucky blackjack stool, who's probably out yacht-shopping by now, nagged by a faint sense of illegitimacy he's drinking hard to mask.

I'm almost out the door and MythTech-bound, heading for a rear exit to miss Craig Gregory, when I fix on a familiar profile alone at a corner mini-baccarat table. They got him. I'm devastated. They waylaid Pinter. There he is, stubbly, strung out on the odds, a monk who ventured from his cell just once and plunged straightaway down Lucifer's rabbit hole. It's my duty to try to haul him out.

It takes him a moment to see me once I've sat down. This game of no skill and one binary decision—Player or Banker; an embryo could do it—has fossilized his nerves. The whites of his eyes are the color of old teeth, and so are his old teeth.

"I was just getting up to come hear you speak," he says. Optimistically.

"I was up against CEO-to-be-announced. I bowed out. How's it going over here?"

"Better and better. I'm almost back to even." He wets his gray lips and commits two chips to Banker, then has an epiphany and shifts to Player. If he wins this, he'll think he has the touch. If he loses he'll think he *had* the touch, but doubted himself. He'll resolve not to doubt himself and keep on playing.

"Have you thought any more about the Pinter Zone?"

He smashes out a hand-rolled cigarette. "I've decided to license those rights to Tony Marlowe. I'm sorry. I planned to tell you at your talk."

"May I ask why?" As if I don't know, and as though I care now. Marlowe's a smiler. He grooms. He follows up. The perennial philosophy.

"You may, but my answer would only make you feel bad."

Fair enough. But he stabs me anyhow. "You're a graduate of my seminars," he says. "Marlowe's not. His brain's not full of goop. He sees me for what I am, another businessman, not an avatar. It takes the pressure off. You, I would have disillusioned."

Wrong. Watching him kill himself to get "back to even" (where but in Las Vegas is reaching zero considered an accomplishment?) has already done that job.

"You seeing the general this afternoon?" he says. "This man won a massive set-piece desert battle. Imagine the confidence that must instill."

"I've heard him. I've gotten all he has to give. I'm off to Omaha. Spack and Sarrazin."

"Say hello to them for me."

He chooses Banker. Loses. The El Dorado of evenness recedes before a new grail: bankruptcy with dignity. I buy a few chips. I'll join him in his ruin.

"I'm not even sure I still want to work for them. I might live on my savings for a year. Read the classics."

"The classics will just depress you. I fled a country nurtured on the classics and everyone there was drunk or suicidal. Keep occupied. Work. Earn money. Help others earn money. Ignorance of the classics is your best asset. If MythTech shows interest, accept. Don't ponder Dante."

I've won two hands, that fast, and I can see the swinging pocket watch of last night's trance. I collect my chips and scoot my stool back, rise.

"Stay. You're the charm," says Pinter. "Five more hands. I'm back within striking distance of where I stood when I felt I was starting to catch up."

Too sad, that remark. And I owe the old man, too, even if he's dancing with Marlowe now. He did something for me once. He did a lot. The sophisticates may sniff, but it's all true: in the course of certain American lives, way out in the flyover gloom between the coasts, it's possible to arrive—through loss of love, through the long, formless shock of watching parents age, through inadequacies of moral training, through money problems—at a stage or a juncture or a passage—dismiss the buzzwords at your peril—when we find ourselves alone in a strange city where no one lives any longer than he must and all of our neighbors come from somewhere else, and damn it, things just aren't working out for us, and we've tried everything, diets, gyms, jobs, churches, but so far not this thing, which we read about on a glossy flyer tucked under our windshields: a breakthrough new course in Dynamic Self-Management developed over decades of experience training America's Top Business Leaders and GUARANTEED TO GET YOU WHERE YOU'RE GOING!

And we go. And feel better. Because there's wisdom there, more than we gained at our lousy college, at least, and more importantly there's an old man's face—beamed in from California by satellite—which appears to be looking at us alone, the ninety-eight-pound weaklings, and not laughing! A miracle. Not even smirking! Beholding us!

"I win again. Are you watching this?" says Pinter. "Don't move an inch. I'm tripling my wagers."

Only for him would I do this: stand around impersonating good luck when I have a flight to catch.

"I'm there! I'm even!"

"You might want to stop now," I say.

Pinter nods. "Unless you can postpone Omaha."

"I can't."

He pockets the chips he sat down with like golden loot dredged from a wreck. He steps back from the table. Look: no handcuffs.

"I'm sorry about Marlowe. I can't unsign. I can, however, run up to my room and call Mr. Sarrazin and vouch for you and suggest that he send a car when you get in. When's your arrival?"

I tell him.

"You brought me back!" He shakes my hand and won't

stop, and though one dreams of someday being thanked by one's old mentor, one doesn't want him to cling this way. It's painful. My favor was so small. I did so little.

Though I guess that depends on how much he was down.

There's always a change in Denver. It's unavoidable. A trip to the bathroom out west means changing in Denver. If you've done it, you've seen the city at its best. Not because the rest of Denver is dull (I've been told my old city possesses a "thriving arts scene," whatever that is; personally, I think artists should lie low and stick to their work, not line-dance through the parks) but because the airport is a wonder. Along with Hartsfield and O'Hare, DIA is one of Airworld's three great capitals. It's the best home that someone between homes could ever want.

But today is goodbye. I'll change in Denver again some-day—I'll still fly, I suppose, though less often, and mostly for pleasure—but this won't be the same DIA, where I know everybody and most folks at least act like they know me. The ten-minute chair-massage girl who just had twins. The shoeshine guys, Baron and Gideon and Phil. The health-walking retired G-man who shows up every weekday at 6 A.M. to clock his nine miles, shielded from the weather by those soaring conical canopies said to invoke a native teepee vil-lage, though to me they've always looked like sails.

And Linda, of course, whom I had to go and sleep with, perverting the pristine relationship of kind and competent receptionist and busy man who loved being received.

I stare at them as I walk between my gates. If I catch

someone's eye I make a finger pistol and shoot them a big "Howdy" or "Keep on truckin'." A few shoot back, but only one person speaks—Sharon, the quickie massage girl. "Flamingo neck, get over here! You need me!"

I mount her odd-looking chair and rest my head, facing down and forward, between two pads. I watch the floor go by. Nothing stays in place; it all goes by. Floors just do it more slowly than other things.

"Hear that Rice Krispies sound? That's your fascia crackling." She always brings up my fascia. She pities them. She believes that if people, particularly people in power, "would only listen to their bodies," war would cease and pollution would abate—and for as long as I'm in her oily hands, I believe it, too. Imagine the red faces if the answer turns out to be that simple. It just may.

I'd tell her "So long," but I don't want to confuse her. Of course I'm going away; I'm in an airport.

I walk to the Compass Club desk and ask the woman filling in for Linda to pass a note to her I wrote on the flight in. Not much of a note: "Keep smiling, okay? I'm sorry about last night. I'll be away. Tell the boys to expect big parcels on their birthdays and yes, you'd make a terrific nurse. Pursue that."

"Are you Ryan?" the sub asks. "The one she always talks about? You fit the description perfectly. You must be."

"Describe the description."

"Medium short hair. A big vocabulary. Flat but pleasing voice."

"With that, you pegged me?"

"Great West ran your picture in the employee newsletter. They've been updating us on your progress. You'll be our tenth."

I'm flummoxed. "You all know my face then? Nation-wide? The tone of this little article was positive?"

"Try fawning." She points a finger down her throat.

"Really? No kidding."

"Orders from on high," she says. "Treat the man like a prince. That's not verbatim, but that's the thrust."

"Go on!"

"You haven't noticed the little smiles everywhere? The big thumbs-up from your teammates?"

I shake my head. "The newsletter said I'm your team-mate? Do you still have it?"

"You really haven't noticed? You're our Most Wanted."

"I'm finding this very confusing. Morse said pamper me? The future head of pro baseball said pamper me? Not give me flak?"

"That baseball thing fell through. We hear he's shat-tered. He spoke at a prayer breakfast in Boulder yesterday and the word is he sobbed. He lost it for a minute. With the stock price stuck and Desert Air's big fare cuts and new 'Let's Fly Together' ad campaign, my union's saying he's gone within six weeks. Maybe—after that breakdown—even sooner."

"Reliable high-level gossip? Or car-pool stuff?"

"Union news. And believe me, we won't miss him. He's Mr. Bad Faith. Gives an inch, then takes it back, then gives it again later on like he's some Santa Claus or wonderful rich uncle. He'll make out fine. They'll slip him a million and he'll walk off laughing."

"He won't. That not how it feels," I say.

"Whatever."

"He's in for some dark nights, if this is true. Is there a way to contact him directly? How would I get his number? The one he answers?"

"Pray to God. Come on, you hate him, too. All the passengers do. He killed this outfit."

"You're still working here."

"You're still buying tickets."

"Soften up on those more fortunate. It's all a continuum. You're in it, too."

"I'll give her the note. Vocabulary man."

I'm hoping Pinter unplugged the baccarat brainjack long enough to reach a phone and order some runway foam for me in Omaha. A driver at the gate holding a placard with my name only slightly misspelled in sloppy black capitals would add a certain something to my deplaning. It would help my arrival feel like an arrival and not just another departure in the making.

I call for my two percent and, yes, it's true—the flight attendant's smile seems to exceed the parabolic millimetric facial crack diagrammed in her Great West training manual. She's not a free being as you and I are free, and when her behavior varies, it's on purpose. Federal regulations rule her life, dictating shift lengths and rest periods and cycles of alcohol and prescription-drug consumption; her contract with the airline covers the rest. Even the bows in her shoelaces have been optimized. Two loops, just so. If she wore laced shoes, that is. It's forbidden; she might trip on them evacuating, helping some class-ring salesman down the slide.

How I mistook my teammates' grins and backslaps for mockery and obstruction, I'm still not sure. It's as though I've confused a dinner in my honor for a penitentiary last meal. These two events might look much the same, perhaps—undue attention from people who've ignored one, telegrams, reporters, handkerchiefs. Maybe it's not all me.

Omaha looms in my window, but its looming stems from my expectations, not its grandeur. On past trips the city has struck me as forlorn, a project that's outlived its founding imperatives and hung on thanks to block grants and inertia and handouts from one or two civic-minded billionaires. This time it may as well be the risen Atlantis. The stubby, aging skyline snags on cloud. The spotty late-morning traffic seems darkly guided. Omaha, city of mystery. Home to MythTech, who guides our hands through supermarket freezers toward rising-crust pizzas and bread-crumbed mozzarella sticks that seem overpriced and skimpy, but what the hell. It's our money. We'll spend it as we please.

I want to be in on that thing, whatever it is. To be safe from them one must be one of them. We dock with the Jetway and I join the line. It's not a job I'm seeking, it's citizenship, a seat inside the Dome. Key modules in the canopy hang from cranes and not every duct is flanged and sealed, but unless I get in before the structure's dedicated, I'll be a spectator. A mark. If MythTech turns out to be seven twenty-five-year-olds shooting wastebasket hoops and munching protein bars, I'll still want in, if this is where it's going. Even the big stuff starts in the Garage.

Sam lets me call him Sam. I ride up front with him. He's not a veteran, like Driver, but he tries, and I suspect he bills clients electronically and doesn't grant show tickets on the honor system. He's in college, no doubt, and this is just a sideline; that Penguin Classics *Bleak House* is no breeze, and half the pages are tabbed and paper-clipped. Sam nods at the sights. A famous jewelry store favored by British royals and software titans who know their Color, Cut, and Clarity. Warren Buffet's first office—see that broken window? It's the one directly above it, with the pigeons.

Someone must want me to feel at home in Omaha, and just in case Sam is reporting back to him, I show interest in salvaged toolworks and thoughtful greenways and redbrick loft districts zoned for art. I'm restless, though. We're leaving downtown along the sluggish Missouri. Paddle-wheel casinos, stacked raw lumber, the home of the nine-dollar T-bone, the eight, the seven. Big dreams and low rents can make beautiful music together, but as the steak dinners give way to dollar Buds, I start to wonder. Does MythTech have no pride?

"Where's world headquarters?"

"For what?" Sam says. "They gave me an address, not a press release."

Low pay, long hours. I don't take his snapping personally.

He looks from side to side, then at the sky, his chin out over the steering wheel. He's lost. Searching the sky while driving on the ground is like kicking the dropped fly ball that ended the game.

"Did they give you a time to get me there?" I say.

"In my glove compartment there's a phone."

Sam dials yet keeps driving; I lose faith in him. Once in the soup, persistence is no virtue. Muffler shops now. Unaffiliated churches. A Dairy Queen rival from the early seventies with a listing discolored cone that doesn't spin. MythTech hired this car, and by a firm's subcontractors you shall know its soul.

"We passed it. I knew it!"

Sam's illegal U-turn ends at an old low warehouse that I'll admit has definite rock-and-roll capitalism potential but could use a few satellite dishes on the roof to close the deal. I open my door; I wish I'd kept my briefcase. Sam tells me he needs to deliver a late tuition payment but promises to be back within the hour.

The intercom panel beside the vault-like door is promisingly rich in lighted buttons but none of them are labeled or even numbered. I hold them down four at a time and in response a buzzer sounds and a hidden latch clunks open. I snatch at the door handle, having never been told how long to expect such bolts to stay retracted. It's always a panic, this moment, for us nervous types.

The space is well-lit thanks to banks of vintage skylights honeycombed with reinforcing wires and remarkably free of bird droppings and dust. There's an old-fashioned gallery or mezzanine of frosted-glass offices served by iron stairways that horseshoes around what must have been the floor of some grand factory from Omaha's golden age as a center of whatever industry—boilermaking?—that survives in the names of its high school football teams. But there's no one around and no visible reception center where one might inquire where they've gone. The rough plank floor is as empty as a rink and hasn't been lovingly sanded and refinished to the customary retro luster or painted with foul lines to afford young geniuses those crucial brainstorming games of lunch-break basketball without which there'd be no Internet, no HandStar.

The only object evoking work or purpose is a sheet metal cube painted army surplus green and the size of an industrial air conditioner. It's featureless, with no rivets or vents or panels, but the sheen coming off it suggests it's well maintained. It's evidence of my investment in MythTech's legend that despite a stint in a high-tech field that taught me what supercomputers really look like—nothing much; they're no bigger than a dishwasher—I insist on seeing the cube as a huge cyber-brain capable of predicting how and when America's recently rekindled romance with the traditional station wagon will end. It's a drab-olive thinking monolith, that thing.

"Hello down there. Can I help you?"

"It's Ryan Bingham!"

The man at the rail of the mezzanine withdraws into the warren of glass offices and out pops a new face, young but very pale. The kid has on an orange Hawaiian shirt that's probably an expensive tribute to the Hawaiian shirt of old, since this one is louder and busier and brighter than any I ever saw my father wear at his annual company picnic in the Lion's Park. The kid's wearing flip-flop sandals, too. Encouraging. This is the look of the new-class robber barons.

"Can I help you?" Same question, but spoken with more authority, even a faint ring of profit participation. The kid considers this strange domain his own.

"This is MythTech, isn't it?" I say.

"Sure is. I'm sorry, though—no more odd jobs. We finished the packing and loading two days ago. Are you from Manpower?"

"I'm dressed like I'm from Manpower? Is Spack or Sarrazin here? It's Ryan Bingham."

"They're already up in Calgary," he says. Why won't he come down the stairs and make this civilized? "It's just me and four temps and two security guys until we can hoist that thing there on a truck. Then we're gone, too. Are you the one I sent the Town Car for?"

"Someone did. That was you?"

"I got a call from one of our old backers," the kid shouts down. "Send a car to meet a plane, he said, and when I asked why and who for the guy got snippy and told me I'm too low to ask him questions. I had to remind the old snot we're not top-down here. We're horizontal."

"Sandy Pinter?"

"One of those guys with all the wrong old concepts, the ones that put General Motors in the tank."

"Pinter's a MythTech backer?"

"From the old days. He got in early third quarter of '98. You haven't said how I can help you yet. Adam called you out here?"

"Indirectly."

"Back-channel stuff?"

"Right."

"It's all back channel lately. Did they contact you via microwave or radar? Or AM radio?"

This is not a high point in my life. I'm being teased by a mental inferior who thinks that America didn't get off the ground until September 1999, or whenever he opened his first IRA. But I deserve his jeers. What do I tell him? That they summoned me on an airport loudspeaker using a mini-mart pay phone?

"What's in Calgary?"

"Tax breaks. Lax accounting standards. Who knows? Strict banking privacy laws. Skilled immigrants. It's not like we're quarrying Nebraska sandstone—we can run this shop from Djakarta." He snaps his fingers and the echo pings around the space. "Unless you can tell me how to be of service, though, I've got an office swamped with cords and cables that need some pretty serious untangling."

"The name Ryan Bingham means nothing to you?" I say.

"Right now it means frustration. An hour ago I probably would've thought it was my senator. I mean it: I have big-time wire to spool, a jumbo commercial coffeemaker to clean. I also have two large guards on antipsychotics. Insanity defense? They've got it memorized."

"What's your name? I'm going to write it down."

"I can give you my log-in. I go by that," he says. "2BZ2CU."

I shift my center of gravity toward the door, but technically I hold my ground. I glance at the cube; it pulsed just now. It scanned me. I have sensitive mitochondria, rubbed raw by X-rays. I know when I've been scanned.

"I came to see that," I say, pointing. "Over there. My assistant took Sarrazin's call. He screwed the dates up. I worked on its prototype in Colorado."

The young man cocks his body skeptically and folds his thin white arms. He's bluff, all bluff, just another Starbucks M.B.A.; a fashion-forward brat in a VW who probably says he admires the Dalai Lama, but inside he's all stock options, all wireless day trades. I've felt these kindergartners at my back for going on a decade, and they scare me. Time to confront that. Kid doesn't know crap. Suspects he's not going to Calgary, either, I bet. These outfits don't go cross-border and non-dollar so they can haul along their slacker trash.

This needn't be pure humiliation, this errand. I can alpha this geek and exit in big black boots. So no one here was expecting me? That happens. I'm used to it by now. But I can at least view the cube and ride off tall into my million-mile sunset flight.

"Professional courtesy call," I say. "Get down here. Give me a tour or Pinter's calling Spack and Spack'll pay your severance in rubles."

2BZ shows Ryan his downy throat. He hits the stairs and flip-flops down in quick-time. The skylights dim as clouds slide over the sun but the cube holds its own in the gloom. It's homeostatic. 2BZ sets us up at a distance from the thing and won't fully face it; he just gives it his profile. He's acting like he's wishing for a lead apron.

"Is it turned on?" I say.

"Huh? It's always 'on.' "

"On inside quotation marks?"

"I'm really not the expert," says 2BZ. "We work on a need-to-know basis in this firm. It's horizontal, but layered-horizontal. I'm infrastructure. I'm shipping and receiving. I can tell you it's insured and that it's fragile and that it travels on a special flatbed that should have been here half an hour ago. I can tell you they already got in touch with Customs and that it wasn't your shortest phone call ever. I think they made two calls, in fact."

"So what's its nickname? Around the central office?"

"This was the back office. People work at home. This place was mostly support and storage," he says. "I'm not sure I have a job once it's cleared out. Who do you work for?"

"Myself. Like everyone. So basically you're ancillary and clueless."

"They told me I was critical. You smoke? Mind if I do?"

2BZ hand-rolls one from a pouch too fragrant to hold mere tobacco. Cloves or dope? These kids smoke all sorts of mixtures, and they should know better. I ask for one, too, but I won't inhale, just steep myself. I've worn a few Hawaiian shirts myself.

"I do have a few ideas about it," he says. "It's pretty skeletal here, there's not much company, just FedEx and UPS, so I spin out sometimes. Whole place was wired for sound once. Sequenced amps. I pirated off the Net and blasted everything. Tried to see if I could break those skylights. Or get myself fired. You know how all the shrinks say that children now are crying out for firmness and discipline and clear-cut values? I think it's true. I always got positive evaluations, but what I wanted was someone to storm in here and kill the music and kick a little butt."

"What ideas?" I'm inhaling some. You think you won't, but in practice it's hard not to. Just three hundred more miles to go, so I deserve it. Forty thousand feet above the wheat, and no one will even look up. As long as *I* know.

"It's the world-record random automated dialer. It skims off the fractional cents from savings accounts and forwards them to some bank in the Grand Caymans. It's where erased voice mails end up."

"Don't kid."

"I'm not."

"They have such devices. On decommissioned air bases. Don't believe it when they say some base is decommissioned. More like 'recommissioned.' "

"That's half this state. Drive through Nebraska sometime. It's all old Air Force. Half the Great Plains is military surplus."

We smoke and behold the cube. We think our thoughts. Is this where the miles are stored before they're paid?

A shuddering noise turns us both and we look on as a broad automated garage door rides its rails segment by segment and opens half one wall to views of the Missouri and western Iowa. We hear the beeps of a vehicle backing up and then we see the flatbed. It's rigged with about a dozen orange triangles and a "Flammable" sticker from some other job, perhaps. Three workmen walk backwards behind it and guide the driver with hand signals aimed at his flared-out rearview mirrors, and all wear emerald jumpsuits with drawstring hoods and trouser cuffs that cinch around their boots. The bed of the semi bristles with tie-down eyelets. Hoops of braided cable hang from the truck and now it's so close that we have to step aside. I can see by 2BZ's squint and brittle posture that he's witnessing his obsolescence here and I wish I knew someone to call on his behalf. My job recommendations pull no weight, unfortunately; the people know that I'm in CTC and am always trying to sell some exile as the Next Big Thing.

The boom on the flatbed is swung over the cube and two new workmen pile out of the cab, one with a walkie-talkie against his cheek. There may well be a helicopter somewhere, but I don't hear blades.

I ask 2BZ for his card and give him mine, though I'm afraid they're both outdated by now. His title is—was—"Associate." I thank him.

"The Calgary location is a campus. They're calling it a campus. It's vast, I hear. An old defunct seminary on the outskirts. No more home offices. They're consolidating."

"If I'm not at one of those numbers on the card, try information, Polk Center, Minnesota. You want me to write that down for you?"

"I'll remember," he says.

"You *tell* yourself. I'm writing it on another one. Take this one."

"You know what I think it is? I think I guessed. It goes outside, on the campus. To welcome visitors."

The workmen swarm and two of them boost one of them onto the top, where he widens his stance and bends. Everyone wields some cable or some hook and radiates safety-conscious professionalism. This baby is reaching Canada intact.

"I think it's probably art," says 2BZ. "It's corporate art. A thing to put out front."

seventeen

"n Omaha, boarding," I answer—accurately. They've worn me down. It's best just to give these women what they want when they ask me where they're reaching me.

"Julie's cut all her hair off," Kara says. "She'll be bald at the altar. I thought you set her straight."

"Waning powers." It's tough to keep my mind on this. My audience is assembling in first class and I intend to remember every face.

"When the salmon never came," says Kara, "Mom got some idea that she could smoke a turkey by putting a pan of wet wood chips in the oven, but underneath she wanted to burn the house down. No one's helping me. It's Shakespeare here. Luckily, the extinguisher had pressure left after four years of not once being checked."

"Did Tammy get in okay? The maid of honor?"

"She's Shakespeare too. She took a bump in Detroit for a free ticket and now we have to wait till almost midnight for her to show her hostile little face. A total play for attention.

Infantile. Her best friend is on her third husband, just about, and she's still single—not because she's a chilly neat-nik, naturally, who bolts every therapist we recommend the minute she finds a stray hair on their couch and the doctor won't let her spray it down with that antibacterial crap she totes around, but because her parents wouldn't buy her braces. She blames her teeth—like mine are any better. *I* got a man."

Someday, when I'm not paying for the call, I'll ask her to tell me exactly how she worked that.

"You there?"

"If you're planning to meet me, you'll have to set out now. You're already late."

"Your voice," she says. "You're loaded. I need you, Ryan. I'm dragging this whole celebration up a hill and I'm doing it alone. Don't drink. It sours you. You get all quippy."

"Big day for me," I say. I watch them file in and hand off wardrobe bags and tussle with the overheads and sit, but the attendance is sparser than I'd pictured and the group less representative, and older. I'd guess that just a third are fly-ing for business and will fully appreciate the feat that's com-ing and that most of the rest are aunts and uncles and granddads off to help video births and blow out candles, or else they just did those things and they're slouching home.

"Bigger day tomorrow," Kara says. "If people can just look within for twenty seconds and get ahold of their spin-ning little gears. Hey, Mom needs to know if she should make a room up or if the hide-a-bed is all you'll need?"

"Room," I say.

"I figured that already. You forwarded your mail here," Kara says.

So that's where it's going. The mist just keeps on lifting and soon I'll be able to see all the way, as far as the earth's curvature allows. It's a blessing, that curvature, that hidden hemisphere—if we could take it all in at once, why move?—and it may be the reason why one-ways cost the same as round-trips. They're all round-trips, some are just diced up in smaller chunks.

"Pick something up for Mom. Some souvenir. She senses the truth, I think; that this whole thing of yours is all about avoiding her. Some knickknack."

"A two-time loser is trying for her third tomorrow. Give your clarity a holiday. And whatever happened to 'Just bring yourself'?"

"The gift's insurance. In case you don't quite manage that."

"We're set to taxi and you need to start driving."

"Got you, brother. We're already in the Suburban and on our way. I'm holding the phone up. That snoring, all that wheezing? Your entire family sacked out, leaving Kara to do the driving, as usual. So don't drink a drop. Don't celebrate too soon."

"I'm drinking," I say. "Odometer set to turn over soon."

"Oh, that."

She's the master of small words, so I took the big ones.

"Get in safe," she says. "There's weather here. There's

black sky to my south and tons of grass and crap is starting to blow, pretty fast, across the road."

I arrange my materials as we thrust and rise. On the empty seat to my left I set my HandStar, displaying our flight path as a broken line on its amber credit-card-size screen and programmed so I can advance a jet-shaped icon by toggling a key. Fort Dodge, Iowa, is the milestone, as it's always been—I like the name—and though it's all an estimate, of course, and I may already have swept across the line, I've always been comfortable with imprecision when it's in the service of sharpened awareness. Factoring in leap years and cosmic wobble, our anniversaries aren't our anniversaries, our birthdays are someone else's, and the Three Kings would ride right past Bethlehem if they left today and they steered by the old stars.

Next I unpocket the single-use camera I bought in a gift shop at McCarran this morning. It has no flash, and I wonder if it needs one, though how could any place have more light than here? I'll let someone else snap the shot, I'm not sure who, though it will be one of the businessmen, naturally, so the photographer knows what he's commemorating, its size and mass and scope, and will make sure to aim squarely and hold still and not let his thumb tip jut across the lens. I'll want at least five shots from different angles and one from directly behind me, of my hair, which is how other flyers mostly see me and how I see them. If there's too much glare I'll lower my shade, though now, as the plane icon crosses a state border and in the real sky clouds accumulate,

I see that I'll have no problems from the sun, which is nothing but a corona around a thunderhead.

And of course I set out the corny story I wrote after he died and before my sad sabbatical studying the true meaning of train songs. After the other students were done abusing it, I stashed it in the pocket of my travel jacket, where it's been graying and softening ever since. I honestly don't remember how it goes, just that I wrote it the night I understood that rowing the uncomprehendingly unwanted across deep waters was not my heart's desire and needed a limit placed on it, a stop sign. The night I hatched this whole plan, wherever that was, bubble-bathing in some Homestead Suites with a cold beer on the tub that fell and smashed when I reached for it with soapy hands. I had to get out and towel off and drain the tub and feel for silvers, because the glass was clear.

"Excuse me. I was back in the wrong seat. This one with the stuff on it is mine, I think."

It's a voice I've only heard in dreams, where it was usually half an octave lower and transparently that of my father at fifty, when he first ran for representative and adopted the hands-off approach to gas delivery that emboldened a ruthless competitor based way off in St. Paul but spreading west. The face, though, I know from pictures in his magazine. That sun-kissed golf-and-tennis ageless skin I liked to think had been softened in the dark room, but appeals even more in person, I now see. The worry lines around the eyes are new, though, and there's an acrid top note in his breath—of failure and drift and working for one's self.

I gather my things and pouch them in my seatback and

start to stand, though he motions me back down. "You're it today. You're on your throne. Don't move. It's Soren. I feel like we know each other, Ryan. Christine, a bottle of white. No stingy miniatures."

"Yes, sir."

"Cold, not lukewarm."

"Don't carry that kind. Sorry." A joke between them. Everyone knows the service has fallen off and no one, not even the chief, knows what to do. More money, and a shower in his office, but on the whole he's in this with the rest of us.

Morse nestles in beside me and we shake hands and then we stretch out a little and touch elbows. He pulls his arm away first and lets mine rest. The plane skims over what feels like washboard gravel and rumbles some, and glasses chatter on trays.

"The way our best math minds have tallied it," he says, "as of today, you're our tenth. Congratulations. You expected a private lunch, I realize, but this'll have to be our date, right here. My board and I came to terms a week ago and I'm moving on effective six October. It's more meaningful this way. Share the living moment."

"Yes. It is." I'm back the way I started; single syllables. They get the point across.

"Funny story. We counted wrong before—" Christine arrives with a bottle, glasses, napkins, and as we unlatch our trays more rumbles come and then a tricky atmospheric pothole that lasts just a second but jostles pretty Christine and forces her to stiff-arm Morse's seat corner. The glasses ring together in her hand and down floats a napkin, onto Morse's knee.

"We thought the big trip was Billings-Denver," he says. "We had a party set up in the crew lounge. We paged, but I guess the speakers weren't so clear. We'd estimated wrong, so it was fine."

The man's unemployed now. His next step won't be up. It's over the instant they tell you, not the moment you go.

"You did it again in Reno this week," I say. Christine is decanting, but shouldn't be on her feet—not with the seat belt sign lit. It just came on.

"I'm not aware—"

It's a big one and it's lateral, like a shark shaking meat in its jaws. Our topped-up goblets slide over my way, but we snatch them somehow. Warm Chablis sloshes over on my sleeve and Morse and Christine exchange looks that don't reflect a master-and-servant imbalance but meet head on. Somehow this sight alarms me more than anything. Christine goes forward bracing hands on chairbacks—not to her fold-down jump seat, but to the cockpit, closing the door in time for a new lateral, though this one has a pitch and stronger swim. My oval window streams diagonally, then milks up and fogs; as crosswinds drive the droplets straight at the plastic. Off and down and forward there's white-green lightning, not bolts, but blurs. Morse buckles himself in and I do, too. The sight of a man of his stature, or former stature, strapped in across the thighs and struggling to feed more belt through for a snugger hold, disorients more than the turbulence.

Our captain speaks and, as usual, minimizes, and I can see mottling on Morse's wrists and a coiled desire to shout at someone and demand results this very minute, but the huffy, flushed look seems childish under the circumstances, and Morse knows this, it seems, and won't look me in the eye but mentally shuts himself inside his office, refusing to take calls. We bronco again and then bang down an escalator that must floor out somewhere but keeps not doing so, and then we're on a whole new ride, even steeper, and my wineglass ejects a column of solid liquid that hangs for a time directly before my eyes and actually shows inner particles and bends light.

Our keel evens but it's a trick and no one's buying and yet it remains even, just to torture us, though level is level, I see after a while, and normal is the most usual condition, so why question normal? Normal's what got us here. There's also more light now, both under and ahead, and light somehow speaks more reliably than flatness about the prospects of its own continuing.

Morse unbuckles to show us all the way, back in the lead and comfortable again, because during normal his orders must be obeyed and his moods are the collective rudder. The episode is over, his face declares, and already he's revising its severity and telling a little story to himself of uninterrupted control. His airline not only lies to customers, it deceives itself. We're steady on now and we always have been.

"Christine, two new glasses. These ones spilled," he says. "Take them away, please."

Already concealing evidence. The continuum would include him, but he won't let it, though soon he'll have to work harder to stand alone, when he's cooling his heels in an office in D.C. as just another aviation lobbyist or whenever a baseball game comes on TV while he's at home with his new and plainer mistress after another long day at the trucking line or the regional frozen foods distributor. Not me, though. I know when I've come through a rough patch and voiced silent prayers that promised deep reforms—the same reforms everyone else was pledging, too, with the full knowledge that we'll dishonor them the moment we're down and safe.

I can see to the ground now between white disks of cloud that meet in the pattern four dinner plates would make if pushed in against one another on a table. The pattern repeats and repeats, and through the breaks shaped like perfect diamonds with curved-in sides I notice that we're no longer above the west. I recognize the tic-tac-toe green fields and the corner placements of windbreak maples. There's a definite American longitude dividing the cottonwoods and scrappy desert trees from the wet shady maples, and we've passed it.

I check my watch to confirm, but I don't have to. The plane icon is well beyond Fort Dodge and in a few minutes I'll be on top of Kara, casting a shadow on her eastbound car. Which means that I missed it, as I was bound to miss it. But I still crossed. I hand Morse the cheapie camera and instruct him to shoot me front and back and from the sides, though of course he can't stand on the wing and shoot from that side. How kind of my family to come pick me up. Will they be able to see it on my face? Morse looks silly snapping that little button. It was worth it to watch this. "From below," I say. I'll tramp along the Jetway, in my boots, and see them all there at the gate, where they've been waiting, though I wonder why. Will we last a whole week together? We just might. Everyone's exhausted. Exhaustion soothes. It's a fable now, anyway. We've used up our real substance. In a fable, you find new resources, new powers. Pick an animal, then take its shape.

Morse runs out of film and begs my pardon: he needs to check in on the cockpit and exercise what's left of his authority. Two more weeks and the pilots will shut this airline down. He's getting out just in time, and so am I.

"My miles go to children's hospitals," I say.

"That's great. What a gesture. We should get this out. I'll contact press relations when we land. You're serious?"

"Don't use my name. No name. It's not a gesture. It's barely charity. I'm sick myself; I can't use them anyway. Plus, I've been everywhere you people fly."

Of course I've had seizures. Why skirt it any longer? One after another, some mild, some not, but nothing one talks about if one wants a job—and didn't I land in the perfect one. Too perfect. My family knows, but we've learned not to discuss it. It started when my car went in the lake. We tried medications, and some worked better than others, but what worked best was lowering my standards for what was not a seizure. And forgetting. I'm not there when I have them, so really, what's to say? How can I tell you a secret I don't know? The spaces between them are getting shorter, though. The signs all agree. The mental gaps are widening. I made my appointments at Mayo before the trip and Mayo has wonderful instruments, so we'll see. I'll drive down alone, in case it's not good news.

There's one last item and this will feel complete. I slide my credit card through the airphone slot. I sense the account's being drained on several continents, but it brings up a dial tone, which is all I need. I punch in my own number and get my voice mail, then press more buttons to reach the little message I recorded . . . when? Three weeks ago? Or was it four? It was after I saw the specialist in Houston, the one I haven't mentioned, since no one's asked.

"You're there," the message says, then tapes my answer.

"We're here," I say. Just that. No more. "We're here."

a b o u t   t h e   a u t h o r

walter kirn is currently the fiction editor for *GQ* magazine and a contributing editor to *Time* magazine. His work has appeared in the *New York Times Magazine*, the *New York Times Book Review*, *GQ*, *Vogue*, *New York*, and *Esquire*. He is the author of three previous works of fiction, *My Hard Bargain: Stories*, *She Needed Me*, and *Thumbsucker*. He lives in Livingston, Montana.